Down & Dirty: Axel

Dirty Angels MC®
Book 5

Jeanne St. James

Copyright © 2018 by Jeanne St. James, Double-J Romance, Inc.

All rights reserved.

No part of this book may be reproduced in any form or by any electronic or mechanical means, including information storage and retrieval systems, without written permission from the author, except for the use of brief quotations in a book review.

Editor: Proofreading by the Page
Photographer/Cover Artist: Golden Czermak at FuriousFotog
Cover Model: Michael Scanlon
Beta Readers: Author Whitley Cox & Krisztina Holló

---

www.jeannestjames.com

Sign up for my newsletter for insider information, author news, and new releases:
www.jeannestjames.com/newslettersignup

Dirty Angels MC® is a registered trademark.

Warning: This book contains explicit scenes, some possible triggers and adult language which may be considered offensive to some readers. This book is for sale to adults ONLY, as defined by the laws of the country in which you made your purchase. Please store your files wisely, where they cannot be accessed by under-aged readers.

This is a work of fiction. Any similarity to actual persons, living or dead, or actual events, is purely coincidental.

Dirty Angels MC, Blue Avengers MC & Blood Fury MC are registered trademarks of Jeanne St James, Double-J Romance, Inc.

Keep an eye on her website at http://www.jeannestjames.com/ or sign up for her newsletter to learn about her upcoming releases: http://www.jeannestjames.com/newslettersignup

Author Links: Instagram * Facebook * Goodreads Author Page * Newsletter * Jeanne's Review & Book Crew * BookBub * TikTok * YouTube

Prologue

AXEL COULDN'T REMEMBER the last time he'd been with a woman.

It'd been way too long, and it was all her damn fault.

Bella climbed into her purple Dodge Challenger and within minutes, pulled away from the bakery's back parking lot.

Just like he did almost every night, Axel hit the starter on his custom Harley and headed the other direction, so she wouldn't spot him following her. Because if she did, she'd have a shit-fit and punch him in the fucking nuts if given half the chance. And he happened to like his balls the way they were. Though, right now, they could be considered blue since he hadn't done anything with them in a while except found relief with his own palm.

He rounded the corner and hit a side street, riding parallel to the one she was traveling. He knew where she was going. He knew exactly how she'd get there.

He only wanted to make sure she arrived safely, then he'd head home.

Like normal.

Because he had no fucking life.

Nope. He'd go home, crack open an Iron City Beer and kick his feet up to watch some TV.

And she'd go home, double lock her front door, check to make sure all her windows were secure, set her security alarm, then make something to eat and climb into bed.

Without him.

She never dated. Never brought a man home. She always went to bed alone.

Although, that should make him happy, it didn't.

Not that he wanted her to be with another man, he didn't. But it also didn't give him much hope for his own chances.

Not at all.

It wasn't like he hadn't been trying. He had. Every chance he got. But she resisted, and she was downright stubborn.

Which was to be expected.

Tenacity ran deep when it came to the women of the Dirty Angels MC and Bella was a biker chick through and through. Born and raised within the club, she was third generation Dirty Angels MC.

Years ago, she had even married into it, became an ol' lady, a biker's claimed property. That day had been one of the darkest days of Axel's life.

Although not the darkest. No, that day came later.

After the worst day of both of their lives, she became "Property of No One." No longer claimed by anyone. And she shouted that to the rooftops. She made that statement loud and clear, even wearing it on her tank tops and sweatshirts. He was surprised she didn't have Crow tattoo it across her forehead.

But he didn't want her to become his property, no.

Yes, he was a biker, but he didn't want her to be his ol' lady.

Yes, he rode a Harley and wore a cut, but he wasn't DAMC.

No, he wasn't that type of biker, even though the club's blood ran thick through his own veins, as well.

No.

Instead, he belonged to the Blue Avengers MC.

Because he was a cop.

BELLA PEEKED out of the window pretending to check the latch, but in all reality, she already knew it was secure.

Axel didn't think she knew what he did way too often, which was follow her home after she finished working her shift at Sophie's Sweet Treats. She noticed him doing it after the trouble with the Shadow Warriors, a rival MC, had become more frequent.

Sometimes he was in his patrol car, sometimes on his sled, sometimes in his truck.

But she knew he was there.

He was always there.

He'd always been there.

She wished he'd give up.

She *needed* him to give up.

But no matter what she said to him, no matter how shitty she treated him, no matter how many times she'd told him to "get gone," he never did.

Yes, he'd back off but only to give her space. He'd always be there waiting on the outskirts of her anger.

It wasn't him. It was her.

She didn't want any man.

Not a biker. Not a doctor. Not an accountant.

Not even Axel.

Or at least, that's what she tried to tell herself.

With a sigh, she leaned her forehead against the window pane and could see him sitting on his Harley, the custom one Jag built for him, in the shadows just outside the circle of the street light.

He probably thought since he didn't have illegal straight exhaust pipes that she wouldn't hear his sled outside her house. But, hell, being raised in an MC meant she could easily recognize the deep rumble of his Harley, legal pipes or not.

So many times she'd pushed him away. But he never gave up. The man was tenacious and determined.

And as much as she wanted him, she couldn't have him. For more reasons than one.

Sucking in a ragged breath, her nipples tightened at the thought of having her way with him just for one single night.

Only one night.

Maybe then she'd get him out of her system. And her out of his.

She needed to prove to him and to herself that this wasn't meant to be, no matter what their bodies said.

No, she couldn't crack that shell to let him in, even for a split second.

Her feet moved without her permission and suddenly she was at her front door punching in the security code, turning the deadbolt, and removing the security chain. Everything her cousin Diesel, the club Sergeant at Arms, had installed for her safety. Before she could stop herself, she ripped open the door.

Barefoot, she stepped out onto her front stoop, put her hands on her hips and stared directly at him.

What was she doing? Why couldn't she fight his pull?

Within seconds, his sled roared to life and he rolled into her driveway, heeled the kickstand down, quieted the engine and stared back at her.

Without saying anything, Axel dismounted, took long strides in her direction and bumped her backwards with his chest against hers until he pushed them beyond the threshold enough so that he could slam the door shut.

Then her back was pinned against the wooden door, his chest to hers, effectively trapping her as he took her mouth.

Her lips parted on a whimper and he took advantage of this by shoving his tongue deep to explore the recesses of her mouth, to tangle his tongue with hers. She moaned as his fingers dug deep into her long, loose hair, pulling hard, imprisoning her head against the door so he could take the kiss even deeper.

A moan bubbled up from the back of her throat but he held her still, his cock hard and long as it pushed against her belly.

It had been a long time for her and she so wanted to accept what he offered but she couldn't.

She shouldn't.

He finally released her mouth, his breath beating rapidly against her parted lips. "Bella," he whispered raggedly.

Then his face was buried against her neck, his tongue tracing along her throat, along the artery that pounded so violently that it might escape. She stared at his dark head, his tightly trimmed hair, as he moved farther down, brushing his lips along her skin, over the large shoulder cap tattoo that ran from the bottom of her neck and down her left arm. He kissed each colorful rose, each lily, each daisy that Crow had inked permanently into her skin in an attempt to make her feel beautiful again.

His thumbs swept lightly over her beaded nipples that pushed against her snug camisole. The one she wore to remind herself and others that she belonged to no one but herself.

As he kneaded her breasts, he pushed a knee between her thighs, separating her legs just enough to cause a rush of wetness that she hadn't experienced in ages.

Tentatively, she brushed her fingers over the shaved sides of his head then over the slightly longer hair at the top as he murmured her name against her skin, working his way back to her lips.

After another long, deep kiss, his forehead pressed against hers and they both panted as their gazes met and held, his blue eyes darker than normal.

His fingers slipped down over her waist to her hips, then snagged the bottom of her cami, beginning to tug the stretchy fabric up her belly. As soon as she felt the air against her bare skin, she froze, turned her head to break their connection and moaned for him to stop.

He didn't. Instead his warm fingers traced along her bare waist and up her ribs, pushing the fabric higher.

She pressed her palms against his chest and screamed, "Stop!"

He went solid, his breathing harsh, and she couldn't bear to look at him, so she closed her eyes and let the darkness behind her eyelids calm her racing heart.

"Bella..."

His voice was gentle, not angry, which made her heart squeeze and her chest tighten.

She shook her head slightly, still unable to look at him.

"Let me in, Bella," he said softly.

"I can't," she whispered back, her voice breaking, her eyes stinging even behind her lowered eyelids. She sucked in a breath to gather her strength since she needed to be strong to turn him away, to say no to this man.

A man who knew her secrets, her past. A man who knew her better than anyone. And he shouldn't.

Knowing what he did, he certainly shouldn't want her.

Not only did Axel know things about her no one else did, they were complete opposites, with families that didn't accept each other. Like the Montagues and the Capulets in *Romeo and Juliet*.

She was DAMC. He was a cop.

She was not accepted in his family, and he wasn't in hers.

Her lips trembled as she repeated, "I can't. You need to let me go. Let this go."

He slowly smoothed her camisole back down until it covered her completely, then stepped back.

Bella mourned the loss of his solid frame, of his burning heat against her. Something that brought her both solace and anguish.

"Look at me," he urged softly.

Reluctantly, she opened her eyes and studied the man she'd known all her life, the one who looked so much like his older brother, Zak, the former president of the DAMC. Like his father, Mitch, a veteran cop.

Sadness softened his strong features as he traced a thumb over her bottom lip, admitting, "Like you, I can't."

A long moment later, he stepped back as his gaze raked over her, then reached for the knob. Bella quickly moved away from the door to let him leave.

Because that was the smartest thing for her to do.

Let him go.

After she heard his sled roar to life and race away, she finally took a complete breath.

Chapter One

Three months later

BELLA STOOD behind the bar at church and eyeballed Zak, the current club president. And, hopefully, the future president since officer elections were coming up in a few weeks.

After ousting Pierce from the top spot a couple months ago, since the man was a complete fucking asshole, Zak had stepped back into his former role, leading the club. And she figured just about everyone, except for Pierce, was relieved.

"Can you do this shit?" Z asked her. "I'd ask my ol' lady, but since she's knocked up, rather not put more pressure on 'er than she already got with the bakery."

"We're hiring two more people to help with the holiday rush, Z."

"Fuckin' know that. Suggested it."

Bella pinned her lips together to fight the temptation to knock his block off. She loved Z, but he'd been on a rampage lately being overly protective of Sophie and his unborn kid.

She understood why, but it was getting to be a bit much. Especially since the couple still lived above the bakery and he was there way too often checking on his wife. Hovering. Keeping an eye out for those asshole Shadow Warriors in case they wreaked havoc on the shop.

The Warriors did it once before, they could do it again. The rival MC had even tried to kidnap Sophie a while ago. Though that attempt failed, it didn't mean they wouldn't try again, especially now that Z was back sitting at the head of the table. And the other club definitely had a hard-on for him.

Even worse, it wasn't like they'd failed on all their kidnapping attempts. They hadn't.

Kiki, Jazz and Jewel had all suffered at their hands.

"Yeah, I can do it, Z."

"Get all the women to help."

"Are you going to tell me how to do it or are you going to let me do it?" she snapped.

Z frowned and picked up the pint glass that Bella had slid in front of him. He downed the beer, then slammed the glass back on the bar before swiping the back of his hand over his mouth, removing any trace of foam from his lips.

Hawk moved behind her and placed a hand on her shoulder. "Don't mind him, his hormones are ragin' like Sophie's."

"What-fuckin-ever," Z grumbled into his glass.

Hawk, Bella's cousin and club VP, snagged a nearby bottle of Jack and poured himself a double shot. He downed it in one swallow, then hissed through the burn. "Assumin' he just asked you to head the Toys for Tots drive?"

He picked up the bottle again and tilted it toward her in invitation. She nodded. Snagging a second shot glass, he poured them each a double.

Bella stared at the amber liquid in the tiny glass. "Yeah. And I'll be glad to do it. I'm happy the club's getting back on track now that Pierce's been replaced."

"Long time comin'," Hawk mumbled, then tilted his head back while downing his double. He slammed the shot glass on the bar and then scrubbed a hand over his short mohawk. "Kiki'll help."

"We're *all* going to help," the redhead, who sidled up to the bar, announced. Bella gave her sister, Ivy, a look of thanks. "We haven't done one in years. It's about time."

"You mean all you *women* are gonna help," Jag, Ivy's old man, clarified. He lifted his chin toward Hawk. "Take one of those."

Hawk grinned and poured the club's Road Captain a double. "Too bad it's too fuckin' cold for a toy run."

Jag shrugged. "Maybe next summer I'll set one up. Or we can wait 'til someone gets their ass arrested an' use it toward community service."

Z snorted. "Like yours, Chicken Hawk."

"Done my time," Hawk reminded his club brother.

"An' benefitted from it, too," Jag laughed. "If your ass hadn't landed in jail, you wouldn't be snugglin' up with the club attorney."

"Don't snuggle," Hawk grumbled.

As if on cue, Kiki came through the double swinging doors of the commercial kitchen that sat between the private clubhouse and The Iron Horse Roadhouse, the club's public bar that Hawk ran.

"Don't believe him," she called out as she approached wearing her tight, sexy business attire and her typical stiletto pumps. Her dark eyes snapped with mischief. "He snuggles. He's a pro at it."

A hand slamming on the bar made Bella jump. All heads turned toward the end of the bar where Grizz, the oldest member of the club, sat nursing a beer. "Fuckin' bitches," he grumped.

They all waited for him to finish his thought, but he didn't, instead he just raised his beer to his mouth, which they could barely see with all his scraggly, overgrown gray beard, and downed a healthy swallow.

A few raised eyebrows later, Kiki slid in between Hawk and Bella. "I'd love to help. I'll set up a collection box at my office. We can set one up at the bakery, too."

"Don't forget the garage and pawn shop," Ivy added. "I'll build a website to help fundraise."

"Get one to Crow an' Dawg, too," Jag added.

"Think the strip club's a good place to ask for children's toys?" Bella asked with a smirk.

Jag shrugged. "Who cares? A bunch of Dawg's girls got kids an' with the fuckin' tips they get, I'm sure they'll donate. I'll tell Dawg to set up a night where the patrons gotta bring a toy to get in the door as a cover charge. You're gonna have fuckin' more toys than you'll know what to do with."

"Prospects'll drop the boxes 'round town at local businesses, too," Zak added.

Bella nodded. That was a good idea.

Z continued, "Gonna reach out to the Knights to see if they want in."

"If they do, let me know. I can reach out to Magnum's ol' lady," Bella told Z.

He nodded, then rapped his knuckles on the bar before pushing himself off the stool. "Goin' home to my woman."

Bella watched Z cross the large, open common area that held a few pool tables and a whole bunch of old, disgusting couches. The swing of his hips was always a sight to behold since the man just oozed chill. His brother, Axel, didn't quite have the same loosey goosey movement. But then, he was a cop and a bit on the uptight side so he tended to move a little more methodically.

Z flicked two fingers over his shoulder as he exited the door.

"We're headin' out, too," Hawk said, grimacing as he downed another double.

"I guess I'm driving," Kiki said, rolling her eyes.

Hawk smacked her on the ass and murmured something in his woman's ear, which made her smile softly and her eyes flash.

Bella did not want to know what her cousin whispered. She shuddered at the thought. "I'll set up a couple donation boxes at The Iron Horse, Hawk."

Hawk gave her a sharp nod. "Yep. Do that." Hooking his arm around Kiki's shoulders, he guided her from behind the bar and in the same direction Z disappeared.

"Who's watching the bar tonight?" Bella yelled out.

"Slade an' Linc," Hawk yelled back over his shoulder.

Bella was glad she no longer had to work late nights at the bar. She'd slung drinks for years and now that she was a partner in Sophie's bakery, she was much happier and got home a lot earlier. Sometimes she still worked late, trying out some new things in the bakery's kitchen, experimenting with new flavor combinations when it came to their locally famous cupcakes, but that was all a labor of love.

It turns out that baking was her calling, just like Sophie's.

She was happy Sophie came into the club family by the way of Zak, who had mistakenly thought one night that she was one of Dawg's strippers and had dragged her kicking and screaming into his life and heart.

Bella smiled softly. Her eyes slid to her sister, Ivy, who was tucked between Jag's legs, leaning into him. Her hand laid on his chest and his arm wrapped around her waist, holding her close.

The club brothers were dropping like flies. First Z, then Jag, then Hawk, and recently Diesel was brought down hard to his knees by Jewel.

No one ever saw that last one coming. Especially D.

Now with Sophie being pregnant, the new year would bring about the fourth generation of DAMC.

She wouldn't be surprised if Kiki was knocked up next. Or even Ivy.

Bella couldn't imagine being an aunt.

The thought should make her warm and fuzzy, but it didn't.

Instead, the idea of being around babies made her reach out and grasp the bar, her nails digging into the wood.

"You okay?" came a deep, low grumble next to her. She turned her head enough to glance up at Diesel.

"Yeah," she forced out. "Fine."

He grunted as if he didn't believe her. Because he didn't. He knew her way too well. Almost as well as Axel.

After that night so long ago, Diesel appointed himself her protector. Her cousin was always looking out for her. Like Axel.

However, the two men hated each other's guts. D would love to do nothing more than pound the cop into the ground if he could get away with it. But that had more to do with Z than Bella. It all stemmed from Z's family, including Axel, not wanting anything to do with their blood relative since Z went the direction of DAMC against his father's wishes.

While Mitch pulled his family away from the club, Zak embraced his grandfather's legacy instead, which resulted in his family leaving him out in the cold.

"I'm heading home, too. Tell Jewel I'll need her help with this Toys for Tots drive, okay?"

D grunted and grabbed a beer bottle from the cooler. He knocked the cap off on the edge of the bar using his meaty paw.

She rolled her eyes. Good thing she understood biker speak and could differentiate what each grunt meant.

Grabbing her keys, she headed out the back door.

THE JINGLE from the bells over the bakery's door sounded, making both Bella and Sophie glance up.

Right on time. The man was nothing if not predictable.

Axel navigated his tall body through the door of the shop, his duty belt hanging off his lean hips and his uniform neatly pressed, making the man look like a well-wrapped birthday present. He slid off his dark sunglasses and tucked them into his breast pocket.

Sophie stopped what she was doing, which was boxing up a cake, and reached into the display case to grab a cream cheese stuffed red velvet cupcake. She held it out to him until he approached the counter and nabbed it.

"Thanks," he murmured, his eyes not leaving Bella's.

Almost every day he stopped in for a cupcake, either before or after his shift, depending on what time he worked, and sometimes he'd even come in on his days off.

Those were Bella's favorite visits, because he'd come in wearing soft, worn jeans that hugged his long legs and now that the weather had turned cold, usually a long-sleeved Henley that fit snuggly across his lean, but muscular torso.

Today he wore a heavy patrol jacket, so all she could do was admire his legs. And his ass. When he wasn't looking, of course.

Despite eating a cupcake on an almost daily basis, the man seemed to stay in shape.

"Bella," he greeted softly, his gaze traveling over her hair—which was pulled up and away from her face into a bun—down her throat, then paused on her chest, which was covered by a white apron that had Sophie's Sweet Treats embroidered on it.

Her nipples peaked immediately under his heated gaze.

Sophie cleared her throat and finally drew his attention. "How's the kid?" he asked her.

His sister-in-law's hand automatically dropped to the slight rise of her belly as she smiled warmly at him. "Great, your niece is growing like a weed."

"Shit," Bella muttered. "Don't let Z hear you say it's a girl."

Sophie laughed. "That's why I do it. Drives him crazy." She tilted her head, her green eyes sliding from Bella to Axel. "I, uh, have to grab something in the back." Then she was gone before Bella could stop her.

Bella busied herself by picking up where Sophie left off, boxing the cake that would be picked up later for a birthday party.

"Bella," Axel murmured, getting closer to where she stood, the glass display case the only thing separating them. "Did you make this?"

Her gaze rose to him before she could stop it. He'd peeled the paper cupcake liner away and was now tonguing the cream cheese icing she'd piped over the top.

All the breath left her as the tip of his tongue swirled through the white frosting. *Jesus.*

He did it to her every time. She should be used to it by now.

"You know I did," she answered, pressing her thighs together and dropping her gaze back to the sheet cake in front of her. She fiddled with the box, trying to get her mind off what he was doing with his mouth on her cupcake.

Fuck. Fuck. *Fuck.*

Three months ago was the first time they'd ever kissed. Though they'd been close to doing it in the past, they'd never followed through. And that one time in her house, with her pushed against the door, his hard-on pressed to her stomach, she'd been kissed like she'd never been before.

Unfortunately, she hadn't been able to forget it.

She tried.

But she couldn't.

She peeked up at him from beneath her lashes. Staring directly at her, the corners of his lips curled wickedly as he now dipped his tongue into the center of the cupcake, slowly savoring the sweet filling.

She groaned.

"What?" he asked, a little bit of frosting stuck to his bottom lip.

If he didn't take his cupcake and go, she was going to leap over the display case and take him down to the ground to lick it right off of him.

She shook her head to clear it. "Nothing."

"I thought you said something."

"Nope."

"You sure?"

"Axel..." she breathed.

"Yeah?"

She curled her fingers into her palms, digging her nails into her flesh to stop her wicked thoughts. "You have schmutz on your mouth."

He smiled and ran his thumb over his lower lip then sucked it into his mouth to thoroughly lick it clean.

Fuck!

"You got your cupcake, don't you need to get back on patrol now?" she asked as she turned away, bracing her hands on the back counter and dropping her head to stare at a smudge of flour.

"You heard 'er, overstayed your welcome. Get the fuck out," Zak said, his voice as cold and hard as steel as he barreled through the swinging door from the back kitchen, Sophie hot on his heels.

"*Brother*," Axel greeted with a soft growl.

Z took a menacing step forward. "You keep callin' me that but it ain't true. Got your shit, now get gone."

"Zak," Sophie murmured, putting a hand on his arm.

"Have to pay yet," Axel said, not moving a muscle, his spine now straight and stiff as the brothers squared off.

"On the house, get the fuck out."

Axel nodded sharply, then, after digging into his pocket, pulled out a couple of wrinkled dollar bills and tossed them on top of the display case.

Bella snagged the money and headed to the cash register, glad to have something to keep her busy until he left.

But he still hadn't moved. Instead, his gaze was pinned to the Toys for Tots box Bella had tucked into the back corner of the bakery.

"How did that get here?" he asked.

Bella frowned. "I put it there."

Sophie pushed around Zak, getting in between the two brothers. "Bella's running the Toys for Tots drive that the club's holding."

Bella knew exactly when Axel's heavy gaze landed on her. She hit the button on the register and the drawer sprang open. Smoothing the money as best as she could, she then shoved it into the drawer, ignoring him.

Or at least until she felt his presence close. Too close. Her nostrils flared as she picked up his scent. She closed her eyes and breathed deeply. Whatever he wore, whether it was aftershave or cologne, was unique and it fit him. And it was a nice change of pace from the exhaust, fuel, smoke, beer and booze that clung to some of the club brothers. She couldn't forget the smell of pussy, either. That was especially strong after a night of heavy partying.

His deep voice nearby made a shiver run down her spine. "How about that? The PD's doing it again this year, and I got stuck organizing it. Might have to compare notes." The last part he said so softly only she could hear it and it made her raise her eyes to his.

"Axel, get gone before Z shoves a fist down your throat," she said just as softly.

Axel shot a look in his brother's direction. "He knows I come in here every day; he should be used to it."

"Doesn't mean he likes it."

Axel gave her a sharp nod, but still didn't move to leave.

The front door to the shop was almost ripped off its hinges as Diesel shoved his big body inside, his eyes heated as they landed on the cop.

"Shoulda fuckin' known that pig mobile out front was yours, asshole."

Axel stepped back from the counter, his hand resting lightly on the butt of his gun, luckily still tucked safely in its holster.

"When you gonna learn you ain't welcome here?" D barked practically in his face, but Axel didn't react. And having a man as big as Diesel shouting in your face was enough to make anyone flinch.

"D," Bella said sharply. "He's just leaving."

"Don't see his fuckin' feet movin'. Get gone, pig."

Even from where she stood, she could see Axel's nostrils flare, but he miraculously held his temper. "The day Sophie says I'm not welcome, I'll stop coming. Until then, you have no say, D."

"Fuck I don't," D barked even louder, his face a threatening mask, his fingers curled into fists.

"Going to hit me, Diesel? While I'm in uniform?"

"Don't give a shit what you're wearin', pig. Don't matter to me."

"Axel, get gone," Bella said softly, then raised her voice to address her cousin. "D, stand down. It isn't worth getting arrested over."

D's eyes flicked to her and then back to Axel. He shoved a finger in the cop's direction. "Back off, Axel. Go sniff elsewhere. Ain't ever gonna happen."

With his eyes never leaving Diesel, Axel murmured, "You don't have a say in that, either."

"Fuck I don't," D repeated.

"Just like I didn't have a say about you and Jewel."

"Got nothin' to say 'bout DAMC property, pig. Remember that."

"She's still my cousin. Like Bella's yours. Still family."

Diesel snorted. "Family. You don't even know what that fuckin' means."

"Axel, go," Bella said more firmly, when she noticed Z moving closer to his brother. She was beginning to think the man had a damn death wish. Nothing good would come out of challenging both Zak and Diesel. So, she whispered, "Please."

That got his attention.

His head spun toward her and he studied her for a long moment. "We'll talk later."

She shook her head. "No, we won't. Please leave."

With a glance over his shoulder at Sophie, he said, "Take care of my niece," then he bravely pushed past D and went out the door.

Bella finally breathed when the bells stopped jingling. She turned toward the big picture window and watched as his cruiser pulled away from the curb, his eyes meeting hers for a split moment.

"You heard 'im, ain't gonna stop comin' here 'til your ol' lady tells 'im to stop," D muttered to Zak.

Sophie moved around Z and stepped up to Diesel, reaching up to plant a hand on his broad chest. "D, I love you like family, but I'm not stopping Axel from coming here. Sorry. Whether you or Zak like it or not, he's still blood. He's still my baby's uncle. And he…" Her voice drifted off as her gaze slid to Bella. "He's a good… customer."

"I need to remind you that you're Z's ol' lady an' this shop now belongs as part of the club?"

"D," Z murmured moving toward Sophie as she dropped her hand from D's chest and took a step back, her face a hard mask.

Diesel shoved a finger in Sophie's direction. "She's DAMC property, Z. You're the fuckin' prez. What you say goes." He swung an arm out. "This place is DAMC property, too."

Bella picked up her gaping jaw, hurried down the counter to the hinged portion and came out onto the shop floor, rushing to step between Sophie, Zak and Diesel.

"Fuck, D. What the fuck is wrong with you?"

Diesel's dark eyes dropped to hers. "Tired of that pig's ass sniffin' 'round you. It's gotta stop. Shoulda stopped it a long time ago. If all it takes is a word from Z's ol' lady to keep his ass outta here, then she needs to say those words. Got me?"

"Brother," came a low warning from Zak. It was hard to miss his raised hackles. "You're overstepping' right now."

"No. My job's to protect this club. To protect everything that belongs to this club. That's her." He jabbed a finger in Bella's direction. "Her." He turned it toward Sophie. "That kid in 'er belly, an' even you, brother. As well as this business. That's my job an' I'm gonna fuckin' do it 'til it ain't my job or I'm dead. Got me?"

"I think you both need to cool the hell down," Bella said, her gaze bouncing from one man to the other. "I'm not sure what the hell's up your ass, D, but picking a fight with Zak isn't going to make it better."

"And you're both going to regret it later," Sophie spoke up. "Let me remind you, Zak, that even if you no longer consider Axel your brother, you *do* consider D as one. Think about that."

Both men said nothing for a moment, then finally Diesel grunted and so did Zak. Suddenly, the tension in the air dissipated and Bella sighed in relief.

"I'll tell Axel to stay away from the bakery," Bella finally said.

D's gaze swung toward her. "Stay away from 'im."

Bella pinned her lips together and headed back behind the counter before she kicked her cousin in the nuts. She was tired of bossy alpha men and her life was full of them.

Now she understood why Ivy had chased geeks and nerds for the longest time, resisting Jag's advances for what seemed like forever. Her sister didn't want to be saddled with a biker for good reason.

She was staring at two of them.

And the other one who had walked out the door just minutes before wasn't much better.

But to keep the peace she would have a word with Axel and ask him to stop coming around. And, while she was at it, to stop following her home every night.

If Diesel knew the man did that, he might end up in prison with Doc and Rocky for murder.

And that wouldn't do anybody any good.

Chapter Two

BELLA PULLED her car into the driveway, scrubbed her hands down her face and sighed. She really wanted to scream instead.

Watching Diesel and Zak at each other's throats had disturbed her more than she was willing to admit. She loved them both and the two men were normally close, so it was up to her to make sure that conflict didn't happen again.

Which meant getting Axel out of her life once and for all. He needed to stop coming to the bakery practically every day. He needed to stop teasing her with his tongue on her cupcakes. He needed to stop licking her frosting.

She squeezed her eyes shut and screamed, "Fuck!" inside the empty, quiet car.

Muttering "Fuck, fuck, fuck," she shoved open the driver's door, yanked her keys from the ignition and got out. Stomping down her short paved driveway, she walked right up to his truck which was parked at the curb, still running. Since that night three months ago, he no longer bothered to hide the fact that he followed her home.

She yanked open the passenger side door of his truck and climbed in, slamming it shut. Staring out of the windshield, she took a moment to gather her thoughts.

After a few heartbeats, she said, "He wants to kill you, you know."

"He's not going to kill me."

"But he wants to."

"Maybe so."

She twisted in the seat to face the man. The cab of the truck was dark, the only light coming from the glow of the dash. Music played at a low volume from the radio and the heater fan running created a steady hum as it chased the late fall chill out of the vehicle.

She studied him, even in the dark. "You have to stop coming to the bakery."

"I'm not going to stop, Bella."

"You need to stop following me home."

His voice was like warm dripping honey when he answered, "I want to make sure you're safe."

Bella gripped her hands together in her lap to keep from shuddering as his words washed over her. She dug her fingernails into her palms to keep herself on track. "I have Diesel; he makes sure I'm safe."

"Diesel didn't keep you safe," he reminded her softly.

She sucked in a breath. She didn't need that reminder. And it wasn't Diesel's fault; he'd had no idea what had been going on. If he had...

"I'm not seeing anyone. There's no one to keep me safe from."

"Shadow Warriors. They're not done with the Angels."

"And they never will be," she answered. Which was true. Until the last Warrior or the last Angel was dead and buried, they'd always be a threat. "If they want to get to me, neither you nor D will be able to stop them."

"I could if I'm in your bed every night."

She sighed. "Let me start from the beginning since you're apparently not getting it... He wants to kill you, you know."

Axel huffed out a breath. "He's not going to kill me."

Bella pressed her hands to her face and shook her head. "You're so fucking stubborn."

"So are you."

She dropped her hands back into her lap and they stared at each other for a few heartbeats in the dim light of the truck cab.

"Bella," he whispered, his voice holding a promise that she needed to ignore.

But she couldn't ignore it.

She leaned forward and shut his truck off before pulling the keys from the ignition. The interior went completely dark.

"Once and done," she murmured.

"What?"

"Once and done," she said louder and with more conviction.

"What are you talking about?"

"You know exactly what I'm talking about. We're going to do this once and then we're done. Got me?" She tossed his keys into one of the cup holders in the center console. "Get out of the truck."

When he didn't move and just sat staring at her in the dark, she closed her eyes, gathered her strength and shouted, "Get out of the fucking truck!"

Then she heard the driver's door open and him get out. She finally opened her eyes and opened her door, climbing down. She left the door open and pointed to the passenger seat as he came around the front of his Dodge, his face an unreadable mask. "Get in."

"Bella," he whispered again, but did what he was told, pulling himself up into his truck and settling into the passenger seat.

Even with just the distant street light, she couldn't miss the bulge in his jeans.

"Are you sure—"

"Get it out."

"Bella..."

"Get. It. Out." If he fought her, she would die right there on the spot. They needed to do this without argument. Just do it and get it over with. Once and done.

He could stop coming to the bakery. He could stop following her home.

She could get rid of him from her life. From her...

Fuck.

He could stop causing turmoil in her life because of the club, the brothers and from him being a fucking cop.

It would never work between them. So this just needed to be once and done.

Get it over with and he could move on. So could she.

Only he wasn't moving. He sat like a fucking statue in his truck, staring at her. He was going to make her do everything!

Standing next to the open door, she ripped open the top button of her jeans then tugged the zipper down. She shimmied out of them, not giving a fuck if any of her neighbors saw her outside on a cold November evening pulling her pants off.

She didn't give a fuck about anything but getting this over with.

After kicking off her boots, she peeled her jeans down her legs one at a time, leaning on the door for balance. Once her feet were free, she whipped the jeans and her boots over his lap into the truck and climbed in only wearing her heavy, loose sweatshirt, panties and socks. She got in and straddled his lap, facing him.

"Shut the fucking door."

Without a word, he pulled the door shut and hit the power locks, closing them in together.

"You didn't get your dick out," she said, sitting back on his thighs and reaching for the waistband of his jeans.

He grabbed her wrists and stopped her. "Bella, I don't have..."

She shook her head and ripped free of his grip. "I don't care." She found the top button and unfastened it, then snagged the zipper.

"But..."

She froze, her fingers still on the zipper tab, his hot length against her palm under the denim. "You know my uterus was destroyed. You *know* that. Don't pretend you don't."

He released a harsh breath. "I don't want you like this."

"This is the only way you're going to get me, Axel. Take it or leave it." His mouth opened, but before he could speak, she cut him off. "This is your one and only chance. It's this or nothing."

"I need to touch you everywhere."

"No."

"I want to see all of you."

She shook her head. "No. You don't get that."

"I'll get it. Maybe not this time, but I will."

"No, Axel."

His broad hands cupped her face as he pulled her closer, capturing her lips. Lightning shot through her as his tongue forced its way inside, sliding against hers, teasing gently. She moaned and tilted her head enough to let him take the kiss deeper. She rocked her pussy against his thighs as he reached up and tugged her hair free from the bun she wore while working at the bakery.

Her long hair spilled down over her shoulders, then he dug his fingers in tightly, grabbing handfuls and pulling her away.

"I want you," he whispered.

"I know," she whispered back.

"Not like this."

"I know."

"But if this is all you'll give me, then I need to take it."

"I know."

"Will you be mad at me for taking what you're offering?"

She closed her eyes for a second, then opened them and regarded him in the dark. She could make out his features clearly enough but not enough to read his expression. "No. I told you to take it or leave it."

He nodded, releasing her hair and reaching down to finish unzipping his jeans. With a buck of his hips, he pulled his pants down far enough to release his erection between them.

Then his palms slid up her bare thighs until they met at her panties. "I want these off."

"No, just pull them to the side."

He fisted her panties in his hands and jerked them, ripping them apart.

"Axel," she groaned.

"Fuck, Bella. *Fuck.*"

His fingers found her center, sliding between her folds, pressing, exploring, then circling her clit. She moaned, dropping her forehead to his collarbone. She inhaled his too familiar scent as he continued to stroke her plump, slick flesh, and teased her now hard nub with his thumb.

She gasped when he slipped two fingers gently inside her. Rocking her hips, she rode his fingers, surprised at how wet she was becoming. She didn't think that could happen anymore. She hadn't tested the theory since she hadn't been with anyone since that fateful day.

Not one person.

Until now.

And when his fingers curled deep inside her, he awoke something she had forgotten all about.

Desire. Want. Need.

Urgency.

Desperation.

She rocked her hips faster, encouraging him to keep it up. She cried his name against his throat when his hand snaked up under her sweatshirt and into her bra. She arched her back as he tugged one aching nipple then the other.

"Take it off, I want my mouth on you."

She shook her head. "No. Leave it on."

"Bella... I know."

Her heart thumped heavily in her chest at his confession. "I know you do."

"I don't care."

"I do."

He blew out a harsh breath but said, "Next time."

There wasn't going to be a next time. She already told him that. Once and done.

"Next time I want my mouth on you everywhere."

She ignored him, instead concentrating on what his fingers were doing to her, the response they drew from her from being both deep within her core and kneading her breast.

God, it felt so good. How could he feel so good?

"You're so wet. I want to taste you."

She wanted that, too, but it was impossible in the cab of his truck.

When he twisted her nipple roughly, she gasped and ground down onto his hand and then something wondrous happened. He crushed his lips to hers as she gasped again when an orgasm ripped through her.

Her toes curled, and her fingers grasped his shirt as she held on for dear life. Every muscle in her body went liquid as she shuddered on his lap.

As the last of the waves waned, he slipped his fingers from her and pulled his mouth away enough to whisper, "Holy shit."

Yeah, she had the same thought.

She couldn't remember ever having a reaction quite like that coaxed from her before. She had only been dominated in the past by a man who couldn't care less if she enjoyed their contact. In the end, it wasn't important to him if she got satisfaction from their sexual encounters or not. It had been all about his release, never about hers. She had been his property, his to do with what he wanted.

Unfortunately, she had been the fool to allow it, to put up with it for so long.

Axel murmuring her name against her lips drew her thoughts back to the present. His breathing was ragged, his chest rising and falling at a rapid pace. Reaching between them, she encircled his cock with her hand, running her thumb over the crown to find silky precum beading at the tip. He was hot and velvety smooth within her fingers.

He groaned when she squeezed him gently. "If you keep doing that, I'm going to make a mess between us. I want to come inside you."

She wanted that, too.

His hands gripped her ass cheeks and he jerked her forward and up, until the tip of his cock was at her opening, sliding between her folds.

"It's all you, baby," he moaned, his head falling back against the seat, but he kept his eyes tipped to her.

She shifted slightly to make sure he was lined up perfectly and sank down onto his lap slowly, until there was nothing left of him. He filled her completely.

Biting her bottom lip, she closed her eyes, reveling in the fullness, the stretch, the relief of him finally being inside her. All these years of wanting him, needing him, but keeping him at arm's length washed over her. He was finally hers if only for this brief time.

Once and done.

His fingers dug deeply into the flesh of her ass as he encouraged her to move, to lift and lower on his hard length. She followed his lead, going slowly, savoring his scent in her nostrils, his taste on her lips, as she rose and fell on his lap, taking her time, appreciating everything that made up the man she'd wanted for so long.

She wanted—no, needed—to draw this out, to take this slow, because this was the only chance she would get with him. This was the only opportunity she would allow.

Once and done.

"Fuck," he groaned. "You're so tight, baby. So tight," he hissed, then grunted as she began to move faster. "I've wanted you so much for so long…"

"Ax."

"I've wanted you to be mine forever…"

"Axel, stop."

"You're finally mine."

"Stop! Stop. Stop. Please."

He needed to be quiet, he couldn't say those things to her. She couldn't let him slip through that crack she opened only to let him in temporarily, just for this one time. If he slipped in, she'd never get him back out. And she couldn't allow that.

His hips bucked off the seat as she increased her pace, trying to let the motions drown out his words.

"Bella…"

She clamped a hand over his mouth and rode him harder, at a more frenzied pace, ignoring the kisses he placed into her hand, ignoring the tip of his tongue tracing her palm.

When he nipped her, she jerked her hand away, balling it into a fist.

His hands slid from her ass up her back and under her sweatshirt. He snagged her bra, unfastening it. And before she could stop him, he forced both the front of her sweatshirt, along with her bra, up and over her breasts, dropping his head quickly to capture a nipple in her mouth.

"Nooo," she groaned.

He didn't stop, and the pulling sensation on her aching flesh made her back bow in an attempt to press herself deeper into his mouth.

While her mind fought him, her body didn't. It encouraged him to take more than she was willing to give.

Sucking hard on one nipple, he rolled the other between his forefinger and thumb, no longer being gentle, instead giving her what she didn't realize she even wanted.

"Bella," he murmured against the damp, heated skin of her breast.

"Don't. *Please*... be quiet."

He shifted the two of them on the seat so he sat up straighter and he drove his hips up harshly, the denim of his jeans rough against her bare thighs and her sensitive flesh.

He sucked a nipple deeply into his mouth and the sharp scrape of his teeth against the tight tip made her shudder against him, made her core clench tightly around his length.

A noise escaped deep from within his throat and he dropped his hands back to her ass, grabbing handfuls of her flesh to hold her still above his lap. He was no longer letting her keep the pace. He controlled it now with the lift and fall of his hips, fucking her hard and fast. She wrapped a hand around the back of his neck and squeezed, while her other cupped his cheek as she pressed her forehead to his and gasped for breath.

"Axel," she groaned. "Yes..."

"Yes," he grunted, pounding her relentlessly until he said, "Baby, you're soaking me." Then his body stuttered, lost its rhythm, and he sank down onto the seat, allowing her to follow.

She ground her hips in a circle, needing to feel him as deeply as possible, unable to take any more of him inside her, even though she tried desperately.

Once and done, she reminded herself, as she felt the crack begin to split wider.

No, no, no.

Here and now. That's it.

That's all she had to give him.

She shoved her face into his neck and bit him hard. With a sharp curse, he shuddered beneath her, dragging his hands through her hair until he had a good hold and jerked until her neck arched and he took her lips again, swirling his tongue into the recesses of her mouth. She raked her nails down his chest, her fingers getting caught in the cotton fabric of his shirt. Tugging it up frantically, she raked her nails down his chest once again, this time into his skin. He broke off the kiss and stared into her eyes.

"Jesus, Bella."

"Make me come again," she panted. "Once more... Please."

All the breath left him as he thrust up and she ground down to meet him. He dropped one hand between them and, finding her clit, he pinched it hard.

She cried out, rocking her hips back and forth against his hand, driving his cock deeper.

She was there. He took her right *there*. To that elusive edge and then without hesitation he shoved her over. Her body became boneless, weightless, and she cried out his name as she free fell, pulsating around him. Everything about her melted against him, the pieces of them fitting together almost perfectly.

Not quite, but almost.

With a groan, his fingers dug into the flesh of her hips as he stiffened beneath her and lifted his hips once more, his cock twitching and throbbing as he spilled himself within her.

For the longest time, his body remained hard, stiff, his eyes closed, and his lips parted. Then he collapsed into the seat once more, wrapping his arms around her, holding her close, not letting her retreat.

His breath came as harshly as hers as she tried to slow her breathing, her heart still pounding a rapid beat in her chest. When he cupped her face softly, she closed her eyes to avoid what she knew she'd see in his... even in the darkness of his truck cab.

"Bella," he whispered.

She shook her head, then turned it away from him before opening her eyes. She spotted her jeans and her boots on the driver's seat and she pulled them to her chest, putting up a wall between them even though they were still connected intimately.

"No. You got what you wanted." She twisted in his lap and shoved open the truck's passenger door, letting the cold night air rush in.

"Bella," he said more firmly, grabbing at her arms, trying to keep her on top of him.

She pushed away, breaking their connection, scrambling out of the truck, even though she was naked from the waist down. Even though she could begin to feel him sliding from her, the warm silky fluid rolling down her inner thighs.

She shook her head, holding her clothes tightly against her pelvis.

"No, Axel, you got what you wanted. Now stay away from the bakery. And stay away from me."

She shut the passenger door before he could get out and ran to the house. Unlocking the door, she rushed inside, slammed it shut, twisted the deadbolt, slid the chain home, then punched the code into the alarm's keypad.

Slamming her back against the door, she slid down to the floor, and pressed her face against her bent knees.

A long, low wail escaped her before she could contain it. Then she sat there for the longest time, Axel slipping from her body one drop at a time until she felt empty once more.

Chapter Three

Axel yanked his heavy duty belt up, trying to adjust it more comfortably on his hips, as his father entered the empty patrol room.

"The captain wants you to take all the toys collected to Store-All Storage out off Route 23. The owner's donating a large unit for everyone in the area who's taking part in the toy drive."

"And the captain couldn't tell me that himself?" Axel asked, annoyed.

The same blue eyes that were in his own head stared back at him, only his father's had narrowed. "Since I'm your Corporal, I'm passing on the order. You have a problem with that?"

Axel scrubbed a hand over his short hair. He was acting like a miserable bitch and he couldn't help it. He not only got corralled against his wishes into this Toys for Tots thing, but he hadn't had his cupcake fix in a week, and he couldn't get the memory of Bella as she rode his cock out of his head. That played on a continuous loop almost twenty-four, seven.

And all of that made Axel a cranky boy.

What he needed was to climb on his bike and go for a long ride. However, unless he wanted to freeze his nads until they cracked off like a nuts-icle, that wasn't going to happen.

He blew out a breath and began to pace the small room, ignoring his father planting hands on his hips and staring at him with his eyebrows furrowed.

"What the hell is wrong with you?"

"I'm giving up sugar. It's harder than you might think," Axel growled.

"Right before the holidays?"

"Yes," he hissed.

"Well, you're acting like you're on your period. So, knock it off and eat a damn cookie or something."

"I need to go out on patrol."

"Right. Check the donation boxes while doing so, say hello to the business owners, thank the citizens of Shadow Valley for donating toys, and do a little goddamn community policing while you're at it." Mitch stepped into his path. "And if you can't resist stopping at Sophie's and shoving a cupcake down your gullet while mooning over Bella, I'll stop there later and check the box myself."

Axel halted mid-stride before he plowed right into his father. "What box?"

"At the bakery."

"I didn't put one there."

"Why the hell not?"

"Because Bella did."

Mitch's bushy eyebrows shot up his forehead. "Why? Is she helping you with the drive?"

"No. The club's doing one, too."

"Are you shitting me?" Mitch growled.

At least now Axel wasn't the only cranky male in the room. "No."

"Was this Zak's idea?"

Axel shrugged. "I don't know, but I would assume so since he's now back as president."

"I was afraid of that."

"I thought I told you."

"No, you seemed to have forgotten."

"Right. Well, they did a coup to oust Pierce and Z took back the head of the table."

"Jesus." Mitch dropped his head to stare at his patrol boots for a moment. "The prodigal son is definitely going places in life."

"Pop."

"Don't start." Mitch shook his head. "At least I have two other kids to be proud of."

"Pop."

"Once Jayde settles down and lands a decent job..."

"Pop," Axel tried again.

His father frowned at him. "What?"

"You know Z wants what's best for the club. And they're getting back to helping out the community. Look how successful the *Dogs & Hogs* event was last summer."

Mitch's eyes widened, and he barked, "They only held it because Hawk got his ass thrown in jail for *assault* and he needed to do *community service*. Did you forget that?"

"No."

"And have you forgotten what a cluster it all turned into when the Warriors rode through the fairgrounds wreaking havoc, beating up women and stealing the money?"

"No." He couldn't forget the day that Bella chased one of the Warriors through the grounds as he escaped with some of the donation money. She was on foot, the outlaw biker was on his sled and even though there was no possible way she'd catch him, she didn't give up until Axel had caught up with her and snagged her ass to take her home. Though, she fought him the whole way. He actually thought he might lose an eye that day.

He didn't, though he did end up with a couple bruises in the process since she was furious that he stopped her.

"And now my grandson or granddaughter will be born and raised in that mess. Your mother's beside herself."

No, Axel didn't believe that. Not one bit. It was his father who was beside himself. His father who cared that Zak had patched into the club as soon as he turned eighteen. His father who lost it when Z became president of the club at an unheard of early age. And it was his father who went ballistic when Z got arrested, convicted, and thrown in prison for ten years.

No, his mother still loved Z as much as she did Axel and Jayde. His mother only followed his father's bidding to keep Z out of their lives because she desperately wanted to keep the peace and keep her marriage on solid ground.

If anything, his mother was beside herself because she'd be forbidden from having anything to do with her future grandchildren.

He looked directly at the reason why. "Maybe once the baby's born, she should go buy a cupcake every day."

Mitch's nostrils flared as he stared at his youngest son. His so-called pride and joy. Axel snorted at the thought.

"Pop, you might have escaped the DAMC, but you still act like one of them."

"I don't."

"Yes, you do. You boss Mom around like she's your property and you're overly protective of Jayde."

"She's my daughter."

"She's in her fucking twenties." Not that he needed that reminder.

"So?"

Axel threw up his hands. "Do you want to lose her like you did Z?"

"What are you talking about?"

"She's got an itch to be a part of the club."

Mitch shook his head. "No. She's college educated and sending out resumes. She's going to have a good, solid, successful life."

"Pop, she's got that itch. That itch that runs through all of our blood."

"No."

"Yes! Why are you the president of the Blue Avengers? Why am I the VP? Why the hell did you name me after a bike part?"

"Because we like to ride—"

"No shit," he cut off his father. "It's in our blood. It's coursing through our veins. You just think our club's different because it's made up of law enforcement."

"It's legit. It's a family-based club, a social club."

"Pop, you grew up in the DAMC. You know their MC's more of a family than ours is."

"It's not the same."

"Maybe not in the past. Especially after your father was killed and vengeance reigned back then. But now..." Axel shook his head. "Pierce is out, Zak's in. Old school versus new school. Like I said, Z wants nothing but the best for the club. And now he's ready to raise his children like you were raised before all the murder and mayhem broke out between the Angels and the Warriors."

"That will never go away."

"Maybe not," Axel murmured.

"And the club will never be completely legit."

"It can be."

"Diesel..."

Axel sighed. Right. Diesel. The Enforcer. The go-to guy to clean up messes and to exact revenge. To provide protection by whatever means necessary.

"That crew of his..." Mitch added.

Right again. D's In the Shadow Security business. His crew of questionable former special ops guys. His "Shadows."

"They aren't DAMC," he reminded his father.

"Close enough." Mitch narrowed his eyes at him. "Why are you defending all of them?"

"I don't know."

Jesus. He did. He knew exactly why.

Bella.

If he was ever going to have a shot at her, she needed to be accepted by his family and he needed to be accepted by hers. Or it would never work.

Somehow, he had to heal the break between them all while trying to help heal her.

"Leave her alone, boy. You'll only court trouble. You know how protective D is of her. He'll kill you and then I'll have to do the same to him."

"He's not going to kill me." He'd stated that one too many times recently, though he couldn't be sure about anything the club's Sergeant at Arms would do.

Mitch snorted. "No, maybe not him. But somehow one of his so-called crew could make you mysteriously disappear."

Like that prospect Squirrel. Like the Warrior Black Jack. Just to name a couple.

Though, if anyone deserved to "disappear," it was those two rapists and violent criminals.

At this point, he couldn't care less if the investigation was ever closed on both of their disappearances and Diesel's resulting gunshot wound.

"Gotta go," Axel finally said, grabbing his patrol jacket from where it hung on the back of a chair.

Mitch only nodded his head and grunted in answer.

One side of Axel's mouth curled up as he strode from the patrol room. That DAMC blood ran deeper than his father wanted to admit.

A*h, fuck.*

After the owner handed Axel the keys, he pulled his patrol car up to the storage unit he was directed to. He had a trunk full of new, unwrapped toys that had been left in the boxes he'd dropped off at some area businesses. Though, when he had gone on his rounds, stopping to check the boxes, he'd found more than Shadow Valley PD's there. Someone from DAMC had placed their boxes right next to his. And theirs always seemed to be overflowing with toys while the PD's were only half full.

Whatever.

He knew who that someone was. He was staring right at her ass as she was bent over, digging out toys from the trunk of her car.

Since she was parked blocking the opening to the storage unit, he pulled up behind her and sat in his car, his eyes glued to her ass cheeks as they flexed while she shifted and gathered.

Fuck him.

She wore thin, tight black pants that looked like some sort of leggings similar to what his sister wore, knee-high black leather boots with a small heel, and from what he could see, no panties. Nope, that fabric was stretched tight over that luscious ass without a line or crease marring it. Well, except for the crease that ran north to south that he'd like to get more familiar with.

Axel pressed the heels of his palms into his eye sockets and ground them hard. What the fuck was he doing, eyeballing her like one of her red velvet cupcakes.

When she straightened, he could see she wore a black leather jacket that was fitted to emphasize her narrow waist but didn't in any way hide her curvy hips.

He closed his eyes as he once again pictured her rising and falling on his cock in the cab of his truck.

Fuck!

Dropping his hand to his lap, he adjusted his now raging erection to a more comfortable angle.

He took one last look at the ass that wet dreams were made of before she turned around, her arms full of packages. Her eyes widened when she spotted him, then they narrowed before she stomped into the open unit.

With a sigh, he turned off the ignition, grabbed his portable radio, and climbed out of the car. He hooked the radio onto his duty belt and the mic onto his shoulder, not bothering to pull on his jacket.

Before closing the door, he popped the trunk latch since she wasn't the only one with a trunk full of toys.

Instead of heading to the back of his cruiser, he went to her car and gathered up an armful of "loot" before striding through the open garage door. The storage unit was one of the biggest ones on the property and it was sectioned off by group. It appeared as though DAMC had the back section of the cavernous concrete block unit and their area was already filling up.

Jesus. That didn't look good for the SVPD. Shaking his head, he walked to the rear of the unit and stood behind Bella as she now bent over sorting the toys into large cardboard boxes by age and sex.

"Fuck me," he said under his breath before he could contain it.

She popped up and turned to face him, her long dark hair falling loosely around her shoulders. Hair he wanted to fist tightly while he was fucking her up against a wall.

"Why's that?" she asked. "Because the club is out-collecting the PD? Do you think it's a competition?"

Hell no, that's not why those words slipped from his mouth, but he wasn't going to tell her that. "You want to show the community how much the club is on the straight and narrow, get all in their good graces, then you knock yourself out doing so. I got nothing against it. You 'out-collecting' us isn't going to make me lose any sleep, Bella. It all goes to the kids just the same."

Her head tilted and her dark brown eyes studied him for a second before traveling down his body and landing on the hard-on that was pressing against his zipper.

Fuck.

"Sure hope you don't have that because of being around kids' toys." Then she pressed her lips together as her eyes crinkled deeply at the corners.

What the fuck.

"There's only one thing giving me that."

She reached out and snagged a couple of the packages from his arms, checking the age ranges listed on the toys and placing them in their appropriate box.

"Should I ask what?"

"Doubt you need to."

She nodded, avoiding his eyes, taking a couple more packages from him. "Doubt I need to remind you that we agreed that it was once and done."

"I don't remember agreeing."

She turned to take the last two packages from him and moved away. "Thank you for staying away from the bakery."

Axel didn't answer. He couldn't. It took every fiber of his being to stay away from the bakery. And not because he loved the cupcakes.

"Thank you for not following me home anymore," she continued.

That had been even harder for him than staying away from Sophie's Sweet Treats.

He swallowed hard. "I worry about you, Bella."

She lifted a leather covered shoulder. "Don't."

"Easier said than done."

She went to move past him, to head back out to her car, but stopped barely a foot away from him and stared up into his face. His nostrils flared as he captured her scent. Sweet, like her delicious cream cheese icing.

"What are you doing here, Axel?" she whispered.

"Same thing as you."

She nodded slightly. "Why now, though, while I'm here?"

"I didn't know you were here until I drove up."

"Would you have waited if you knew?"

He hesitated, then spoke the truth. "No."

"If I'd known you would be here, I would've brought you a cupcake."

"It was never about the cupcakes, Bella."

She nodded again, then walked away. He followed her back out to her car in silence and let her load the last of the toys from her car into his arms. She slammed the trunk closed, and they went back inside the unit. One by one she picked a toy from his arms and stacked it neatly into the appropriate box. When his arms were empty, he continued to stand there watching her move, double checking everything one last time.

"Thanks," she finally murmured, then bit her bottom lip which made his cock twitch in his pants.

He thought his erection was finally subsiding but when she sank her teeth into that plump lip of hers, it decided differently.

"Can you lock the unit up when you're done?" she said softly, her voice a bit breathy, color tinging her cheeks.

"Yeah," he grunted. Their gazes locked, and he was unable to break away from her spell.

Then his feet were moving, and he was pulling on the chain to the overhead garage door, closing them inside.

"Axel."

He ignored her and turned the latch to secure it. He spun on his heel and strode back to her, where she stood frozen in place, her eyes wide, her body solid, her hands fisted against her thighs.

Going toe to toe with her, he stared down into her face and when she dipped her head to avoid his gaze, he snagged her chin and lifted it back up.

"You're like a fucking addiction, baby. I can't get you out of my head."

He reached down and grabbed her wrists, pulling her hands away from her thighs. She was stiff and tried to jerk away.

"No," she moaned, blinking up at him, something moving behind those dark brown eyes of hers. "Once and done, Axel."

"No," he echoed her. "Never."

He raised her wrists and held them to his chest, drawing her even closer, until he could feel her warm breath beating against his throat over the collar of his uniform.

"I don't want this."

His eyes raked over her face. "Liar," he whispered.

She shook her head, not breaking their locked gaze. "We can't do this."

"The only reason we shouldn't do this is because I'm in uniform and my shift isn't over."

"That's not the only reason."

"Fuck the rest of them."

"It'll make life messy."

"When has it ever been neat?"

Her eyelids slowly lowered, and he took advantage of it by dropping his head and sliding his lips across hers. Then he did it once more, pressing harder, taking more. She kept her mouth closed until he captured her bottom lip with his teeth and tugged. When she gasped, he went for it, sliding his tongue inside. She tasted as sweet as she smelled. A mix of chocolate, icing and cinnamon. A groan escaped from the back of her throat as he took the kiss deeper, tangling his tongue with hers.

He released her wrists when he felt her fists flatten against his chest, when she stopped pulling away and leaned closer, her tongue sweeping over his lips and entering his mouth as she took control of the kiss.

And he let her.

Grabbing one of her hands, he placed it over his erection, holding it there. He pulled his mouth away just enough to tell her again, "It was never about cupcakes, baby."

He released her hand, but it remained as she traced his length through his pants with her fingertips.

If she kept touching him like that...

He blew out a breath and stepped back, needing some space.

Slowly, he unclipped the mic from the shoulder loop on his uniform and removed his portable radio, turning the volume low before setting it aside. Then with a slight tremor to his fingers, he unsnapped his belt keepers, unfastened his duty belt and carefully laid it on the concrete floor next to the radio. After releasing the Velcro on his trouser belt, he slipped it through the loops, dropping it at his feet.

In the quiet of the storage unit, he heard her unmistakable shaky inhale. Then she breathed out his name.

Suddenly she was on him, tearing at the fasteners of his trousers, ripping his zipper down, her hand diving into his boxer briefs.

"Fuck," he muttered as she wrapped her fingers around his cock and squeezed. "Jesus Christ." All the breath in his lungs escaped him as she freed him from his pants and fell to her knees at his feet.

He tried to say her name but nothing came out except a groan as she took him into her mouth. Her warm, wet tongue swept over the crown of his cock and he threw his head back and dug his fingers into her long hair.

"*Jesus... Bella... Fuck...*"

She traced the tip of her tongue up and down his hard length, then took him almost completely into her mouth. His hips shot forward, and she encircled the root with her fingers squeezing tight as she sucked him hard and fast. He dropped his head forward to watch her moving back and forth each time she sucked him deep then pulled away until only the tip was between her lips. Gripping her hair tighter, he thrust forward until he hit the back of her throat, then pulled back slightly as she hollowed her cheeks and sucked him hard.

Jesus fuck.

Holy Jesus motherfuck.

He forced out her name, "Bella."

She continued sucking him, teasing him, licking him, squeezing the root, cupping his balls.

He couldn't let this continue. Otherwise he was going to lose it.

"Isabella!"

She stopped, his cock still in her mouth. Her eyes tipped up to his. And then she smiled.

Fucking smiled. He shook his head to clear it. "On your feet." He struggled to make his demand sound like one. He hooked her under her arms and helped her up. "To the wall. Face it. Palms flat against it. Legs spread." Something he wasn't sure of moved behind her eyes. Fear? Excitement?

Her husband had been a bastard, demanding, rough and violent. Axel didn't want to be like that, didn't want to evoke those memories, but even so, he needed to take control.

When she didn't move, he said, "Now!"

Finally, she moved to an open space along the concrete block wall. Facing it, she did as she was told and raised her hands above her head, placing her palms flat on the wall, she cocked her hips back and spread her legs.

She had assumed the position.

Then he was there, kneeing her legs farther apart, sliding his erection against her ass, pressing his mouth to her ear. "I want to take you like this."

She said nothing, but he could see her pulse pounding in her neck. He swept her long hair away and pressed his lips to it, feeling the rapid beat with his tongue. She ground her ass against him, a moan slipping from her lips.

Sliding his hands around her, he found the zipper to her leather jacket and slowly tugged it down. He let one hand fall to her mound to cup it. It was hot and he could feel the dampness at the apex of her thighs.

"Are you ready for me?"

"No."

"Liar," he said softly.

His other hand slid under her shirt and then her bra, his thumb brushing over the tight tip of her nipple. He pressed his face into her neck and nibbled along her skin.

"Next time you're going to be naked against me. I want to feel your skin against mine."

"No."

He smiled. "You want me."

"No."

Releasing her mound, he pulled at the waistband of her stretchy pants and pushed his hand past the elastic and down. Just as he suspected. She had no panties on.

He lost his breath as he slipped a finger through her slick folds. "Liar," he whispered against her ear.

Her head dropped forward and he could hear her panting as she ground her ass harder against his cock.

"You want me to fuck you."

"No," she groaned.

He slipped one finger, then a second inside of her, testing her wetness. "You're such a fucking liar."

Pinching and plucking at her nipple with one hand, he fucked her with the fingers of his other. A whimper escaped her as her hips followed his movements.

"Are you going to come?"

"No."

He smiled again. "Do I need to prove you're a liar?"

"Yes."

"Come for me, Bella."

"No," she groaned again.

"Come for me," he murmured directly against her ear. "I want to feel how wet you can get for me. I want to feel you climax from my fingers. Next time it'll be my tongue and my mouth. I'm going to watch you come when I eat you. I want to hear you scream my name when you do it."

"Noooo."

"Yes. You want this."

She shook her head.

"Tell me you don't want this."

She couldn't. She didn't. Because she wanted it. She wanted him.

And he wanted her like no other.

"Come for me, baby." He twisted her nipple harder, and she arched against him and cried out.

Then he felt it, the rush of wetness, the waves of orgasm as her body clenched around his fingers and he didn't stop, he kept moving, drawing them out of her, supporting her body with his, pinning her against the wall when her knees buckled. Then she became a rag doll. The only thing holding her up was his knee between her thighs, his chest against her back, his hand on her breast and his fingers inside her.

"Did you come?" he asked, already knowing the answer.

"No."

"Pretty little liar. I'm going to make you come again when I fuck you."

"No," she moaned.

The only problem was he had no idea how to get her pants down far enough so he could do just that. Her legs were spread wide and even though her leggings, or whatever the hell she wore, were stretchy, there was no way they would stretch enough to roll them down her thighs.

Fuck.

Then she shoved him back a step with her butt, wiggled and shimmied her hips, pulling her pants down her legs. He stared at the pale globes of her ass as they were exposed and his dick kicked hard. She rolled them down to her knees, then planted her palms back on the wall and shoved her ass out.

She turned her head enough to glance over her shoulder at him. "Fuck me."

She didn't have to say it twice. Grabbing his cock, he shifted forward, slipped the head up and down her slick, plump folds to gather her natural lubrication, then pushed inside her.

He stilled, and neither said a word. Their breathing was loud, quick and hitched. Digging his fingers into the flesh of her hips, he began to thrust in and out of her soft, wet heat.

His eyes rolled back as she squeezed him tight, pushing back when he pushed forward, their bodies slamming together, the sounds of their fucking, their breathing, her soft mews the only thing surrounding them.

Her pussy felt like heaven.

But he wanted more from her. She was not a once and done for him. She was not a twice and done for him, either.

She made him lose his mind. Enough so, that he was in uniform, on duty, having sex in a storage unit surrounded by toys for needy children.

He wasn't doing this anymore with her. Only pulling his pants down enough to get his cock out. Only getting her naked enough for her to ride him. This wasn't how he wanted her. Not against a wall, not on the seat of his truck.

He wanted her spread out in his bed, so he could take his time, appreciate every inch of her, explore every nook and cranny. He wanted to savor her scent and her taste until he forgot every woman that ever came before her.

Because they no longer existed. They never existed.

It had only been Bella for him. Always been her.

He only bided his time with the others.

He watched from a distance when she became a biker's ol' lady, stepped back once again when she needed time to heal her physical wounds. Left her alone while she worked on the emotional ones.

But he was done with that. That all stopped here and now.

He reached around her to press a thumb to her clit, his fingers brushing against where they were connected, him unbearably hard, her unbelievably soft. His rhythm hiccupped for a split moment, then he drove harder, teasing her clit until she cried out and then he felt it…

Her tumbling around him, grabbing onto him, pulling him with her as he shoved his hips forward, until he couldn't get any farther inside her and, when his balls tightened, he lost it. He couldn't tell where his throbbing began, and hers ended.

He closed his eyes, his chest heaving as he sucked in oxygen, tried to slow his pulse. She released the wall and leaned back into him, keeping that connection between them. Wrapping his arms around her, he held her tight because he didn't want to let her go.

Even though where they were wasn't the most ideal place, he didn't want the moment to end.

But it had to. In moments, reality would set in.

For her. For him.

She'd go back to keeping him at a distance. He'd go back to chasing her like the stupid fuck that he was.

"I'm sorry," he whispered.

"For what?" she whispered back.

He wished she was facing him, he wanted to see her face, kiss her. But he also wasn't ready to break their connection.

"For this. For here."

She shook her head, a thick strand of her silky dark hair sliding over his cheek.

He continued, "We're not doing this anymore."

Her body jerked against him. It wasn't much, but it was enough that he felt it.

"That's for the best," she said softly, though she couldn't keep the sadness from her voice.

His nostrils flared at her assumption. "No... No more quick fucks. Next time we're doing it right."

"No."

"Yes, Bella, yes!"

"No."

"Stop saying no to me, goddamnit. I fucking love you."

She froze in his arms. He closed his eyes and cursed himself for being so fucking stupid. For revealing it in a storage unit when he wasn't even facing her.

With a noise that sounded like a wounded animal, she pulled free of him, yanked up her pants and shoved him away, her hair hiding her face.

"Bella."

"No, Axel!" she screamed as she ran to the garage door, unlatched it and pushed it open just enough for her to scoot underneath the large metal door. She slammed it shut while he still stood there, his pants wide open, hanging off his hips.

As he tucked his dick back into his pants and pulled them up, he heard her tires spinning on the gravel outside the storage unit.

He dropped his head back and screamed, "Fuck!"

Fortunately, no one heard him but a bunch of boxes and stuffed animals.

Chapter Four

"With all the help the Dark Knights have givin' us this past year with the Warriors, we're gonna do somethin' different an' invite 'em to the Christmas party. Anyone got a problem with that?" Hawk shouted over the crowd.

The common area was packed since everyone was there after the monthly church meeting, including the DAMC women, who were only allowed to enter church once the meeting was over. Because they certainly weren't allowed to take part in it. Otherwise, they might hear club business. Which wasn't for women's ears.

Bella shook her head and snorted.

"Problem?" Hawk asked, looking down at her from not only his height of six-foot-four but he also stood on a wooden box in front of the club's private bar.

"Nope."

"Got your permission to continue then?" he asked her with a cocked brow.

"Sure," she murmured with a smirk.

"'Cause thought you might be tryin' to take over," he said, sarcasm dripping from his tone.

She gave her cousin a wide smile and the middle finger at the same time.

He grunted and went back to bossing around the membership. "'Kay, well, prospects an' the women will get their orders, then."

Of course.

The only thing lower than a woman was a prospect. At least a woman could provide a receptacle for the brothers to bust a nut into.

Bella snorted again.

Kiki sidled up to her and whispered, "Are you *trying* to get him worked up? Some of you women might like angry sex, but I prefer it when he's not pissed off."

"You gotta live with him," Bella answered with a shrug.

"That's right. What you see here and what I see at home are two different people."

"Don't let him hear you say that," Bella warned.

Kiki laughed. "I know you'll keep that between us."

Kiki and Bella both gave Hawk an innocent smile when he scowled in their direction.

"Gonna close down The Iron Horse to the public so Dirty Deeds can set up in there, an' it'll give us more room since their club's 'bout as big as ours. Gonna be a crowd."

"They already know they're invited?" someone yelled out. Bella thought it sounded like Crash.

"Yep. Comin' with bells on."

"With both clubs here, at least we don't have to worry about the Warriors while everyone's eating and drinking themselves into a coma," Ivy murmured as she leaned into Bella, wrapping an arm around her waist.

"Why are you hanging on me?" Bella asked her.

"I can't hug my sister?"

Bella frowned as she looked her sister up and down. "Why are you being mushy? Are you knocked up or something?"

"No!" Ivy's eyes widened. "At least, I don't think so."

"Oh shit," Bella groaned. "Better find out before the party."

"I'm not."

"Right."

"If anyone's going to be knocked up next it's going to be Kiki," Ivy insisted.

Kiki sucked in a breath. "No, it's not. I'm still establishing my law firm in town. I don't have time to have a kid hanging off my hip."

"Hawk will do it. I could see him at The Iron Horse with one of those baby holster-thingies strapped to his chest, spit up on his cut," Jewel said, then laughed as she came up behind the group of women.

"Will you bitches shut up? The man's talkin'!"

The group's eyes swung to Grizz sitting two stools down from them, nursing a beer and yanking on his long, gray beard in agitation. Their eyes swung back to Hawk, who was scowling in their direction.

"Do you think he heard me?" Jewel whispered.

"You work with D's crew, Jewelee. No one should scare you more than those terrifying motherfuckers," Diamond reminded her, stepping behind the bar to join them.

"When did you get here?" Jewel asked her sister.

"Just now."

"Where's Slade?"

"Don't know. Don't care."

Bella curled her lips under and bit them to keep from calling her out on her lie.

"Watching the bar," Sophie announced with a sigh, her hand to her lower belly as she joined them, too.

"Are you holding onto that kid for a reason?" Diamond asked, grabbing a beer from the cooler.

Sophie grabbed a ginger ale and popped the tab on the can. "I don't want to miss it when she starts moving."

"You're only going to feel gas if you don't stop drinking carbonation," Diamond warned her.

"It helps settle my stomach."

Bella grabbed a bottle of whiskey. "Jack's going to help settle mine."

"Pour me one," Ivy said.

Bella shook her head. "Not until I know you're not pregnant."

"Who's pregnant?" Jag said, coming up to the bar and settling on a stool near them.

"No one's pregnant," Ivy told her old man quickly.

"I'm pregnant!" Sophie practically yelled.

"That's old news," Bella said.

"Baby, pour me a double," Jag said to Ivy.

Ivy snagged the bottle from Bella and poured two doubles. Then she slammed the bottle onto the bar and downed her double shot with a wince.

Facing Bella, she said, "See? Not pregnant."

Jag's eyebrows shot up his face. "You're knocked up?"

"No!" Ivy shouted.

"Thank fuck. 'Cause I'd have to spank your ass if you just did a shot with my kid in your belly."

"Holy fuck," Ivy grumbled, pouring herself another one and downing it quickly. "My belly's empty except for whiskey right now."

"Better be," Jag grumbled back.

Bella shook her head and sighed. Then she looked up at Hawk. "Are you going to finish?"

Hawk seemed to have misplaced his happy face. "Just waitin' for you all to quit your yappin'."

Bella raised her shot glass to him. "Carry on."

Hawk frowned at her and shook his head.

Bella didn't even bother to listen to everything else her cousin yelled out. It was the same old, same old. Prospects are going to do this, the women are going to do that, Mama Bear would prepare the food with help from the sweet butts and the line cooks, the band was going to play, the booze was going to flow, Dawg's girls would give lap dances, head jobs and whatever else they can be talked into. Basically, people were going to get drunk, high, and fuck.

Typical club party. Christmas or not.

The only difference would be a pine tree in the corner and that this party would be held inside instead of the church courtyard because of the weather.

Bella would probably just stay behind the bar and sling drinks all night for the brothers and their ol' ladies or their lays for the night.

If she was smart, she'd tie one on, grab one of the better looking, recently-bathed hang-arounds—if she could find one—and fuck his brains out to get Axel out of her head.

That's what she needed to do, but probably wouldn't.

Instead she'd tie one on, fill her belly full of good food, maybe dance a bit with the other DAMC women, then get a ride home before climbing into her empty bed.

Because that's what her life consisted of... the club, the bakery, and a cold, empty bed.

And she just couldn't see a man who wore a badge fitting into her exciting lifestyle. Z's brother or not.

AXEL STEPPED out of the shadows of the bakery's back parking lot. "We need to talk."

"What the fuck," Zak growled, spinning on his heels to face him. His hand went automatically to his back pocket.

Axel quickly widened his stance. "You got a knife?"

Z dropped his hand though it remained curled into a fist. "No."

"'Cause you know you can't carry a weapon. Even a knife."

"Fuck you."

Axel nodded. "You fucking hate me, and I get it."

"Don't know shit."

"No, I get it. Not one of us visited you once during those ten years you did at Fayette."

"*Your* brothers threw me in there. *Your* brothers fucked up the investigation. *Your* brothers fucked up the evidence. Neither you nor our father said a fuckin' word durin' the trial or even at the appeal. Neither of you believed that I was set up."

"Yeah," Axel said simply, because there really wasn't much more he could say. Everything his brother said was true.

"What're you doin' here, cop?"

"Said we need to talk."

"Past talkin'. Nothin' left to say. Makin' my own family now with Soph an' my son on the way. Got the club. More loyal than you an' our sire."

Axel pressed his lips together and inhaled deeply through his nostrils. "Got it."

"Good. Then nothin' to talk about."

"No, you're wrong."

"Think we're gonna kiss an' make up? You're fuckin' dead wrong on that one, *brother*."

"You have a good woman."

Z didn't answer.

"I want one, too."

"Bella," Z said softly, then shook his head. "If you're lookin' for my permission as prez, the answer's no."

"Why?"

"She's DAMC property. You know that."

"I'm not going to take her away from the club. I understand that's her family."

"You're 5-0. Ain't gonna happen."

"I'm not going to give up my career."

Z gave a sharp nod. "Even if you did, you ain't welcome in the club. Ain't welcome in her bed. Even if she wanted you."

"She wants me, Z. I want her."

"Ain't gonna happen. Fuckin' D would kill you."

His words drew a sigh from Axel. "She'll never be with a biker again, Z. You know that."

Z stared at him for a moment. "That's her choice. Not yours."

"She'll end up alone. She deserves to be loved."

"Not by you."

"She deserves better than what she had."

Z planted his hands on his hips. "Why the fuck am I still standin' in the dark talkin' to a fuckin' pig?"

"You're talking to your brother," Axel said softly.

Zak shook his head. "No. Know what a real brother does? Picks me up from prison after doin' a decade in a fuckin' concrete box. For a fuckin' crime I didn't do. That's what a real brother does. Know who picked me the fuck up? Know who my real brother is? Diesel. Not you." He snorted. "Conversation's over." He turned and headed toward the back of the bakery, to the door that lead up to his and Sophie's apartment.

"Z!"

Zak stopped but didn't turn around.

"We need to try to work this out. If not for Bella and me, then for Mom and Jayde."

Zak didn't move for the longest time, then he spat on the ground and went inside, slamming the door behind him.

"Dad know you're inviting her for Christmas?" Jayde asked, shoving a cupcake into her mouth. Her eyes rolled, and she moaned as she chewed.

He had sent his sister to the bakery to buy a dozen cupcakes because he couldn't resist not having them anymore. And he was hoping she'd run into Zak.

"Did you see Z?"

"Yeah."

"Did you talk to him?"

"Of course. And I got to touch Sophie's belly. I can't wait to be an aunt!"

Axel fought the roll of his own eyes. "Think you're going to be able to hang out with that kid the way things are now?"

Jayde's blue eyes hit him, and she frowned. "I'm sick of this fucking mess, Ax. Dad's such a stubborn old coot. I'm telling you right now that I'm going to the club's Christmas party. If you tell him, I'll never get you another cupcake from the bakery again. You'll just have to suffer."

"You're not going. Everyone will have a shit-fit." He snagged a red velvet cupcake from the pink box and peeled the paper baking cup back to take a bite. Jesus. Sinking his teeth into that moist cake was almost as good as sinking his dick into...

He eyeballed his sister and swallowed hard.

"Telling you right now, I'm going." She shoved a finger in his direction. "Don't be a snitch."

"When is it?"

"The twentieth."

Axel tucked that bit of information away for his own use.

"So, you didn't answer me... Dad know you're inviting a DAMC bitch home for Christmas?"

He shot her a frown. "Don't call her that." He took another bite of the cupcake, this time with some of the sweet cream cheese frosting.

"That's what they call them."

He cocked a brow toward his sister. "Who?"

"The brothers."

Axel snorted. "*The brothers?*"

"It's in our blood, Axel."

"No shit. You're not telling me something I don't know. And no, he doesn't know."

"Mom knows, right?" she asked.

"Of course, it was her idea."

"Oh shit. *Ding, ding, ding*, the fight is on."

"You think?" He popped the last bite of red velvet into his mouth and swirled his tongue around, savoring that sweetness. Jesus. He couldn't eat red velvet without thinking of Bella.

"Well, of course. Dad's going to be pissed that it was Mom's idea."

"I'll tell him it was my idea."

"You might find yourself outside looking in." She laughed and rubbed her hands together with glee. "And I'll be standing at the window by the warmth of the fire, waving at your cold ass with a big smile on my face as I get to open not only my gifts but yours. Yeah, so go ahead and invite her."

"Why are you such a smart ass?"

Jayde smiled. "That's in the blood, too." She finished off her cupcake and wiped her hands down her jeans. "I like Bella."

She wasn't the only one.

"Don't think she can have kids, though, after what happened to her." She raised a brow in his direction. "Might want to reconsider your choice."

That he wasn't going to do.

"Not only that, but what's it going to be like when you take her to the policeman's ball and she has to wear a gown and all her bad-ass tats are showing? How will that look to the other cops when you have a biker chick on your arm?"

Axel looked in disbelief at his younger sister. "First of all, there's no 'policeman's ball.' And, second, I don't give a shit if her whole body is tatted up."

"You don't know? Haven't you seen her naked yet?"

Axel shook his head. "Fucking Jayde."

She laughed. "I'm just messing with you. I've seen that shoulder tat of hers. It's beautiful with all those flowers and stuff. I want one just like it. I'll have to talk to Crow."

"You're not getting ink from Crow."

"Why not?" she asked with a mouthful of her second cupcake.

"Because Pop wants you to lead a respectable life."

She swallowed. "You can lead a respectable life and have tattoos, *Dad*."

"I know that. But, remember, you're still living at home."

"Better than this shitty-assed apartment."

That may be true. But at least he had his own place, unlike his sister. It was only supposed to be temporary, but five years later, he still hadn't moved into anything nicer. It was fine for what he used it for, which was a bachelor pad. He just needed a kitchen, a bathroom, and a comfortable couch with a large screen TV. He didn't need much. "At least I don't get an allowance."

"I don't get an allowance!"

"Oh, did you get a job I don't know about?"

"I may have something lined up."

Axel eyed her suspiciously. "Like what?"

"Working for Kiki."

"Doing what?"

Jayde shrugged. "Doing whatever she wants me to do. And I think Jewel's spot is open at the garage, too."

Axel shook his head. "No, Diamond took that."

"Huh. You sure keep up with the club news."

Well, he used to when he stopped at the bakery every day. Sophie would share a lot of information to keep him up-to-date on what was going on with his brother and his cousins.

"Dad might not like you working for Kiki."

"Why? She's a lawyer."

Axel held up a finger. "One, she's the club's attorney." He held up a second one. "Two, she's a *defense* attorney. She defends the people we arrest." He held up a third. "Three, she's Hawk's ol' lady."

Jayde shrugged. "He'll get over it."

"Just like he will when Bella comes over for Christmas dinner."

Jayde laughed. "Right. Looks like we're both going to piss off Dad." Suddenly, her head twisted toward him, her blue eyes wide. "Wait. Does Bella know she's coming to dinner?"

He grabbed another cupcake and took a bite.

Chapter Five

"You shouldn't be here, Axel," Bella said as she opened the door, using her body to block him from entering.

The man stood on the concrete stoop of her small rental house looking good. *Way* too good for comfort.

And that was exactly why getting her brains fucked out by a club hang-around wasn't going to help get Axel out of her mind. She'd have to have a lobotomy for that to be successful.

"I have something to ask you." His blue eyes swept over her face and down her body, pausing only for a split moment on the hard peaks of her nipples she knew must be visible through her baggy, off-the shoulder, boat neck sweatshirt. When she had arrived home from church, it was the first thing she did... ripped off her shoes and bra and threw on a comfortable top along with a pair of black yoga pants.

"You couldn't text me?" she asked, knowing full well that he probably didn't even have her number. If he did, he didn't get it from her.

"No, I needed to do this face to face."

Her eyebrows furrowed. "What?"

"Can I come in?"

"I don't think that's a good idea."

"Why?"

She sighed loudly. "You know why."

He nodded then peered over her shoulder into the house. "You're going to let all the heat out."

"Then ask quickly."

"Bella," he murmured at her stubbornness.

"Axel," she snapped back. "Ask your question and get gone."

"Please let me in."

Bella had a feeling that meant a whole lot more than just letting him into her house. "Can't do that."

He snorted. "Why? You can't resist me?"

Whether he was trying to be funny or not, Bella forced a fake laugh, even though what he just asked was true. If she let him into her house, she might not be able to resist him. Not tonight. She'd had one too many whiskeys earlier. A warmth filled her belly, her guard was down, and her inhibitions were lacking from the liquor. Not a good combination when trying to resist a man she should not let into her house.

Not if she wanted to keep him at arm's length.

Not if she wanted to keep from dragging his lean, but muscular, ass—one that without a doubt looked fucking hot in the Levi's he wore—into her bed.

Not if she wanted to keep that protective armor she wore in one piece. Because the last two times she let him peek inside, poke around, she ended up full of his cum.

And the thought of that stoked the fire in her belly more than the whiskey.

"Let me in, Bella."

She shook her head. "It's not smart."

"I just need to talk to you about something."

She arched a brow at him. "I thought you had a question."

He closed his eyes and blew out a breath, planting his hands on his hips and tipping his head down. She wouldn't be surprised if he started tapping his toe with impatience.

She shivered as the winter chill crept through the door. Releasing it, she wrapped her arms around her middle.

Big mistake.

Suddenly she found herself pushed two steps back, and the door slammed shut. The only problem was that Axel was on the wrong side of the door. He now stood inside when he should be outside, returning to his truck and getting gone.

She tossed a hand his direction. "Come on in," she muttered, then shook her head and left him by the front door to move closer to the gas fireplace in her small living room. The whiskey was no longer making her warm, but if she continued to stand that close to him, something else would.

She waved a hand over her shoulder in the direction of the couch. "Have a seat," she said, staring into the flames.

"Come join me," came way too close to her ear, making her jump. How could he be that quiet?

She looked down at his boots... which were missing. What the hell?

"Make yourself at home," she said, laying the sarcasm on thickly.

When his hand landed on her bare shoulder, she stared at it. His fingers were long, the nails neatly cut, not a speck of grease or oil underneath them. She inhaled, taking in his familiar scent that always made her body tingle. If she was a dog, she'd want to roll and cover herself in it. In him.

Fuck.

Her hard shell was beginning to split. She needed to seal the crack and do it fast.

"Bella, please come sit with me."

She shook her head, refusing to meet his eyes. "Again, Axel, not a good idea." When his fingers squeezed her shoulder, she whispered, "Please don't touch me."

"Maybe you can resist me, but I can't resist you."

I can't resist you.

She squeezed her eyes shut for a moment, then spun on him, breaking his hold. "Why? Why, Axel? Why do you want me? I'm broken. Why do you want someone so broken?"

Something she didn't recognize crossed his face. "You're not broken."

"You know just how broken I am. You know better than anyone."

"I know how strong you are."

"All show."

"It's not."

"What do you need to ask me? Please ask and get gone."

"I'm not going to leave until you sit down and talk to me." He moved to the couch, sat down and held out his hand.

Ignoring it, she went to the other end of the couch and sat, leaving a gap between them. If sitting on the couch was going to make him leave quicker, well then... "Ask."

"I want you to come to my parents for Christmas dinner."

Her eyebrows shot up. "What? Have you lost your mind?"

"No. My mother wants you there. Jayde, too."

"Really?" She didn't believe it.

"Yes, really."

"Why would they want that?"

"Because they know how I feel about you."

The air left her lungs as she remembered his statement in the storage unit. "What about your father?" When he didn't answer, she twisted to face him.

"We'll deal with that when the time comes."

"Oh no. No, we won't. I'm not going anywhere I'm not wanted. And we're not a thing, Axel. There's no reason I would come to your family's house for a holiday. None."

"It's a start."

"A start of what?"

"Us."

Her heart squeezed painfully. "There is no us."

"But there can be."

She scrubbed her hands down her face. "No, there can't. Your father will never accept me. I'm biker trash."

"Not true."

Whether he wanted to hear it or not, if his father couldn't accept his own son, who was blood, then he'd never accept her, who wasn't.

She sighed and tried again because she had to get it through his thick skull that they would never work. "I don't want you, Axel."

"Again, not true."

"You shouldn't want me."

"But I do." His chest rose and fell slowly as he inhaled deeply, like he was steeling himself for battle.

She broke their gaze to stare back at the fireplace. "Though your invitation wasn't exactly a question, my answer is no. You can go now." She pushed to her feet and before she could round the couch to head toward the front door, his hand snaked out, grabbing her wrist to stop her.

"I'm not leaving." His voice was low and gruff, his tone forceful.

She fought the shudder that wanted to run through her. She couldn't show any weakness. She needed to stay strong. Yanking her arm, she tried to break his grip. "Let me go."

"I'm not letting you go."

Her heart thumped wildly in her chest at the double meaning of his words. "You have to," she whispered on a shaky breath.

"Give me a good reason why." Without releasing her, he rose to his feet, and she avoided his searching gaze.

Jesus Christ, he was killing her. Why couldn't he make it easy and just go? "Because…" Her words got stuck in her throat. She swallowed hard and tried again. "Because you saw me… like that."

"So what?"

"So what!" she exclaimed in disbelief.

"If it doesn't bother me, it shouldn't bother you."

She squeezed her eyes shut, the past flooding over her, bringing her back to the night all those years ago that changed everything.

"That's not up to you."

Suddenly, he grabbed both of her shoulders and shook her. "The fuck it isn't! I have a say in this! I was there for you, Bella." He slapped his chest. "*Me*. I'll never forget what I saw, what he did to you. You wanted no one to know the extent of it and I've kept it locked deep inside of me. But I was the one who was there. I was the first one on the scene."

Fuck! She couldn't do this with him. Not now. Not ever.

She pointed a shaky finger toward the door. "Get gone, Axel! Get the fuck out of my house!"

"It tore me apart," he said softly, ignoring her demand.

The blood rushed into her ears and without thinking, she slammed both palms into his chest, shoving him backward. "You? It tore *you* apart?"

He caught his balance before falling back onto the couch. "Baby, if I could take that pain from you, I would."

"You can't. Just like you can't forget. Just like I can't forget."

"Bella—"

"You want to see why I'll never forget?"

Stepping back, she grabbed the bottom of her baggy sweatshirt, yanked it over her head and threw it at him. He caught it, balling it up in his hands as he stared at her, his nostrils flaring, his eyes heated.

A crazy sense of relief swept through her at his look because it would have hurt so much more if she saw pity in them instead.

She held her arms out, making sure he could see her clearly. So he could see everything. "You see that? You see how ugly he made me? He wanted to ruin me for anyone else."

"He didn't ruin you. He was the ugly one. You're still beautiful, Bella. Now more than ever."

She shook her head violently. "Don't lie to me. I'm not beautiful. And it's certainly not beautiful to be reminded every day of what I lost."

"I'm not lying. And you need to stop lying to yourself."

"I can't do this, Axel. I can't," she whispered painfully.

He cupped her cheek and asked softly, "What can't you do, baby? I'm just asking you to give me a chance."

"I can't..." She couldn't let herself ever be that vulnerable again.

He blew out a breath. "You can't love me?"

No. That wasn't it. Not at all.

She sucked in a shaky breath, then confessed, "I've loved you my whole life, Axel. My whole life."

. . .

Axel stumbled back, his head spinning at her words, the air rushing from his lungs. He struggled to collect himself. "Then, what were you doing with that asshole?"

Bella closed her eyes and whispered, "I was never good enough for you."

The pain in her words made his chest squeeze tight. "What are you talking about?"

"We weren't good enough for you, Mitch, Jayde... Hell, your family turned your own brother away. Your own blood."

"He didn't want us growing up in that mess. The constant conflict."

"It's family, Axel. You deal with the good along with the bad."

She was so right. Only it took him until recently to realize that.

"Now, you need to go," she said softly. She held out her hand for her sweatshirt. "I need to cover up."

He held it behind his back out of her reach. "No, you don't. I want to see you... Let me love you, Bella."

A small sound escaped her as he took the two steps forward and cupped her face in his hands.

"I don't care how many scars you have on the outside. I don't care how many are on the inside. I love you... scars and all."

"Axel," she whispered. He couldn't miss the trembling of her bottom lip.

"Bella, please." He pressed his lips to her forehead, then both eyelids, down her nose until finally he took her mouth hard, deep and wet until her groan bubbled up between them.

He pulled away, breathing hard. He brushed his thumb over the inch-long scar right below her left shoulder. He knew exactly where each and every scar was on her body without even looking. It wasn't because he'd seen them after they healed.

But because he saw every bleeding stab wound that fucker had caused. Because he was the first one on the scene. He was the one who found her crumpled in a corner of the kitchen, bleeding out. He was the one who rushed in, falling to his knees in a puddle of her blood to check her pulse and press his hands to the wounds in a futile attempt to stop the flow. But there were too many wounds for him to stop them all. He was the one who screamed into his radio mic to send all emergency responders, code three, to her apartment.

He was the only one who knew she was pregnant after she begged for him to save her baby. He'd hardly heard her plea since she was only half conscious. But his blood had frozen in his veins when he saw the stab wounds along her abdomen.

No one ever knew she was pregnant. Only her bastard biker husband, Axel and the medical staff who did the emergency surgery and who cared for her afterward in the hospital.

No one knew. Not her family. No one in the club. Not her husband's family.

Not even Diesel.

It was something he had to live with, to tuck away when she begged him not to say anything to anyone. Everyone thought she had to have the emergency hysterectomy due to the multiple tears in her womb. She had hardly been showing so it was easy for her to keep her secret.

But it wasn't so easy for him. He kept picturing her child. Maybe a little girl with her dark brown eyes and equally dark hair, with her spirit. A miniature of Bella herself.

It took everything he had not to hunt the bastard down before Diesel did. Neither of them got the chance. The asshole was arrested, charged, and eventually ended up in SCI Greene where Doc and Rocky were both doing life. The former Dirty Angel was murdered in his cell. Though it was ruled a suicide, everyone knew better.

And no one cared. Death had been too good for Bella's old man. But at least she was finally free of him.

While free of him legally, she was still not free from the damage and heartache he caused.

Dipping down, he hooked her behind her knees and along her back, holding her close to his chest as he strode out of the living room. Her bedroom was easy to find since she only had one, her single-story rental house smaller than most apartments.

After gently laying her in the center of the bed, he turned on the lamp that sat on the nightstand. The Harley bandana draped over it gave the room a soft orange glow.

Her bed was small, possibly a double. It was as if she never planned on anyone joining her in it. But tonight, that was going to change.

Standing at the end of the bed, he peeled his Henley up and over his head, tossing it aside. His cock twitched in his jeans as her eyes raked over his chest. This was the first time she was seeing him without a shirt on since they became adults. And this time he was definitely taking his jeans all the way off, so he could feel her against him.

This was not going to be a quickie. No fucking way. He wanted it all tonight. He wanted all of her.

"Baby, you can say I shouldn't want you a million times but that doesn't change the fact that I do. It's only ever been you, Bella."

Unfastening his jeans, he pushed them down his legs along with his boxer briefs and pulled everything off in one shot, including his socks. He dropped them to the floor and stood, his cock hard and ready as he climbed onto the bed.

She didn't move, she didn't try to escape. She didn't say a word as he moved over top of her.

He dug the fingers of one hand into her hair and tipped her head back. She closed her eyes as he lowered his. "It's only ever been you," he whispered again against her lips.

Her fingers wrapped around the back of his neck as he crushed his lips to hers. Her other hand trailed down his chest, over his belly, until she encircled his cock, gently stroking him.

With a groan, he broke the kiss and shoved his face into her neck as her fingers worked their magic, sweeping over the head of his cock, sliding along his length, brushing against his sac.

He sucked in a breath as her hand moved faster. He couldn't let her do that. "Bella, don't. Let me take care of you first."

Her hand stilled but didn't let him go, her breath coming in pants close to his ear. He kissed along her collarbone, over the colorful flowers of her large tattoo, over the thick, raised scar on the other side. He continued across her chest, placing a light kiss on each nipple, then the puckered scar on her right breast, then the one at her ribcage. He brushed his mouth across her belly, stopping at the two ragged scars above her navel and the one below it.

He pushed her pants down far enough to trace his tongue along the long horizontal scar above her pelvis. The incision which removed both the life she'd created and the possibility of creating any future life within her.

She whimpered as he did it again. He expected for her to tell him to stop, but she didn't. Instead, she lifted her hips slightly and began to shove her yoga pants down farther. He pushed her hands away and grabbed the elastic waistband to tug them down her hips until her pussy was barely exposed. Pressing his nose into the apex of her thighs, he inhaled her scent and suddenly he was impatient to taste her.

Scrambling back onto his knees, he yanked the pants down to her ankles and over her feet, tossing them to the floor. Starting at the tip of her painted toes, he kissed each one, over the top of her feet, up her calves, letting his fingers trail over her skin following the path of his mouth. Then he was there, settling between her legs.

"Open for me, baby."

When she didn't, he pressed her thighs apart gently, encouraging her to bend her knees.

"Axel," she groaned.

"Beautiful," he whispered, before taking her with his mouth, dipping his tongue inside her. "Sweet in the center just like your cupcakes." He swirled his tongue around her clit. "As delicious as your icing." Running his tongue through her folds, he captured her slick arousal. With his own groan, he sucked on her clit, making her hips jump off the mattress.

He lifted his head. "As much as I love your responsiveness, we don't have a lot of space here, baby. Don't knock me off the bed."

"No. More."

With relief that it was two sentences and not one, he smiled against her soft, swollen flesh and continued to do whatever he needed to do to make the mews and whimpers escape her, to make her dig her fingers into his hair, her nails into his scalp. Her cries were music to his ears when he slipped two fingers inside her, finding her center hot and tight. Curling them, he stroked her spot until her body shuddered, and she slammed her palm on the bed, her hips shooting up, dislodging his mouth as she came hard. As soon as her hips returned to the bed, he was up and over her, plucking at her tight nipples with his lips and teeth.

She was driving him crazy. He couldn't be gentle anymore, he couldn't hold back any longer. He had to make her his.

He tweaked one nipple hard and her back arched off the bed. Sucking the other one deep into his mouth, he reached down and lined himself up against her entrance.

He struggled to get out his question. "You want me?"

"Yes," she cried out, her head back, her eyes closed.

"Bella, look at me."

After what seemed like forever, she opened her eyes and met his.

"You love me?" he asked.

"Yes."

With a tilt of his hips, he thrust home.

Home. Right where he belonged.

This wasn't in the dark cab of his truck. This wasn't in the cold, stark storage unit. He was in her house, in her bed, in her.

She had finally let him in. She had finally let him come home.

Digging his hands into her hair, he pulled her head back and scraped his teeth along her throat then kissed the hollow of her neck.

He began to move faster, harder, her wet heat surrounding him, drawing him deeper. He couldn't get enough of her.

Not nearly enough.

When her heels dug into the back of his thighs, he realized she was saying something.

"Harder, fuck me harder."

The last two times he had held back. He lifted his head. "You sure?"

"Yes... please. Give me everything you've got."

Taking her mouth again, he did just that. He twisted both of her nipples between his fingers and began to pound into her as hard as he could. The sounds coming from her throat encouraged him to keep going. Her nails raked over his ass and up his back.

She twisted her head to break his kiss. "Fuck me harder."

"Bella..."

"Do it, Axel. Do it. Make me feel alive again."

Jesus. His pace skipped a beat, and so did his heart at her words. "I don't want to hurt you."

"You won't. I'm not going to break."

Fuck, he hoped not. But he did what he was told, even though he knew it would push him to his limits, that if he fucked her at a frenzied pace, he wouldn't last.

"You might not break... but I will..."

"Then make me come again before you do."

Right. Easier said than done. He was already hanging by a thread. The harder she clenched down on him, the wetter she got...

Fuck, he just wanted to let go inside her, but he didn't want to leave her hanging. He wanted this to be about her, to please her. For her to see how they fit perfectly, how they belonged together.

That no matter the differences in their lives, they should tackle them together.

He pressed his mouth to her ear. "Come for me, baby. Feel how hard I am for you. That's all you, baby. All you. That's what you do to me."

"Axel..."

"What, baby?" he murmured, hoping like hell that she was getting close.

"Shut up."

He froze, then realized her body shook beneath him in laughter. He smiled into her hair.

"Just for that, I should just come and say to hell with you."

Bella grabbed his ass, digging her nails in. "You'd better not!"

He tilted his hips, driving into her hard. "Oh, yeah. That's what I'm going to do."

"No, you won't..." she said, but this time her demand was breathy.

He winced as she dug her nails even deeper, encouraging him to thrust faster. "No... you... won't... ah, fuck, Axel."

"Uh huh. You want all this Axel goodness," he teased, grinding his hips in a circle.

She snorted. "You're supposed to be making me come, not making me laugh."

"I love hearing you laugh, baby. Even more than I love being inside you."

"Axel..." she breathed, her humor fleeing her. "*Fuck*, Axel, right there."

"There?" He thrust again. "Right *there*?"

"Yes... *oh, please...*"

"Please what?"

"Please stop talking!"

He chuckled. "Guess I'll need to keep my mouth busy."

"Mmm hmm," she murmured against his mouth as he took hers. But he didn't have it very long, because moments later, she threw her head back, crying out as her orgasm raced through her.

"Oh, thank fuck," he muttered as he grimaced and finally let himself go with a groan. His cock jerked deep inside her as he emptied himself, his balls thanking him for the relief.

He pressed his damp forehead to hers, her eyes still closed. "Baby, look at me."

When her eyelids fluttered open, he murmured, "Everything's going to be fine. I promise."

Chapter Six

WITH HIS HEART pounding in his chest, Axel sat straight up in bed to something that sounded like a large redwood crashing to the forest floor.

Bella rolled away from him, gathering the sheet to her chest. "What the hell was that?"

"Stay here," he told her, scrambling from the bed and trying to find his boxer briefs where he'd thrown them on the floor earlier. Instead, his fingers brushed against denim. Tugging his jeans up and over his hips, he didn't bother to fasten them. He headed toward the bedroom door, but quickly returned to the bed to grab his .38 off-duty revolver from the nightstand. He unholstered it as he rushed to the door. Pressing his body to it, he listened carefully.

"Axel," she called softly, the tremor unmistakable in her voice.

"Quiet," he whispered.

Then he heard a rush of heavy footsteps and the bedroom door crashed open, knocking him back into her dresser. The corner of it caught his ribs, and he grunted from the impact, his gun slipping from his fingers.

The sudden overhead light blinded him for a moment, then he heard Bella's gasp and before he could react, a big, beefy hand grabbed his neck and hauled him out of the room, throwing him across the narrow hallway.

"What the fuck!" Axel yelled as he slammed into the drywall across from her bedroom door, cracking it.

"Fuckin' pig! Stickin' your dick where it don't belong."

Oh fuck.

"Diesel!" Bella screamed.

"Fuckin' stay there," he barked over his shoulder, not taking his eyes off Axel.

Axel's chest heaved as he tried to retrieve the air that had been knocked out of him for the second time. He took in the larger man and all his fury.

This was not good. It was even worse than coming face to face with an armed intruder.

Then Diesel's finger was in his face. "Told you to stay away. Told you not to touch DAMC property. Fuckin' did it anyway. Now you gotta pay."

Axel brought his palms up. "D..." he started as if reasoning was going to work.

Diesel shook his head, his brows low, his jaw tight, a vein throbbing in his forehead. "No. No fuckin' way. Nothin' you say's gettin' you outta this."

When D took a menacing step forward, Axel drew himself up to his full height, which still wasn't nearly as tall as the massive biker. Jesus, he was a good fifty pounds lighter, too. If Diesel wanted to kick his ass, there wasn't going to be much Axel could do about it. And his gun was in the bedroom. He was going to have to say, "Thank you, sir, may I have another?"

Out of the corner of his eye, he noticed Bella rush to the bedroom doorway, the sheet wrapped around her. "Diesel! Get out!" she screeched.

D ignored his cousin as the man's nostrils flared. Axel wouldn't be surprised if he saw smoke and fire shoot from them.

"You're fuckin' dead, pig," came low and menacing from the man he'd known his whole life, but wasn't close to. He'd never been allowed to hang out with any of the DAMC kids. He'd always been kept apart from them, even his own blood relatives.

"Diesel..." Again, he could attempt to reason with the man, but Axel doubted it would do any good. However, he knew it just wasn't feasible to fight Diesel. He would lose and lose badly.

"D, you touch him..." Bella let the warning drift off.

"Then what?" D barked.

"Swear to Christ, I'll leave the club. You won't ever see me again."

Diesel grunted, his dark eyes still pinned to Axel. "Bullshit, woman, ain't goin' nowhere."

"Try me."

Fuck. Axel suddenly felt less than a man, and even less of a cop, by having a woman fight his battles. Sucking in a breath, he pushed away from the wall and took a step toward Diesel. "You want to hit me, D? Will that make you feel better? You can beat the fuck out of me and that still isn't going to stop me from being with her. That isn't going to stop me from feeling how I do. So go ahead. Fucking hit me. Pound the shit out of me. Take all your rage out on me. I don't give a fuck. Because she's fucking worth it."

A muscle in Diesel's jaw ticked, and Axel swore he could hear him grinding his molars. Anger blazed behind his eyes.

"You know I can't take you, even with all of my training and experience. You outsize me, outweigh me, and you're like a fucking raging bull when you're pissed. But you want to take a swing?" Axel raised both arms up. "Then do it."

The huge fist emblazoned with the letters D-I-R-T-Y on the fingers barreling toward his face was the last thing he saw.

"Guess you shouldn't have parked your truck in the driveway."

Axel tried to laugh, but instead he groaned as pain shot up his jaw. He pressed the bag of frozen peas tighter to his face.

"Want me to take you to the hospital?"

"No."

Her fingers swept over his short hair as the back of his head pressed against her collarbone. His nose had finally stopped bleeding but had started to swell, his left eye was nothing but a slit, and, luckily, his jaw wasn't dislocated. He wiggled it again just to make sure.

"Did he break your door down?"

"Yeah," she answered softly, running her palms over his bare chest as he leaned back into her. She wore his long-sleeved Henley, and she had settled him between her thighs on the couch as she tended to him. "He propped it back in place as best as he could. He said he'd get the prospects over here in the morning to fix it."

He glanced over toward the door. A heavy blanket covered it, too, to help keep out the draft. "Landlord's going to be pissed."

Her shoulder lifted and fell. "If so, I'll get D to cover it. Love the man but he can be a complete dick."

He put a hand on her bent knee and squeezed. "Sorry I couldn't defend your honor."

She snorted. "I almost died when you told him to take a swing at you."

"Yeah, me, too," he murmured. Because that was so true. When he saw that fist headed his direction, all he could think was, "Oh fuck!"

Bella said he was out cold for a good ten minutes. Apparently long enough for her to kick Diesel's ass out of her house and at least fix the door somewhat on his way out.

"That was stupid," she murmured, her fingers still brushing over his hair. Now he understood why dogs loved to be petted so damn much.

"I'm not backing down, Bella."

Her chest rose and fell behind him as she took a deep breath. "And that's stupid, too."

He shook his head but then cursed when his whole face began to throb at the movement. "He's going to have to accept me. They all are."

There was a long hesitation before she answered, "Right."

"My family's going to have to accept you."

"You know that won't ever happen."

"It'll be a start."

"To what?"

"Mending fences."

"Mending fences?"

"Z and my father. Z and me."

"Even if your family... your father accepts Zak..." She sighed. "Axel, the brothers are never going to accept you."

"You don't know that."

"I do. You're a cop. 5-0."

"A pig?"

"Yeah." She chuckled. "That, too."

"They don't need to accept me as a cop." Though it sounded good, he wasn't sure it was even possible. But it was worth a shot even if he had to take a few more beatings from Diesel. He groaned at the thought. The man had knocked him out with one punch. Men like him were the reason cops carried tasers and guns. The man's fist could be considered a lethal weapon.

"Then what?"

"As your..."

"Old man?" she asked.

"No." No fucking way would he ever call her his ol' lady. He may love to ride, be VP of the Blue Avengers, but he was not that type of biker. Never was, never would be.

"Then what?" she asked again.

"As your man."

She got quiet, and he wished she wasn't sitting behind him so he could see her face.

"Axel..."

"Bella..."

She sighed.

"When I'm with you, I'll be Axel Jamison, brother to the DAMC prez, grandson of one of the founding members. When I'm working, I'll be Officer Jamison and stay away from the club... unless I'm needed in an official capacity."

"Right. Like arresting one of the brothers."

"If I have to."

"Right, Axel. And there's the rub."

"I'm not giving up my career."

"And I'm not giving up the club. They're my family."

"You threatened Diesel that you'd leave if he touched me."

Silence answered him.

"You were blowing smoke."

"Yeah," she said so softly he wouldn't have heard it if her mouth wasn't so close to his ear. "I was just trying to get him to stop. See reason."

Axel snorted, then winced at the pain it caused. "Diesel see reason? Laughable."

"He's got Jewel now; he needs to start."

Right. Axel's cousin, Jewel, and him were now shacked up. "They get hitched, he and I will officially be family."

"Don't expect that anytime soon," Bella warned him.

He hadn't expected Zak to get married, either. Then Sophie came along, and his brother was suddenly whistling a different tune. And now she was carrying Axel's niece or nephew. "If she gets pregnant..."

"D as a father. Holy fuck."

"I second that."

"Fuck. That could happen, though," she whispered. "Picture it, some toddler calling D Daddy. Holy shit."

"Sorry, I can't see him changing diapers, giving a baby a bottle, and him holding hands with a toddler as he walks the kid over to a swing set to push her on the swings."

"One good push and he'd shoot that poor kid all the way to the moon."

"Fuck. Don't make me laugh. It isn't fun when your nose is smashed."

"Probably broken. You should get it looked at."

He probably should, but he liked where he was currently settled at the moment and that was between Bella's legs on her couch in her house. He wasn't giving that up anytime soon. "I straightened it. It'll be fine."

"Axel…"

"Bella, it's fine. It'll give me some character if it heals crooked."

"I love your face the way it is."

He sucked a breath through his mouth. "Yeah?"

"Well, not right now."

"Fuck! Stop making me laugh."

Her body shook beneath his as she laughed, too.

"He did what?" Diamond screamed.

Bella winced. The meeting of the DAMC sisterhood had officially commenced in Sophie's Sweet Treats.

Bella couldn't stop thinking about what Axel had asked her, so she wanted to run it past her club sisters. She had texted everyone and told them to get their asses to the bakery. Of course, they did, expecting some juicy news.

Which was exactly what Bella was giving them.

"Hold up. Did you guys sleep together?" Diamond asked.

"I don't think she needs to answer that. It's pretty obvious," Ivy said, propping a hip against the bakery counter and crossing her arms over her chest. The redhead gave her a big smile. "Jag's going to shit a brick."

"They all are," Jewel added.

Bella didn't volunteer the fact that Jewel's old man already knew. Though, she wouldn't be surprised if D hadn't told her what he'd done, since he was a man of little words.

"I'm not telling you this so you can run to your men and flap your gums," Bella said, frowning. "I need your advice."

"My answer is hell yes!" Sophie yelled. "About time you two got together. I think it's time to celebrate with a sugar rush."

"I second that!" Kelsea shouted. Bella's youngest cousin snagged a cupcake before Sophie could even pull the tray completely out of the display case.

Sophie offered Bella one, but she shook her head. "I don't think it's a good idea."

"To eat a cupcake?" Kelsea asked with a full mouth.

"No, to go to dinner at the Jamisons."

"I think it'll be a start, Bella, I really do. It could mean healing the rift between Mitch, Axel and Z," Sophie said.

Bella shook her head. "Mitch is pretty damn stubborn."

"And Z isn't? Where do you think he got it from?" Sophie asked. She pressed a hand to her stomach. "This baby needs her grandparents. Her aunt and uncle, too."

"She'll have all of us," Ivy reminded her. "No matter what, we'll all love her."

"Again, if this baby is a girl, Z might cry. Just warning you now. He might even try to shove her back in and tell you to try again," Jewel joked.

Sophie swatted a hand in Jewel's direction. "He won't care."

Bella raised her brows. She hoped Sophie was right.

"If it's a girl, she'll have him wrapped around her finger, just like he is with you," Diamond scoffed.

Ivy looked to Bella. "Why isn't Kiki here?"

"She's working on a case," Bella answered. "She said to save her a cupcake."

"Are we that predictable?" Ivy asked, laughing.

"Hell yes, we are," Jewel said, taking another bite of their newest cupcake concoction, Cookies and Cream. Vanilla icing, Oreo crumbles on the top, and the best part was an Oreo baked in the middle of the chocolate cake. Bella would have to bring one over to Axel's since they both decided it was best if he stayed away from the bakery for now.

"So anyway, I think you should go," Sophie said, getting back to the reason they were all gathered.

"I do, too," her sister piped in.

Bella looked at Ivy. "You're not the one who'll have to spend an uncomfortable evening with someone who hates you."

"Uncle Mitch doesn't hate us," Jewel said. "He just wanted to keep his family separated from the club lifestyle, that's all."

That's all? That was enough.

"Right, we're not good enough for him and his precious family," Diamond added, wiping some stray icing off her lip.

Bella threw a hand out in her direction. "See? Diamond understands it."

"Di needs to get laid," Jewel grumbled under her breath.

Kelsea shot Diamond a look. "I thought you and Slade..." She drifted off since it was hard not to miss the sudden stormy look on the woman's face.

"No."

"But..." Suddenly, Kelsea smiled. "Oh fuck! Can I go for it? He's fucking hot!"

A groan rose from everyone but Kelsea and Diamond.

"Sure," Di answered, even though her answer did not match her expression.

Bella would be sure to pull her youngest cousin aside and tell her that wasn't a good idea. But she would wait until Diamond wasn't around, especially now that Di was shoving another cupcake into her mouth with a vengeance.

She had no idea what, if anything, happened between Di and Slade. The last thing she'd heard was she'd been on the back of his bike on a few of the club runs during the summer, but she hadn't heard anything since. Not that she'd asked, either.

Bella couldn't quite get a bead on Slade, but she had a feeling that he wasn't ready for Diamond to get her claws in him. Being the newest fully-patched member, he probably wasn't ready to have an ol' lady or even someone permanently on the back of his bike.

But being a former Marine, the man had some manners, unlike most of the other brothers. He actually treated the club sisters with respect. Though, Diamond tended to be a bit hard to swallow and probably wore on his patience.

Bella had to agree with Kelsea, though, the man *was* fucking hot!

However, Slade wasn't her problem, Axel and his invitation was.

Luckily, Ivy got them back on track. "Go. Jayde, April and Axel will be fine. You'll just have to deal with Mitch if he decides to be a dick."

"And it's a free meal," Kelsea teased.

"I think it will be not only good for you and Axel, but for Z, too. Like I said, I think it could be the first step into healing that broken relationship," Sophie said.

"So, I'm the sacrificial lamb," Bella murmured.

"Depends. Is he worth it?" Sophie asked softly.

The jury was still out on that one. Was he worth it in bed? Hell yes. Was being with him worth the turmoil between the club and his family? She wasn't so sure.

The only good thing about being with Axel was that he wasn't a biker, so she'd never be treated as property.

She'd been there, done that, and got the T-shirt. And now the sweatshirts and tank tops that all claimed she'd be the "property of no one."

"Wouldn't everyone shit if you brought him to the club Christmas party," Diamond exclaimed.

"Yeah! Tell him you'll suffer through his family dinner if he comes to the party," Jewel said, slapping her thigh in amusement.

"That may be a good idea," Sophie murmured.

Bella's jaw fell open. "For fuck's sake, has everyone lost their mind?"

"Why? He's my blood. So is Jayde," Jewel said. "Why shouldn't they be able to attend?"

"Uh... How's this for a good reason, Diesel came over last night, broke down my door and practically knocked Axel's block off?"

"He did what?" Jewel asked, her face turning dark.

Whoops. Shit.

"Oh fuck," Ivy muttered.

"Is he okay?" Sophie asked. "What the hell's wrong with D?"

"I think his nose is broken, though he wouldn't let me take him to the hospital. He's got a shiner and a sore jaw."

"Damn," Kelsea whispered.

"Fucking beast!" Jewel screamed, grabbing her coat and quickly leaving the bakery.

As the door slammed behind a raging Jewel, they all looked at each other.

"Uh oh," Ivy murmured.

"Probably like Axel, Diesel's not going to know what hit him," Diamond snickered.

"Well, if Axel stuck around after Diesel clobbered him, I'm assuming he's serious about you," Kelsea said.

"He's always been serious about her," Bella's sister said. "She's just ignored all the signs."

"No, she's always felt the same way," Sophie added.

"Um, hello? I'm standing right here," Bella exclaimed. "And my love life, sex life, or whatever this is, isn't any of your business."

"Then why'd you text us all to meet you here?" Kelsea asked.

Good question. Her mistake.

Chapter Seven

"Did you empty the Toys for Tots boxes?" Axel asked as soon as he opened his apartment door.

He stepped back and she stepped inside, shooting him a frown. "Not today. I came directly here from the bakery."

"So you didn't empty the PD's boxes in the last couple days or even the club's?"

"No, I didn't get a chance." Her dark brown eyes narrowed. "Why?"

"Fuck," he whispered to the door as he closed it.

"What?"

He turned and regarded her. He was thrilled she'd agreed to come over after work for dinner and really didn't want to dampen the evening with bad news, but she needed to know. "I checked our donation boxes, and they were all empty."

"Okay?"

"And so were yours. I thought maybe you just grabbed everything at once and took them out to the storage unit." Or he had hoped to hell that she had.

"No, I didn't... Shit!"

"Yeah, shit. When's the last time you were out there?"

"The last time I emptied the boxes... three days ago."

"I'm going to take a ride out there tomorrow. I have a feeling about this."

She chewed on her bottom lip and suddenly he was very jealous of her teeth. "Oh, fuck. Please don't tell me someone stole all the toys."

"Hopefully, not. Or at least, just the ones in the boxes."

"How could someone get away with that? Those boxes sit inside local businesses."

Axel cocked an eyebrow at her. "Just get a biker to say he's collecting for you. I'm sure you sent prospects to do a few rounds."

"Fuck. I... The Warriors!" she spat out.

That was his fear, too. Those fucknuts did anything to screw the Angels and he wouldn't put it past them to steal toys collected for needy kids. He knew the DAMC was done with dealing with the rival bikers' shit and he expected some sort of war to break out at any time. The pot shots they took at DAMC were getting more and more dangerous. Theft was one thing, the kidnapping, rape and assault was another. As was throwing a Molotov cocktail into Sophie's bakery that could have caused great harm and damage both to Z's woman and the business.

If there was any way that the Shadow Valley PD could disband that outlaw MC, he'd be on it. Problem was, they were a nomad club, never settled anywhere and the havoc they wreaked usually was of the hit-and-run variety. Like when they stole the donations at last summer's *Dogs & Hogs* fundraiser.

They were not only an all-around nuisance, but a dangerous one.

Though, when it came to dangerous, so were Diesel's "Shadows" who Axel was sure were hunting down Warriors. He couldn't prove it, but after Kiki, Jazz and Jewel were kidnapped by a Warrior named Black Jack and then Diesel was shot, he knew D wasn't going to just sit back and let something else happen. He'd strike first. Or he'd send the men from his crew at In the Shadows Security to do it.

Axel wasn't stupid. He knew the MC's Sergeant at Arms was keeping the club "clean" by using his own men to do his dirty work.

"I'll do a report, try to get a description from the business owners or employees of the person or people who emptied them, but I have a feeling..."

She groaned. "No. That unit better not be empty. It wasn't just our toys or the PD's donations in there."

He put an arm around her shoulders and squeezed. "I know."

"Thousands and thousands of dollars' worth."

Like he needed a reminder of how great of a loss it would be. The thought made him sick to his stomach. "I know, Bella."

If Bella hadn't agreed to come over, he would've gone out there tonight to check. But there was no way he was letting her back out of his apartment, even to run to the unit with him, now that she was here.

"I'm going to get Diesel on it."

Oh fuck. "No. I'll handle it; the PD will handle it."

"If it's the Warriors..." Her eyes slid to the side.

"Bella, look at me." He waited until she did before saying slowly, "I will handle it."

"Axel..."

Axel switched to his cop's authority voice. "It's not even a discussion. Keep him out of it. Keep them all out of it. Do you hear me?"

Bella said nothing.

He sighed.

"They're going to find out and then what you and I say won't matter. If D wants to handle it, you're not going to have a say, Axel."

"Then we're going to keep it quiet for as long as possible. This will be done the right way. The legal way." He frowned at her when she didn't answer. "Bella, seriously."

She raised her hands. "Not up to me. I'm not going to hide the fact that the toys were stolen. It needs to be addressed. Especially if the Warriors are responsible. The Knights were doing their own collection. I'll have to check with them to see if they were hit, too."

Say what? "You talk to the Dark Knights?"

"They're good allies."

"Are you serious? They're outlaws."

"You know they helped out at your brother's wedding, right? And they helped support the *Dogs & Hogs* event."

"I'm aware of that. I was at the fundraiser, remember?"

"How can I forget?" she muttered.

Axel smiled, then quickly stopped since doing so still shot pain through his face, especially his nose. "Fuck."

"What?"

"My face still hurts."

She smirked. "Yeah, it looks bad."

"Thanks."

Bella shrugged. "Your dick isn't hurting, is it?"

"That's all you want from me, what's hanging between my legs?"

Her smirk widened into a smile. "It's a start."

"Jesus, please don't make me laugh."

"Did you go see a doctor today?"

He sure did, right after he called off from work. He certainly didn't want any of his brothers in blue to see his face in the shape it was in. Though, he knew he couldn't avoid it forever, since it would take a while for the bruises to fade. He'd need to come up with some sort of story other than a big-ass biker doing a single K-O punch. "Yeah."

"And?"

"It's fractured. It'll heal fine. They also did an x-ray to make sure nothing else was broken."

Her dark eyes searched his face with concern. "Fuck, I'm so sorry."

Hell, having her look at him like that was worth getting knocked out. "Not your fault."

"It is. D's only super protective of me because..." She drifted off.

"While that may be a part of it, I know it has to do with me being a cop, too. And then there's the whole Z thing."

"You two are so different," Bella murmured.

True, he and Zak were very different, but polar opposites apparently ran in the family. "Well, so are Rocky and Mitch."

"Yep, nothing more opposite than your father being a cop and your biker uncle doing life in prison for murder. Hmm. Kind of reminds me of you and Z. One brother's a cop, the other did time." When Axel opened his mouth to respond, Bella stopped him by holding up a finger. "For a crime the Warriors set him up for, by the way."

Right. Fuck.

They were supposed to be having a nice dinner, and then, if it was up to him, getting horizontal in a bed much bigger than her tight double. He woke up in her bed this morning with her practically on top of him, her slobber pooled on his bare chest and his back muscles tight and cramping since he pretty much had to make sure they didn't hit the floor during the night.

It probably would have been better to stay on the couch. One thing was for certain, either she was getting a new bed or they were getting together only at his apartment in the future.

However, he knew his apartment was nothing to write home about. It was a typical bachelor pad. Sparse, unkempt, and only held manly things like a big screen TV, the latest gaming system, huge-ass surround sound speakers, an old mismatched couch and recliner, a beat-up coffee table, and a fridge full of beer... but more importantly, his king-size bed. He'd splurged on that. He had a quality mattress, excellent pillows, and it was big enough to do a lot of different positions with his woman while naked.

He eyeballed Bella in her snug-fitting jeans, knee-high boots, and white top that had a deep V crisscrossed with laces that showed off just enough cleavage to give him a chubby. Her long dark hair had been released from the bun she normally wore at the bakery, so it fell midway down her back in soft waves that he wanted to shove his face and fingers into.

"Axel."

"Hmm?"

"Are you going to stare at me all night?"

"Can I?"

She laughed. "I'm sure after a little while it might start feeling a little creepy, just so you know. But my stomach's growling, and you lured me over here with your promise of a good meal."

"Did I say good meal? I should've said good company."

"I'll be the judge of both of those things."

He reached out and cupped her cheek. "Have I told you how beautiful you are?"

Her eyelids lowered and her eyes became heated. "Not today," she whispered.

"I'd kiss you but my face still hurts too much."

"That sucks because you're a good kisser."

"Am I?" he asked softly. He'd never been told that, but as long as Bella thought so, that was all that mattered.

She bit her lower lip. "Yeah. You're good at eating pussy, too, but I guess that's out for now."

Fuck him. His half-chub was now a raging hard-on. "Could I talk you into sex first and then ordering pizza in after?"

She looked at him in surprise. "You consider pizza a good meal?"

"I'm a single man who lives by himself. Pizza is the shit."

Her laughter caused a warmth to spread from his chest down to his gut. Fuck, he wanted to hear her laugh every day for the rest of his life. He wanted to make it his mission to never see her as sad as she was after losing her baby and almost losing her own life.

"Are you hating on pizza? The breakfast of champions?"

"If I stay over tonight, is that what I'm getting for breakfast?"

He tilted his head and stared at her mouth. It was so hard to resist kissing her. "Will cold pizza convince you to stay the night?"

"No."

"Will my awesome king-size bed?"

"Doubt it."

"Then what will?"

She stepped forward and placed one hand on his chest over his heart and then the other slipped down to cup his erection that wanted to punch a hole in his jeans. "Dick?"

"Just any dick?"

She shook her head, her eyes flashing. "No."

He liked this game. "Any particular one?"

She gnawed on her bottom lip and nodded.

"Does it have a name?"

She nodded again and smirked. "Axel rod."

Axel snorted so hard that he ended up crying out as pain exploded through his face. "Fuck! Stop it. That hurts."

She laughed. "Sorry."

"You can make it up to me."

"That I can. So I'm assuming the so-called 'good homemade meal' is out. Just a ploy."

"Do you forgive me?"

"I'll forgive you if you get Bangin' Burgers delivered instead of pizza after I fuck your brains out."

He fought so hard not to smile, but it was tough. "Who the hell needs brains, anyway?"

"Deal?"

"Fuck yes," he breathed as her hand squeezed him over his jeans. He brushed a knuckle over her cheek. "Did I say you were beautiful? Because I was wrong."

She arched an eyebrow at him.

"Because you are fucking goddamn beautiful. And I can't wait to be inside you."

"I can't wait for you to be inside me, either," she whispered back.

BELLA FLICKED his nipple with the tip of her tongue.

"Jesus," he groaned.

"Like that?" she asked as she straddled his hips, taking her time as she rose and fell on his cock.

"I dunno," he murmured.

"Let me try the other side." She leaned over and flicked the other one, then scraped her teeth over the small hard tip.

His hips jumped off the bed. "Fuck."

She dropped her head and studied his face. "See? You do like it." Her gaze roamed over his bruises, dark purples and blues, his left eyelid was still pretty swollen, his nose puffy, his jaw sporting a colorful bruise, too. But she could see past all of that to his intense blue eyes, his thick eyelashes, his perfect mouth. She wasn't lying when she told him he was a good kisser. He was. And as long as she just laid light kisses on his lips, it wasn't painful for him. But the hard part was resisting the urge to take the kiss deeper.

They found that out earlier during their first round of sex. That time he was on top, making her come until her legs turned to jelly. Then she got to lay in bed while he ordered a couple famous Bangin' Burgers, fries and two vanilla shakes. Normally, a meal like that would have put her into a food coma, but she was not passing up round two. No fucking way.

She had wanted Axel for what seemed like forever. Back to when they were teenagers and would see each other at school. She had crushed on him big time but knew he was off limits. Eventually, he went off to college for a couple years, then the police academy, then followed in his father's footsteps of becoming an SVPD officer. So she kept her distance. And found herself looking for love...

In all the wrong places. Or one wrong place. Church. Being constantly surrounded by aggressive men growing up, she was used to them. Actually preferred them because she knew nothing different. Her sister, Ivy, had even fought being with a biker for most of her life since she didn't want to be considered a man's property. Until Jag showed her otherwise.

However, once Bella started slinging drinks at The Iron Horse after turning twenty-one, she was at the club a lot. Between both the public and private side of the club, she practically lived there. She was constantly partying with the brothers. Drinking, having a good time, hooking up for just the fun of it.

Then she caught his eye. Her hips had filled out, her breasts became fuller, and all male eyes started landing on her. Even Pierce's. Like most of the rest of the women, she had to make sure she never found herself alone with the club president.

But it wasn't Pierce who she needed to watch.

No.

It was Rebel.

A big, good-looking brother with smoky green eyes, long blond hair, who'd been patched in years before. He was slick and could talk the panties off any woman. Including hers.

Night after night she'd end up in his room at church after her late shift at The Iron Horse. Until he became more and more possessive every day.

He even tried to talk Hawk into letting her go at the bar. Hawk refused, saying everyone had to pull their weight and help out at the club businesses.

Hawk nor Diesel liked the way things were progressing between her and Rebel. But they both tried to keep out of a fellow brother's business. And at that point Rebel had done nothing wrong since it wasn't abnormal for a brother to be possessive of a woman, ol' lady or not. If she was his regular piece, then it was acceptable.

Even so, Rebel could say all the right words, make her feel good about herself, he was great in bed when he wanted to be, made promises for their future. So when it came time for him to claim her at the table, he did it without telling her first. It was voted on and, suddenly, she was officially Rebel's ol' lady without even having a say in the matter. He immediately moved out of church and into the small apartment she had at the time.

Then he became demanding. He hated that she worked at the bar where other men could ogle or hit on her. She had to have dinner made exactly at the time he wanted. Not a minute before or a minute after. Didn't matter whether he was late or didn't plan to come home at all. Bella lived with it because she thought he loved her, the sex could be somewhat decent when he wasn't drunk or high, and he hadn't done anything to harm her. He was simply a bit on the bossy side. Again, nothing she wasn't used to.

Then suddenly, she had a ring on her finger and a marriage certificate in her hand. And with her future set, she was ready to start their family.

She wanted to be the first one to bring the fourth generation DAMC into the world, so she stopped taking birth control.

And then it began... Out of the blue, bossiness turned to slurs, insults, and demands she wasn't willing to fulfill. When she didn't do as he demanded, it turned physical. A twist of a wrist, a smack across her face, a lit cigarette to the bottom of her foot. Nothing noticeable to anyone else.

She was about to tell Hawk and Diesel, to let the club deal with Rebel's ass, but she discovered she was pregnant. It thrilled but scared her at the same time. She didn't want to raise her child in an abusive relationship. She told him she was pregnant and would leave if the abuse didn't stop. He promised he'd do better.

He *promised*.

But it didn't stop. It got worse. And the night she packed her things to leave the apartment, to leave him, changed her life forever.

Then Axel found her, came back into her life for the worst possible reason. And he never left, no matter how many times she pushed him away.

But he wouldn't let go...

"Let go," he murmured, as she rocked her hips back and forth, taking his whole length then letting him slip almost completely from her. Almost, but not quite.

His thumb circled her clit, making her insides clench around him tightly.

Their eyes met and held. "Where'd you go?" he asked gently.

She shook her head. "Nowhere."

"You never have to lie to me, Bella."

She didn't answer him, instead she picked up the pace. He needed to be quiet and not force any issues or the past. To just enjoy what they had. This moment, this night.

Because nothing else was guaranteed.

Whether he wanted to admit it or not, she was not the one for him. She wouldn't be able to give him a family. She would never be accepted in his. Or him in hers.

Even if they both wanted that, it would never work. She knew that back in high school and that's why she left him alone. She'd catch him sneaking glimpses at her, but he always kept his distance.

It was for the best then. It would be for the best now.

She just needed him to fill her soul for a little while, then she could tolerate going back to being alone. He could fill his need for her and then go find the right woman for him. One his father would be proud of, one that could produce the next generation of Jamisons. Children that would rightfully fill those seats around the table at Christmas dinner.

It wasn't her. It would never be her.

He needed to realize that. Somebody better was out there for him. Someone that would make him whole. Someone who he hadn't seen almost bleeding to death on a kitchen floor after being too weak to leave her abuser. Too weak to protect herself and her unborn child.

He didn't deserve someone like that. He was strong and strength was what he needed by his side.

But she would take tonight and think about what could've been if they'd been raised differently, if they'd had a shot years before she met Rebel. Before the biker charmed her and convinced her life with him would be good. When she was still a woman who went by Izzy and hadn't changed her nickname yet in an attempt to escape her past.

"Bella," he whispered.

She glanced down at the man beneath her and wished things had been different.

But they weren't.

He reached up and brushed at a tear rolling down her check. She glanced at the wetness on his thumb in surprise, she hadn't even realized she'd been crying.

Again, more weakness. She blinked the rest of them away and masked her sadness with a smile.

She was relieved when he didn't ask her what was wrong, didn't insist she spill her thoughts. Instead, he rolled them over, taking her gently, slowly and lovingly.

Which made her want to cry all over again.

She didn't deserve the goodness of him. And he didn't deserve someone with a scarred past.

"No matter what's in your head right now, just know this... I love you."

She closed her eyes at his words, the burn behind her eyelids now more intense.

"Don't shut me out." When she couldn't answer him, he continued, "Promise me that, baby. Please."

She wanted to promise him she wouldn't, but she couldn't say the words. She didn't want to disappoint him if she couldn't keep her promise.

Instead she stared up at him, cupped the unbruised side of his face and whispered, "I love you, too."

Uncertainty flickered behind his eyes and it killed her that she had put it there.

"That's all we need and we can get through anything."

She doubted that was true, but saw no point in telling him otherwise.

She lifted her hips to meet his thrusts as she trailed her hand down his back until she reached his ass. The muscles under her fingers contracted and flexed with each push of his hips as he kept his pace slow and steady, turning the sex into something that was so much more.

To him probably a promise of what could be. For her an acknowledgement of something that may never be.

"Baby, I need to come inside you. But first, you need to come for me."

Bowing his body above hers, he kissed the scar at the curve of her breast, then sucked one nipple, then the other. He teased the tips with his tongue, then nibbled along her skin until he reached the hollow of her throat where he kissed her gently. Rolling her nipple between his thumb and forefinger, she arched her back and cried out.

In a flash his gentleness was gone. He drove hard and fast in and out of her until she tilted her hips to meet his every thrust, welcoming the pounding, the reminder of how this man could be tender one minute then intense the next.

The harder he twisted her nipple the more she clamped down on him, making him hiss out a breath. His fingers found their connection, where they were joined so intimately, then teased her clit until she cried out again.

Seconds later she felt the rush, the wave that spiraled out from her core all the way to the tips of her fingers and toes, then it came crashing back to her center.

"Axel," she whimpered.

"Yeah, baby. Tell me you love me."

When she breathed the words, "I love you," he stiffened and stilled above her. The root of his cock throbbed intensely against her sensitive, swollen flesh as he spilled himself deep within her. Once again giving her a piece of him.

Even if it was only temporary.

Chapter Eight

Slade pushed through the swinging doors of the commercial kitchen that separated the clubhouse from the public side.

"It over?" Bella asked as she slid a pint of beer in front of a customer.

"Yeah."

Bella watched the man as he stepped behind the bar. His hair was still trimmed as high and tight as when he first entered The Iron Horse all those months ago. His haircut reminded her of Axel's, though for him it was a leftover from when he'd been in the military. If it wasn't for the tattoos that crept up his neck and completely covered his arms he could pass for some sort of law enforcement.

Besides being a former Marine, Bella had to admit she didn't know much about the man. Only that he'd patched into another club previously, but bought out his membership when that club began doing some sort of illegal activity.

She also knew Diesel wasn't on board with the way Slade patched into DAMC. Most prospects had to do at least a year before even being considered. Slade did none of that. He just hung around the club for a few months on Z's invitation and then after an executive committee vote, he was handed his cut in exchange for paying his dues.

"You stayin' or am I takin' over?" he asked her, sliding behind her close enough that she could feel his heat against her ass. He wasn't touching her but it was close.

Though she thought the man was hot, she never gave him any indication she was interested. She had never shown any interest in any biker since Rebel. She'd learned her lesson about hooking up with a brother the hard way.

He braced a hand on the bar beside her, practically caging her in. Taking a slow, deep breath, she tried to calm her nerves. She turned, pressing back against the bar to put some space between them.

"Hawk coming?" she asked, keeping the tremor from her words.

He shook his head and stepped back. She was relieved he wasn't pushing for contact. But when he didn't answer, she realized he was a typical brother... A man of little words.

"Is he heading home to Kiki?"

"Yeah," he grunted.

Now that they faced each other, still a little too close for her comfort, he eyeballed her. It wasn't aggressive, but his look definitely held some interest. The brothers knew to leave her alone and Slade was new, but that was no excuse.

"Wanna hang here with me an' come up to my room later?" he asked her unexpectedly.

On the surface it sounded innocent and in the past few months, he'd never disrespected any of the women, so his attention caught her off guard. Maybe he wanted to work his way through the available DAMC women.

"Are you done doing Diamond?" she asked, surprised at his offer.

He frowned and jerked his head back. "Never did her."

"I thought... I heard..."

"She tell you otherwise?"

"No."

He shrugged, his eyes on her neck. She raised her hand to her throat and could feel her pulse racing under her fingertips.

"Had a couple fun times, that's it. So..." He tilted his head as he studied her. "Wanna wait around 'til I'm done here?"

Out of nowhere, Diesel was towering over Slade. He scrubbed his fingers over his ear. "Hearin' must be fucked," he barked. "Thought I heard you offerin' to stick your dick in my cousin. Can't be right."

Slade turned to face Diesel, his shoulders squaring off. "Up to her. She can say no."

Diesel's eyes narrowed and his fists clenched.

Jesus, she did not need D punching Slade out over her, too.

"She ain't takin' your dick. Already got a dick in 'er that shouldn't be there."

Bella's jaw dropped, and she groaned, covering her face with her hands. "For fuck's sake, D."

"Rather you be with a brother than a fuckin' cop, woman. But this ain't the one."

Slade's gaze slid back to her, his brow raised. "A cop? You doin' Z's brother?"

She bugged her eyes out at the two of them in disbelief and shook her head. Then she glanced over her shoulder at the customers lining the bar, all listening with great interest.

"It's no one's business who I'm doing *if* I'm doing anyone." She scowled at Diesel. "Even you."

He grunted.

She rolled her eyes. "Come with me."

Bella didn't even wait to see if her asshole cousin followed her back through the kitchen and into church. When she stepped through the door into the clubhouse, she was dismayed to see there wasn't any privacy there, either. She should've known everyone would be hanging out, drinking and playing pool after the annual club election.

But it would have to do. Grizzly sat at the end of the bar in his usual spot with his perpetual pint of beer sitting in front of him. Crow was sitting at the other end, nursing a whiskey.

His long black silky hair hung loose tonight and her fingers itched to go braid it. She moved closer to him and away from Grizz's nosy ears.

"Hey, baby," Crow greeted her softly, his dark eyes flashing.

"Hey, handsome. Can I braid your hair?"

"Fuck no."

Bella laughed. She always asked, and he always refused. So now it was a regular routine between them.

"Can I just run my fingers through it?"

"Only if you're naked while you do it," he shot back his usual response, then took a sip of his whiskey.

"One of these days when I say okay to that, are you going to fall off your stool?"

"Nope, gonna take you upstairs an' hold you to it," he murmured back with amusement.

Heat crept into her belly at the thought of doing Crow, though she'd never follow through. It was a nice fantasy, but that was all she ever allowed herself.

She felt Diesel's massive presence behind her. She sighed and turned toward him, crossing her arms over her chest.

"Said you needed to talk to me after the meetin', so talk," he grumbled.

She propped a hip against the bar. "Everything go smoothly at the election?"

"Yep," Diesel grunted. "Everythin's as it should be."

Her gaze slid through the busy common area. Pierce was nowhere in sight.

"He show up?"

"Was here an' gone, baby." Crow's voice sounded just like his honey-like skin tone... warm, smooth and delicious.

Bella nodded as she turned her attention to the ink slinger. "Any problems?"

"Nope," Crow answered, lifting his whiskey again and taking another sip. "When you gonna let me finish that sleeve of yours?"

"When you do it naked," she shot back.

Crow gave her a slow, panty-soaking smile. "Deal."

"For fuck's sake," Diesel barked. "Bad 'nough I gotta hear Slade tryin' to get down your pants..."

Crow's head spun toward him, and Bella decided she needed this to stop before it got blown out of proportion.

"He was just flirting."

"No, what you an' Crow do is flirtin', he was tryin' to get his dick wet."

"It was harmless. I'm not interested and I think he knows it now."

"Gonna make sure it's clear," D mumbled, glancing back toward the double swinging doors to the kitchen.

"D, let it go."

He grunted.

She released a long, loud sigh. "Anyway, I do need to talk to you."

"'Bout what?"

"Warriors."

D scowled. "What about 'em?"

"Got a text today from..." She drifted off. Maybe now was not a good time to mention Axel's name. "Got a message earlier today saying all the toys from the donation boxes were taken and the storage unit was emptied."

Crow whistled low while D shouted, "What the fuck!"

"I stopped out there before coming here. It's true. The padlock had been cut off and there wasn't anything left in the unit. It had been cleaned out completely."

"Sure it was those piles of dog shit?" Crow asked, now ignoring his whiskey and his eyes hard like black diamonds.

"Not sure. The PD's investigating it since their stuff was taken, too. They'll be checking with the business owners."

"Toys still in the box at my shop," Crow mentioned.

Bella nodded. There was no way a Warrior could walk into any of the DAMC businesses and take the toys from the donation boxes without someone stopping them, including the one in Crow's tattoo shop. "Good, but you should've seen how much we and the PD had collected. And we weren't the only two organizations using the unit for that purpose."

"Fuck," D grumbled.

"Yeah, D, fuck. Thousands and thousands of dollars' worth of toys for needy children."

"Gonna fence the shit probably," he mumbled.

"Do me a favor and check with Magnum to see if they were hit, too. If so, then we know it had to be those bastards."

"Gonna get my crew on it," D grumbled, sending a text, she hoped to Magnum, as they spoke.

"Keep it on the D.L., D."

He cocked a heavy brow in her direction. "Need a woman tellin' me how to handle shit?"

Bella rolled her eyes at him. "Just saying, SVPD took a report."

"Mean that pig who stuck his dick in you took a report."

"If you mean pig as in Axel, *Z's brother*, then yes."

"What about my so-called brother?" Zak asked, taking a seat on the stool next to Crow.

D jerked his chin toward her. "Caught the fucker in 'er bed."

Crow and Z both shouted, "What?" at the same time.

Normally, she'd find that simultaneous outraged reaction humorous. Tonight, it was anything but.

She whacked D on the arm. "You mind not telling everyone about my sex life?"

"Didn't know you had one," Crow murmured. "Always wearin' that 'property of no one' bullshit."

Bella planted her hands on her hips and turned on Crow. "Do I ask you who you're boning?"

He picked up his whiskey and hid his grin behind the glass.

She answered for him. "Didn't think so. Now, can we get back to Toys for Tots?"

"What about it?" Z asked.

"Wiped out," D grunted.

Z was clearly confused. "What's wiped out?"

"All the toys are gone, Z," Bella clarified. "Might have been the Warriors."

He shook his head, pounding his knuckles on the bar top. "Motherfuckers."

That described them perfectly.

"How much time do we have left to collect?" the club president asked.

"Two weeks? Maybe a little more?" Bella guessed.

"Gives us time to get the word out, try to get the community to step up even more."

What he said was true, but... "Still a huge loss," she murmured.

"If we gotta, we'll take funds outta the club coffers to make up for whatever was lost."

Bella nodded, it was better than nothing. She hoped either the PD or at least D's crew could track those fuckers down, if it *was* them, and recover at least some of the toys.

Axel was not going to be happy that she told D. But he'd have to get over it. Someone needed to recover those toys before they were sold, pawned or simply destroyed.

Zak continued, "I'll spread the word that everyone comin' to the Christmas party gotta bring at least one toy or a cash donation."

Bella braced herself. "Speaking of the Christmas party..." she began.

"AND THEY SAID WHAT?" Axel asked after Bella just dropped a bomb on him.

She shifted her head on his chest and tipped her brown eyes up to him. "Really want to know?"

He shook his head. "I can imagine." Combing his fingers through her long dark hair, he spread the silky locks over his bare skin. She was curled against his side, a bare leg thrown over his, an arm over his waist and her soft breasts pressed to his ribs. "Not a good idea, Bella," he murmured.

"About as good as me coming to Christmas dinner at your parents."

He snorted and was relieved it was less painful this time. The swelling had gone down on his face, including his nose and eye. Though, the bruises looked worse than ever since they had started to change colors. His father and the other cops at the station demanded to know what happened. He vaguely told them he'd been working on his bike when it fell over on him. Mitch eyeballed him suspiciously but didn't call him out on it in front of everyone else.

"It's not the same and you know it."

Attending the club's Christmas party would be like a mouse voluntarily entering a den of vipers. It would be like suicide. Only worse.

They might let him live but they sure would make him suffer and wish he was dead.

He couldn't imagine any of the brothers would be okay with it, especially his own. Or Hawk and Diesel. It was bad enough when one six-foot-four pissed off beast of a man wanted to kick his ass, but two?

"Told them what you said, you'd be coming as Axel Jamison, not Officer Jamison."

That was the other rub. His father aside, he was sure his captain wouldn't be thrilled with him hanging out with the club, whether they were one-percenters or not.

"Oh, I'm sure they started writing out the invitation right then and there."

She traced her fingers back and forth over the wiry chest hairs that lightly covered his pecs. Every once in a while, she'd brush over a nipple. He never realized just how sensitive they were.

She sighed. "No."

"Right."

"You talked about mending fences. It's a start."

"It's one thing to try to mend a fence one on one with my brother, but to walk into a party with at least twenty fucking bikers," he lifted a finger, "who are drinking heavily, by the way, *and* who all hate my guts, it's another."

"Probably more like forty or fifty."

He lifted his head and stared at her. "What?"

"Dark Knights are going to be there, too."

Well, that was even better! His eyes narrowed. "Why?"

She shrugged a shoulder. "Biker bonding."

Axel dropped his head back onto his pillow and studied the ceiling. "Right. And what better way to bond then to kill the sole cop amongst their midst."

Her fingers followed the thin line of hair that lead to his pelvis. "Too many witnesses."

"I'm glad you find this amusing. I could see going into the bathroom to take a piss, the lights go out, my throat gets slashed and one of D's crew hacks my body into small pieces, so it's never to be found again."

She chuckled as she palmed his sac and squeezed lightly. "You've been watching too many movies."

"You told me yourself that D wants to kill me."

"It was a metaphor."

"For what? For him wanting to give me a great big bear hug?"

She placed a kiss over his heart then her tongue came out to flick his nipple. "You said yourself that he won't kill you."

"Well, after he punched my lights out, I kind of had an epiphany." He sighed. "I still don't understand why in the hell they'd agree to me coming."

"A brother's never going to claim me."

"Okay?"

"I think they all realize that now."

That was nothing new, so he didn't understand where this conversation was headed. "And?"

"So unless I'm claimed, I'm up for grabs."

"By who?"

"Anyone."

He swept the hair away from her face to see her more clearly. "I'm confused."

"D's got his hands full with Jewel and..." She paused. "Everything else."

That was clear as mud, but then it wasn't helping that she kept kneading his balls and teasing his nipples. If they hadn't just had a sweaty, noisy, awesome round of sex, his cock would be ready to go. But it wasn't and what she was doing to him was exquisite torture. Not that he was going to tell her to stop.

She continued, "And Hawk has his hands full with Kiki and... everything else."

Everything else. He could just imagine. "Right. And Z has Sophie, Jag has Ivy. Get to the point."

"None of us are easy women to deal with."

He almost let "no shit" slip from his lips, but he caught it in time. When she released his balls, clarity suddenly hit him. "So you're saying they're trying to lighten the load? Less DAMC women to watch since I'd have your back? It would make sense since the Warriors are on a rampage. But still... Can't see any one of them being that reasonable."

She shifted and nipped the flesh near his nipple hard. He sucked in a sharp breath and rubbed his skin when she moved on to another spot.

"First of all, I don't need a babysitter. But I think what happened earlier kind of threw it in their face that they can't be everywhere at all times. That their women make them vulnerable."

"So they need all hands on deck?"

"Sort of, but—"

He lifted his hand. "Wait. Hold up. What happened earlier?"

"Slade asked me to..."

Axel sat up, dislodging her from his chest. "To what?"

"To go up to his room."

Blood rushed into his ears and a muscle in his jaw flexed.

"Nothing I haven't heard before," she added quickly.

"Slade hit on you?"

She sat up, too, pulling the sheet up around her. He hated that she felt the need to cover herself around him. He understood that she felt self-conscious about her scars, but he'd been working hard on showing her that he loved her, scars and all. They didn't make him change the way he felt. And never would.

"Yeah. He didn't force the issue or anything. He was just showing interest and probably gauging what mine was in return. It was innocent."

Sure it was. "I thought he was doing Diamond?" Though anyone in their right mind wouldn't take on Diamond. From what he understood, Slade had been a Marine. So maybe the man liked a challenge.

"Yeah, no. Apparently not."

His chest tightened. "Now he's got his sights set on you?" If so, the man definitely liked challenges. But Bella was one Slade was never going to get to try. Not if Axel had any say in the matter.

"Mmm. I think D kind of cleared that up."

He chuckled. "Oh, fuck. Did he get to read the word 'dirty' before being knocked out, too?"

She smirked. "No. I think he likes Slade more than you. Though, he doesn't like Slade much, either."

Axel's ears perked at that information. "Why doesn't he like Slade?" Maybe he needed to run a background check on the guy and see what legal skeletons the biker had in his closet.

"Not sure. It could be just D being D. Being overprotective."

"So, he was there when Slade hit on you?"

"Yeah, he heard it... at least the last part."

For once, he was glad that Diesel had been around and looking out for Bella when he couldn't be. "You going to be safe around him?"

Bella looked at him in surprise. "Are you going into cop mode?"

Was he? Maybe, but more like protecting his woman mode, protecting what was his.

"He wasn't pushy, he was just testing the waters, Axel. It's over and done with. He doesn't creep me out, he was just being a typical horn dog. Unlike Pierce..."

"Yeah. Glad they ousted his ass."

"Still a brother," she reminded him.

"Right, but he no longer holds any power. That makes a difference for someone with his ego."

"Cops should know all about ego."

"Very funny."

"Anyway, I think it's an olive branch."

It still didn't make any sense to him. He wouldn't be surprised if it was a trap and they invited him to the party so they could string him up and club him like a piñata.

"I still can't see D agreeing to this." This whole thing just made his cop Spidey sense tingle.

"He knows we're sleeping together."

Axel pointed at his face. "You think?"

"Again, I'm sorry about that."

"Do you think he is?"

She grinned. "No."

"So if I do this, you'll come to Christmas dinner?"

"I'll think about it. By the way, Z's going to invite Jayde to the party."

Well, there was another interesting twist. "My sister doesn't need an invitation. She already planned on crashing it."

"Well, there you go. You'll have someone else there who'll tolerate you. Ace, Janice, Jayde and me."

"Sounds like a great time. Nothing like only being tolerated."

"Now you know how I'll feel at your parents."

"It's only my father you'll have to win over."

"I'm not going to do that, Axel. I'm not going to force him to like me."

"No forcing necessary. He'll love you as much as I do."

"Damn, did my bullshit meter just hit red."

"I'm telling you right now, I'm wearing my ankle holster to the party. Hell, I'm wearing two."

"Axel..."

He sighed. "Okay, I'll do it for you." He had a feeling he would regret this. But someone needed to take the first step. And if he had to take a little bit of abuse to move this all forward, then he would.

He sank back onto the bed, and Bella curled back around him. She felt so right being there. In his bed. In his life. So maybe this was a good thing. *If* he survived it.

"You wouldn't be doing it for me. You'd be doing it for you. For Jayde. For Z. For Sophie and the baby." She hesitated. "I guess it would be for me, too, since I don't want to live the rest of my life with that turmoil."

His heart thumped heavily in his chest. "The rest of your life?"

"I can't continue to do this with you, Axel, if these burned bridges can't be repaired."

"Are you saying you want this to continue?"

Chapter Nine

BELLA TOOK a deep breath and thought about Axel's question. If she did want what they had to continue, it was going to be a long road ahead. Even if the brothers started to tolerate him—and she couldn't expect any more from them than that when it came to a cop—it was still going to be a bumpy ride.

The worry gnawed at her when she thought about his coming to the club's Christmas party to the point it turned her stomach. Things could go so wrong.

The only good thing was all the DAMC women would be thrilled he showed up with her, as would her uncle, Ace, and his wife, Janice. She wasn't lying when she told Axel that. Ace had reached out to Axel and Mitch several times, trying to convince them to visit Z while he was in prison. They refused. She understood how it might make two police officers look, having a son and a brother doing time, but even so...

"Why didn't you ever visit Z in prison?" she asked softly.

"That wasn't an answer to my question."

"I know, and you want to avoid mine, too." She sighed softly. "I honestly don't know that answer, Axel. If I had to answer that today, I would say probably not."

His body jerked slightly under her cheek which she had pressed to his chest. "Bella," he whispered, the hurt clear in his voice.

"That's not what you want to hear, but it's the only answer I have if you need to know today."

"And if I ask tomorrow?"

"It's not just us, Axel. You know that. Our lives aren't simple. We don't live in a bubble. We're so different. You and your father don't want to recognize where you came from. What your grandfather built. What *our* grandfathers built."

"Fuck! My grandfather died because of the club. He was murdered by Warriors."

"I know that."

"And my uncle's doing life in prison for retribution. So is your grandfather, Bella. This isn't some game. Those were human lives they took. By doing that, they acted as judge and jury. My father and I swore an oath to help save lives. To keep people safe."

"Exactly my point of how different we are. And it's not only that. I can't..." She didn't want to talk about this, about why he needed to rethink all of this. "Axel, you need to think about the future."

"We're working on that now, aren't we? We're trying to repair some of the damage done from the past."

She shook her head. "It's not that simple."

"No shit."

"I'm not talking about your family and mine, though that's a big obstacle in itself."

"Then what?"

"You know what happened to me."

"Fuck!" he shouted, making her jump. He grabbed her chin and turned her face up to him. "We went through this already."

"No! No, that's not... that's not what I'm saying... I don't... have... a womb."

He blinked at her, his expression confused. "Yeah, which is great because I don't have to wear a fucking condom and we don't have to worry about you getting—" He stopped abruptly. She watched as the emotions changed on his face. From confusion to clarity to what looked like a mix of grief and guilt.

He scrubbed a hand over his hair and blew out a breath. "Fuck, I'm so sorry. That was... a callous thing to say."

She forced herself to swallow the knot in her throat. "But it's true," she said softly. "And if you're talking future, Axel, you need to think about that. I may not be able to give you everything you want or need."

He interlaced his fingers with hers and lifted their joined hands to his mouth. "I want *you*." He kissed the back of her hand. "I need *you*."

She closed her eyes for a moment, trying to slow her pounding heart. It sounded so simple, but she knew it wasn't. He might want her now, but when it hit him later that she couldn't be everything he wanted or needed her to be, he could come to resent her.

And to let herself become emotionally invested in him and to have that happen... It would be devastating. At least for her, if not him.

"There are so many other women out there that would be better for you. Women who would fit into your lifestyle, mesh with your career, make your father happy, give your parents grandchildren. None of those are me. You need to face that, Axel."

"All obstacles we can overcome."

"Holy fuck, are you Jamisons stubborn."

"Right and you Doughertys aren't?"

"I'm a McBride," she corrected him. "Though, only because of my sperm donor."

"Baby, you're pure Dougherty through and through. McBride's just a name. I take it your father isn't invited to the party."

Bella snorted. "Not unless he wants Ace to put a bullet between his eyes."

"You've heard nothing?'

"No, not once. Hell, he didn't want one kid and by the time mom popped out the third one in three years, he turned tail and ran as fast as he could." Neither her nor Dex remembered anything about their father. Dex was two and Bella was only a year old when Ivy was born. Three young children were a lot for anyone to handle but for someone who disliked kids? Impossible. The man just up and rode off on his

Harley with all of their money stuffed into his pockets. If it wasn't for her Uncle Ace, Aunt Janice, and her Aunt Annie, Kelsea's mother, her mom would've struggled to raise three children on her own.

Axel was quiet for a moment. "Want me to find him for you?"

She widened her eyes at him. "Seriously? If I wanted to know where that fucker was I would've asked Diesel. His crew is good at finding people." She thought about D and the Toys for Tots issue. "Which is why we should have him help find the stolen toys."

"No."

"Axel."

"Bella, no. Keep him out of it. I'm on it. No reason to make a bad matter worse. And that's all he'll do."

"But he—"

"No, Bella," he said in his deep cop voice.

Fuck. She wiggled her eyebrows at him. "Can we negotiate?"

"Nope."

Double fuck. If Axel found out she told D, he was going to be pissed. She'd have to remind D to keep a low profile when he was doing his own investigation...

"How's your investigation going with that?" Maybe Axel would give her some leads that she could give to Diesel.

"Sounds like the Warriors. Everyone describes two bikers coming in saying they're DAMC."

"Not wearing colors?"

"No. None. I sent out a press release today and it should be on the news tonight. Now people will be keeping an eye out."

"Too late, though."

"I also mentioned that we're asking the public to step up and donate."

"I hope it works."

"Most people get upset when something like this affects children. We may get more donations now than ever. Everyone at the station has pledged to donate at least five more toys each."

"Time's running out, Axel."

"It'll be fine. We can do this."

"Still want those bastards caught."

"You know they're wily fuckers. Never staying in one place too long. Which reminds me, I do need to stop in and talk to Ace."

"About what?"

"He might have close connections with the area pawn shops. They may be more willing to give him a heads up if the stolen goods show up in their shops than they would be talking to the PD. We did put a notice out to all pawn shops in Pennsylvania and the surrounding states."

Ace. It *was* a good idea to stop in and talk to him. She may have to do that before Axel. She needed to check the boxes she'd set up there, anyhow. She'd left the toys in all the club's donation boxes at the DAMC businesses since they were safer there for now.

"What should we do about storing any of the toys we collect from here on out?"

"We've got an empty office at the station we're going to use. If you want—"

"No. I'll find a safe spot." Like D's warehouse. But she wasn't going to tell Axel that because then he'd realize she told Diesel about the Warriors' thieving asses. "How am I supposed to keep this from the guys?"

"Eventually you're not going to be able to. I'm just asking for you to keep it between us for now, so we at the PD can do our jobs and not worry about a bunch of vigilantes interfering."

"Vigilantes," she snorted.

Axel cocked an eyebrow her way. "How much do you know about Diesel's so-called Shadows."

"Not much."

"When I questioned you in the hospital the day D got shot, you looked like you knew more than you wanted to say."

She avoided his eyes. "Right. Club business and all that."

Axel sighed and sat up, dislodging her again.

She rolled onto her side and propped her head up on her hand. "What?"

He stared at her until a tingle skittered down her spine. It was not the pleasurable type of tingle. Disappointment crossed his face. "You're right. This isn't going to work, Bella. If you're going to hide shit from me, lie to me when it comes to the club and everyone involved, it's not going to work. There can't be any secrets between us."

Her heart thudded in her chest. "You know the women aren't involved in club business."

His blue eyes narrowed on her. "Bullshit. You know more than you let on."

"That's why I said you needed to find someone who would mesh with your lifestyle and career, Axel. There's no fucking way I'm telling a cop—even if it's you—anything about the club that they don't want you to know."

"Bella…"

"No, it's unfair that you would ever even ask me that. I have my loyalties."

He threw up his hands. "And there we go. You're loyal to the club but would lie to me. That's just great."

She sat up, dragging the sheet more securely around her. "You're assuming I lie to you or will in the future. I don't know dick about D's getting shot."

"Nothing about Squirrel and Black Jack's disappearance?"

She hesitated, then studied a loose thread in the sheet. "Whatever happened, they had it coming to them."

"Fuck, Bella. That's the shit I can't get involved in. *You* shouldn't get involved in. That could make you an accessory after the fact. Oh fuck, it better be after the fact and not before. Fuck, Bella." He buried his head into his hands.

"Axel," she murmured, touching his arm.

He dropped his hands and studied her for a moment. "No, this is not good. You need to promise me… You need to tell me when illegal shit happens, and you need to keep your hands clean. I can't be a part of that, Bella. I can't lose my career. It's against everything I stand for. Do you understand that?"

She opened her mouth, but nothing came out. Her mind spun. "I can't do that. I'm not going to turn in anyone from the club. Ever.

Especially Diesel and Hawk. My brother. Zak. Whoever. It's never going to happen."

Axel closed his eyes and groaned. "Then we're done here." His deep voice sounded tight.

Her heart skipped a beat, then began to thump furiously. "Done?" She threw off the sheet and climbed out of his bed, searching for her clothes. She snagged her panties and yanked them on. "I never wanted this to start. You pushed it. You didn't listen, Axel. *You*!" She put on her bra and slipped her shirt over her head, pulling her long hair out of the neckline.

She glared at him. He sat in bed, staring at her, his face pale but unreadable.

"I always knew this would be temporary. I knew it would never work." She grabbed her jeans, hopping up and down as she tugged them on. "You can't make me choose, Axel. I won't do it. So, if you can't accept me for who I am, which is DAMC, then fuck you."

"Bella..."

"No. I've always been DAMC and always will be."

"Even after Rebel—"

All the breath left her lungs and she jerked up a hand. "Don't even go there. Don't you dare use him against me. Don't you use my mistakes against me."

She yanked on her socks and boots, zipping them up. As she straightened, she tossed her head.

Pulling the covers aside, he moved to get out of bed, but she screamed, "Don't you dare get out of that bed until I'm gone." If he came over to her, if he touched her in any way, she was going to break. And she needed to stay strong. At least until she was out of his apartment. She planted her hands on her hips. "Why did you do this to me, Ax? Why?"

"I didn't do anything to you," he said softly, his eyes searching her face.

She swallowed and tried to keep her expression as neutral as possible. She couldn't show him how hurt she was. "Yes, you did. You convinced me to let you in and I mistakenly did. Another bad decision." She bounced her fist on her forehead, then let a "Fuck!" burst out of her.

"Don't compare me to him." His words were harsh and low as he got out of bed.

She lifted a hand to stop him from approaching. "Don't come near me. Not now, not ever again. Stay the fuck away from me." With that, she turned on her heel and left his bedroom, jerking the door closed.

She grabbed her leather jacket on the way out then slammed his front door behind her so hard the wall rattled.

She stomped down to her car just like he stomped on her heart.

It wasn't until she was in her car and halfway home that she allowed the first tear to fall.

Chapter Ten

"How's the Toys for Tots collection going?" Sophie asked, pulling money from the register to make a deposit.

Bella peered over her shoulder as Sophie counted the cash. "Damn. 'Tis the season! I'm glad we hired those two baker helpers. Without them we wouldn't be able to keep up."

"I know. It's nice to be operating in the black. If it wasn't for you buying in and becoming my partner, I'm not sure if the shop would've survived this year."

"Bullshit, we make awesome cakes and cupcakes. Word of mouth is our best advertising."

"And our cheapest. So... Toys for Tots?" Sophie asked again.

"Fine. I'm going to make a round tomorrow afternoon and will take the stuff out to D's warehouse. Thankfully, it seems as though everyone in Shadow Valley stepped up."

Sophie tucked the wad of cash into a blue bank bag and zipped it shut. "How's the PD doing with theirs?"

Bella ignored her question. She hadn't told Sophie what happened between her and Axel over a week ago. She hadn't told anyone. It was still too raw, and she wasn't done kicking herself for letting the man get to her. "Good thing the Knights stash wasn't stolen."

"Maybe next year it's best not to have one location for storing them all," Sophie suggested.

"Agreed."

"Have you convinced Axel to come to the party?"

Bella moved down the counter to avoid Sophie's prying eyes. "No, we haven't discussed it yet."

"Better soon."

"Yeah," she murmured.

"I still can't believe Zak agreed to it. That's good though. I'm glad. It gives me some hope."

Bella didn't want to dash Sophie's hope. They'd find out soon enough when he didn't show up at the party, which was only a week and a half away.

"Oh!" Sophie yelled out, grabbing her stomach.

Bella felt the blood rush from her face and her stomach turn. "What? Are you okay?"

"Oh my God!"

Bella rushed up to Sophie. "What? What's wrong?"

Sophie was leaning back into the counter, the fingers of both her hands stretched along her lower belly. Suddenly Sophie's hand snaked out and grabbed her wrist, pressing Bella's hand flat to her belly before Bella could stop her.

"Feel that?"

No, she couldn't. She couldn't feel the baby. She desperately wanted to feel the baby, know she was okay. But she couldn't feel anything.

Bella's heart thumped heavily in her chest. And then she felt it. Movement of the life within Sophie's womb. She tried to pry her hand away gently, but Sophie wouldn't let go.

Sophie's lips were moving quickly, her eyes wide and holding excitement. She was saying something, but Bella had no idea what. As if in a trance, she stared at her hand trapped on Sophie's baby bump. But she was no longer in her own body, it was like she floated above it, looking down at the two of them.

Then the baby moved again under her palm and she squeezed her eyes shut, her head spinning.

She couldn't see anything, either. Everything was black. Everything throbbed. Her face, her arms, her legs, her belly.

Then her stomach churned and a sharp pain shot through her. Not the dull ache, not the sting. No, this was intense like someone was trying to rip out her guts. Someone was trying to steal the life that was inside her.

The one she had fought so hard to protect, but failed.

She failed.

She failed.

But so did he. He wanted to kill her. But from what she could tell she was still alive, still breathing, still bleeding. Her baby, too.

The baby just had to stay inside her belly where it was safe. It was the only way to keep her safe.

She couldn't let him win.

Because if she died... If her baby didn't survive...

He won.

The darkness crept in and surrounded her as she fell to her knees at Sophie's feet.

A scream cut through her brain like a hatchet.

Was it her? It had to be. She was bleeding, and the pain was unbearable. She couldn't move, her back was shoved into the corner of the cabinets, her hands shaking as she held onto her own belly. The movement beneath her fingers wasn't joyous. No, it was frightening. She glanced up, her mouth agape as she stared up at Rebel.

His face was a mask of rage, his eyes hard, his hands covered in blood as he held the long, thin kitchen knife. He was screaming something at her.

Streaks of blood crisscrossed his leather cut and down his jeans. Was that his? Or hers? She looked down at herself, her white top now blood red as the soaked fabric clung to the small rise of her belly.

"Why?" she tried to ask him. But he didn't respond. Maybe he didn't hear her.

Why? Why would he do this? Only a monster would try to kill his wife and child. She did nothing wrong. She didn't deserve this. This had to be a bad dream. A nightmare.

She just needed to wake herself up.

Because no one in their right mind would do something so horrific. Not to their own family.

She screamed and then clenched her teeth hard when the cramps twisted her insides.

No... No. No!

Wincing in pain, she slowly peeled the bottom of her blood soaked top up and saw three of the deep stab wounds along her abdomen. The ones he placed with a purpose once she was knocked to the floor. She closed her eyes and tried to take a breath, her mind racing. She needed to get help. Someone needed to save her baby.

But she couldn't move. Her muscles wouldn't cooperate; she was losing her strength by the second. Opening her eyes, she saw he was gone. She was finally alone.

But she was unable to help herself. She couldn't scream for help, either. She couldn't suck in enough of a breath to do so. The dizziness began to set in, spots crossing her vision, her body trembled, the sting of the wounds unbearable. The cramping in her gut telling.

Her eyelids felt as heavy as concrete blocks, but she forced them to remain open as she tried to look around, but her head refused to turn, her body refused to cooperate. Then she spotted it. Her cell phone in the puddle of blood she sat in. With a great effort, she forced her hand to drop and for what seemed like hours, she crept her fingers closer until the tips brushed the blood-slickened phone. With one finger she tried to drag it closer. With excruciating slowness, she got it close enough to hit the power button on the side and tap 911 on the screen. She watched the call connect as it laid on the floor beside her.

When she heard, "Nine-one-one. What's your emergency?" she again tried to scream for help, but the word just gurgled from her throat.

Someone help me. Someone help my baby. Someone...

"Hello? ... Do you need assistance? ... Hello?"

As if from a deep well she heard, "We have your location and police are on the way."

No. She didn't need police. She needed an ambulance. Why didn't they know that? Why couldn't she tell them?

The cops could do nothing. They couldn't help her, help her unborn child.

Please. Please. Please. Hurry up. I'm dying. We're dying.

Then she heard nothing. Only darkness and an eerie quiet remained.

AXEL HELD Bella's limp body against his as they lay on her narrow bed. He debated whether to take her to the hospital or just wait out whatever was happening. Which he had no fucking clue what that was. Fear clawed at his gut to see her in this semi-comatose state.

Her eyes were open, but she stared blankly. She couldn't focus on him or anything around her. And he didn't think she could feel his presence, either. Even so, he kept talking to her because he hoped that would bring her back from wherever she had disappeared to.

When Sophie had called him in a panic, he'd driven code three, lights and siren, directly to the bakery. He found Bella curled up on the floor, unresponsive but breathing, and her pulse attempting to beat out of her neck.

Sophie was freaking out, holding onto her stomach, but he didn't have time to worry about her. He just made sure she had called Z to come home to the bakery to be with her.

Then he'd scooped Bella up, placed her gently into the back of his cruiser, took her home and placed her into bed. At first, he had covered her completely with her bedding since she was shivering uncontrollably. But soon she had become flush and overheated so he pulled them all back off.

A feeling of helplessness washed over him.

He was worried that her mind had broken, that she had completely snapped.

All of it was due to feeling his niece or nephew moving in Sophie's belly. Something so simple sparked a reaction like he'd never seen before and never wanted to see again.

Sophie had been scared to death of Bella's reaction. Not that he blamed her. He was, too.

He held her tightly against him and stroked her hair, whispering her name, pressing kisses to her temple and her forehead. "Bella. Please. Don't make me take you to the hospital. Please."

If he did, she would be committed and could be held involuntarily for up to five days. He couldn't do that to her. Not if he didn't have to.

"You need to break free of this." He brushed a knuckle across her pale cheek. "You need to talk to me."

He braced when he heard her front door open and a rush of heavy boots down the short hallway. Then he was there, filling up the doorway with a look Axel had never seen on the man's face before.

Although the man could normally hide any emotions, Diesel couldn't hide his worry when his eyes raked over Bella's listless body. "What the fuck happened?"

"Sophie made her touch her stomach."

His brows shot up his forehead and D took a step into the room. "So?"

"She felt the baby move."

Diesel's gaze slid from Axel to Bella and then back again. "So?"

"It made her... snap."

"Fuckin' cop, get to the point. Why would that make her snap?"

Fuck. "She never told you."

Diesel took another step closer, looking like he wanted to tear Axel's windpipe from his throat. "Told me what?"

Axel shut his eyes and shook his head. He shouldn't tell him. It wasn't his place to tell D her secret.

Suddenly, the massive man was next to the bed, towering over him and Bella. "Tell me what?" When Axel didn't answer, D's nostrils flared, and his eyes got hard. "Don't make me pound it the fuck out of you."

"What she lost," he answered simply.

D's dark eyes pinned him to the bed for a moment before moving to Bella. Even in her state, her arms embraced her lower stomach. His eyes landed there and he said nothing.

Axel knew D wasn't stupid. He might appear to be a dumb biker, simply grunting and fighting his way through life, but he wasn't. He was smart... He ran a business with a crew of former special ops who were as equally cunning. And Axel knew the second that Diesel put two and two together.

His face got dark, his brows went low, his mouth got tight. "Rebel," he grunted. He lifted his gaze back to Axel. "She told you."

It wasn't a question, but more of an accusation. He was clearly not happy that Axel knew something he didn't, especially since it was D's job as club enforcer to protect everyone in the club, to be in the know. He took his responsibilities seriously. And, worse, Bella and D were close.

"Not by choice." Axel took a deep breath. "I was the first on scene that day, remember?"

D studied him. "You knew then."

"Yes."

"You told no one."

"I did what she asked."

D gave him a sharp nod. Was that a nod of respect? Impossible.

"I'm here. You can go."

Axel was not going anywhere. D would have to physically remove him. "Diesel, she needs to snap out of this."

"She will," he answered with confidence.

Axel tilted his head to stare up at the larger man. "How do you know?"

"Done it before. Didn't realize..." He stopped, a muscle in his jaw ticking. "Didn't know it all."

Axel glanced down into Bella's face. She still stared off at nothing. Her eyes unfocused. He'd hoped that D's voice would pull her back to the surface. But it didn't. "She's not going to be happy I told you."

"Didn't tell me. Guessed."

"Right." Semantics. No matter what, Bella would be pissed about it. If she wanted D to know she would have told him years ago.

"Get gone now," D said, but his words lacked any force behind them.

Axel steeled himself, tightening his arm around Bella's shoulders. "I'm not leaving."

"Not your decision," D said, planting those meaty hands of his on his hips.

Axel had no plans on getting up close and personal with one of those fists again any time soon. His face still bore the discoloration from the last time. But, no matter what, he wasn't leaving.

"Not going, D. If you feel the need to hit me again, then I'll take it like a man, but I'm not leaving her."

D's nostrils flared. "In uniform it'll be ag assault."

Axel glanced down his own body. His uniform shirt was unbuttoned from the collar to mid-chest, his undershirt was peeking out, his duty belt was in the corner of the room, and his boots by the bed. He hadn't bothered to undress Bella, either. He'd only removed her shoes before settling in next to her, just in case he did end up taking her to the hospital to commit her.

"She on meds?"

D shook his head. "Right after. Then stopped."

"She needs—"

"Fuck she does," he barked, cutting Axel off.

Axel frowned. "How is she going to deal with the baby once it's born? She and Sophie work together. And this baby isn't going to be the only one in the future for the club."

"She'll deal."

"She's got PTSD, Diesel."

Something flashed behind his eyes, but, again, he hid it quickly. "Yep."

Yep? That's what his answer was? An emotionless "yep?"

"Got us. All she needs."

Axel's fists clenched. He wanted to argue with D. He was starting to rethink how smart the man was. "This isn't a 'it takes a village' type of situation. It's serious."

"Know it. Now, you goin'?"

"No."

D practically bared his teeth. "Fuckin' pig."

Axel sighed. There was the Diesel he knew and loved. He shook his head. "Never changes, does it?"

"Nope. Not when you wear a fuckin' badge. Not when you an' your *brothers* are ready an' willin' to take us down."

"Stay on the right side of the law and there'd be no risk of that."

D grunted. "Time for you to get gone, cop. Got it from here."

"I don't think you do," Axel said low, with warning.

D's head jerked back, then he leaned forward enough to make Axel a little worried. Just a little.

Axel's heart thumped in his chest. "I'm not going anywhere, so fuck off."

D's eyes widened for a split second but he hid his reaction quickly. "Gun's in the corner. Wanna get it so this is a fair fight?"

Was this man serious? Bella was in the middle of a mental breakdown and he wanted to get into it over who was going to take care of her? "Don't need it because you're going to *get gone* and let me handle this."

D cocked a brow at him. "I am." Not a question but a challenge. One Axel was ready to meet.

Axel cocked one back. "Yeah, you are."

D's eyes flicked to Bella, then back to him. When he leaned forward more, Axel braced himself for another ass kicking. But the bigger man just reached out and brushed his fingers along Bella's pale cheek, then he straightened and pinned Axel with his gaze. "Don't fuck it up."

D spun on his heel and strode out of the bedroom.

Axel finally breathed when he heard the front door close.

BELLA'S EYES POPPED OPEN, and she stared up at the ceiling in the dark. She'd done it again. Disappeared. Lost herself. Lost time.

All because of something she should've been able to handle, but couldn't. Because she was weak. Unable to control her emotions, her mind.

She took a deep breath and closed her eyes for a moment to settle her thoughts.

She knew she was in her bedroom but she had no idea how she got there.

Diesel most likely. Throughout the years when she broke down or got lost, he was usually the one to find her and pull her back out from the black abyss. From those dark memories.

But D would never climb into bed with her. If anything he'd hold her in his lap on the couch or the floor until she "woke up."

And whoever was pressed against her in her narrow bed was not nearly as bulky as him, anyway.

She breathed deeply and caught his scent, listened to his steady breathing, his fingers buried in her hair, one arm over her waist.

She was fully dressed still, and it seemed so was he.

Someone had called Axel instead of D.

Sophie.

Bella didn't blame her, the woman still thought that she was seeing Axel. She didn't realize that they'd decided to let things go finally.

Sophie wouldn't have known.

Her head pounded with a headache and she needed an aspirin or three to reduce the pounding pain at her temples. Her mouth was as dry as cotton and she was way too warm from being held so closely to Axel's body. She shifted to break his hold.

"Stay." His gruff voice asked, "What do you need?"

You to leave my bed. For you to stop breaking my heart. "I'm fine. You can go now."

The silence between them grew by the second.

Finally, he said softly, "You scared me."

Bella squeezed her eyes shut, and she sucked in a shaky breath. "Sorry. It happens sometimes."

"What are you doing about it?"

She didn't want to discuss it. She didn't want to reveal her weakness any more than she already had. "I'm fine."

"You're not fine."

"Nothing for you to worry about."

"Bullshit, Bella."

She pushed out of his arms and sat up, dropping her legs over the side of the bed and holding her throbbing head in both of her hands.

"What do you need?" he asked again more firmly, sitting up.

"I can get it."

"Bella," he said, his voice holding a tinge of frustration and anger.

She sighed. "Water. Aspirin."

She heard him get off the other side of the bed. "I'll get it. Stay here."

He switched on the bedside lamp and the room lit up with a muted glow from the bandana draped over the shade.

She peered over her shoulder at him. He was in uniform, though it was not neatly pressed like normal. The fabric of his shirt was badly wrinkled, half of the buttons undone, the tails untucked from the waistband. He was bootless and his duty belt was missing.

She watched him move stiffly from the room. Her bed was way too small for the two of them. She knew it that first night he stayed over. But there was no reason to upgrade her bed. He had said he was done with her. That he didn't want to deal with her connections to the club if they were in any way questionable.

She didn't blame him. So, he shouldn't be here.

What the fuck happened?

He was back in minutes, a bottle of water and generic aspirin in hand. He handed them to her after opening both.

She took a gulp of the cold water, then downed three pills before placing both bottles on the nightstand.

He sat down on the bed next to her, close but not touching. "Want to talk about it?"

"No."

He said nothing for a minute.

"Next time, get Diesel," she said finally.

"He was here."

She glanced at him in surprise.

"He threatened to beat my ass if I didn't leave."

"And you stayed?"

"I wasn't leaving."

"Why, Axel?"

"Because... I couldn't."

"You should have. You should've left and let D handle it."

"I don't think he realizes the magnitude—"

"And you do?" she cut him off. "He does. He knows."

"He didn't know everything."

Her stomach churned. "And now he does? You told him?" she asked, her heart in her throat.

"He figured it out."

"He couldn't have," she whispered, her mind spinning.

"He's not stupid. He put two and two together."

It was bad enough that Axel knew, but now Diesel...

Axel continued, "You should've told him a long time ago."

"Not your business."

He stared at the floor and nodded. "You're right."

Bella didn't expect that answer from him and she was surprised at the ache it caused in her chest. She expected more of a fight from him. "You should go."

His chest rose and fell as he inhaled deeply, then he pushed to his feet and avoided her gaze as he moved around to the other side of the bed. "I have to go back to the station, anyway. I've had the cruiser all night."

Bella listened as he yanked his boots on, laced them up, then grabbed his duty belt and patrol jacket. She didn't watch him this time as he headed out of her bedroom door and down the hallway.

She closed her eyes as the front door clicked softly.

Axel was gone.

Chapter Eleven

"You shouldn't have left," Bella told Diesel's broad back as he helped carry a box of toys into the warehouse. She might as well be talking to a brick wall.

At least she got a grunt as an answer.

"You should've made him leave, D." She rushed past him to open the back door for him. "Are you listening to me?"

"Tryin' not to," he barked and pushed past her and down the hallway. "But hard to ignore you when you're screechin'."

"I'm not screeching."

"Sounds like it."

"Whatever." She followed quickly on his heels as his long strides ate up the floor space. The corridor spilled into a big wide-open area that held a few vehicles, some equipment, and a whole bunch of padlocked containers.

She wasn't even going to bother to ask what was in them. She would be wasting her breath.

He made a sharp right turn to a storage room they were using to house the donated toys until they could get them to Toys for Tots.

She rushed past him again to grab the door. At least being in D's warehouse, she knew the donations were safe. There was no way the

Warriors would break into this location to steal any more. Especially with D's crew coming in and out at all hours of the day and night.

And if the Warriors had any brain cells, they'd want to stay off his crew's radar. Especially since they had a hard-on for the Warriors ever since Kiki and Jazz were kidnapped.

She followed him into the room and as soon as he put the large box down, she began to sort the toys.

"Gonna be in my office. Find me. Gotta talk."

She straightened to ask why, but when she turned, he was gone. With a sigh, she went back to pulling each toy out of the box and organizing them by sex and age.

The community had really pulled through, especially when both the DAMC and the PD put the word out about the theft.

"Gotta find those fuckers before the PD does."

A deep voice behind her, one she didn't recognize, startled her. She straightened and turned toward the door. A tall man, maybe six-foot-three, leaned against the doorjamb. He had super short dark hair, military-type cut like Slade and Axel, had piercing gray eyes and the man would have been extremely good-looking if he didn't have a scar that ran diagonally across his face. With his arms crossed over his chest, it emphasized how big and built he was. He didn't look like a man to mess with.

He had to be Mercy. Though she never met him, she'd heard about him from Jewel, who was now helping D run the security business. She also recognized him from the scar.

Bella nodded. "Hope so."

"Gonna teach those fuckers a lesson they won't forget."

Bella had to admit a chill ran up her spine when he talked. He was scary as shit and she wouldn't want to be on his bad side.

Mercy pushed away from the door and took two steps into the room. Bella's pulse began to pound in her neck. Looking at him was like looking at someone with no soul.

Empty. Cold. Merciless.

"Heard you were stabbed," he said softly, his eyes running down her body. "The fucker dead?"

She wondered if D told him. Though she couldn't imagine why. If Jewel was running her mouth... "Yeah."

He gave her a sharp nod, then tilted his head as he stared at her. "Good. Thought I may have to put him on my to-do list."

That was probably a list you never wanted your name to be on. "Nope. He was taken out in prison."

"Where at?"

"SCI Greene."

His eyes crinkled so slightly at the corners Bella almost missed it. "No." He lifted his chin up and down her body. "Where at?"

"Is this a 'if you show me yours, I'll show you mine' thing?"

Finally, one corner of his mouth curved up. The side that was marred slightly from his scar. "Wouldn't say no if you're agreeable."

He might be a scary fucker, but his rough voice sent a shiver through her. If the man turned on the charm, he might be irresistible. Even with that scar and those intense eyes.

But he didn't and he wasn't, so she shook her head. "No thanks."

"You're a survivor." He tapped his temple with his finger. "Like that."

"Not looking for a date," she said, hoping he'd get the picture.

"Don't date," he answered, clearly not offended at her disinterest.

Of course he probably didn't date. He didn't seem the type to want any attachments. Until Jewel, Diesel was like that for the longest time. Fucking women in the bathroom at church. He didn't even want them up in his room so they wouldn't get any ideas.

Mercy probably did something similar, just pulled his pants down far enough to get his dick out, get it wet and tuck it back in once he was done draining his nuts. No commitments. No noose around his neck. No ball and chain around his ankle.

She nodded. "Good. Then no further discussion's needed."

He smirked. "You're D's family, so if you ever need anything..."

He let the rest of that fade off. Bella had no idea if he meant sexually or protection wise. Either way, she hoped she never needed his services.

"Done here? I can take you to D's office."

She glanced down at the remaining toys. She had more to sort, but she could finish that the next time she did a drop-off. "Sure."

She followed him out of the room and closed the door behind her. As they traveled down the narrow corridor she realized just how big Mercy was. He might be an inch shorter, a few pounds lighter, and not as broad as D, but the man was still someone to take seriously.

He halted abruptly and leaned into an open doorway. "Boss."

Bella heard D's familiar grunt. Mercy stepped back and lifted a hand, indicating she should go in.

As she stepped into Diesel's office, Mercy closed the door behind her at D's chin lift.

Why did she feel like a student going to the principal's office?

She looked at her cousin sitting behind his desk and snorted. "Hard to picture you in an office."

Even so, his desk was a mess. D had never been a neat person. She remembered how he used to keep his room at church; like a complete pigsty before moving in with Jewel. And now his ol' lady was always bitching about how he just threw his clothes and shit everywhere around her apartment, including the floor.

"Try to get Jewelee to do all this shit now," he grumbled.

"How's she doing with it?"

He grunted.

"Keeping you organized?"

D grunted again and leaned back in his office chair.

"You said we have to talk," she started. "What about? If it's about the toys—"

"That pig."

Her stomach dropped. "I already said you should've made him leave."

"Reason I didn't."

Bella waited.

And waited.

She lifted her hands impatiently. "Want to explain?"

"The man loves you."

Bella reached out to grab the arm of the chair that sat in front of his desk. She plopped her ass in it before her knees gave out.

First of all, she couldn't believe D called Axel "the man" and not "the pig" or "cop." Second, it floored her that D would even care how Axel felt about her.

"I know," she whispered.

"Wanted to pound the fuck outta 'im when I saw 'im in your bed again. Fucker wouldn't leave your side, though. Woulda let me do it just to stay with you."

"I know what it looked like, D, but he doesn't want to be with me."

D's brows rose sharply. "Why?"

"He realized that..." She stared at her clasped hands in her lap.

"What?"

Bella closed her eyes for a moment, then opened them before continuing. "That my loyalties lie with the club."

"Yeah. And?" he asked, satisfaction clearly in his voice.

Of course Diesel wouldn't see a problem with that. He lived and breathed DAMC. "He can't be involved with someone who might have ties to... illegal things."

His head jerked back and his eyes narrowed. "Ain't nothin' illegal."

"Right. But... with all the shit that's been going down with the Warriors... Squirrel and Black Jack's disappearance. You getting shot. Plus, you and Hawk getting arrested after that fight in South Side... And he knows your crew's hunting Warriors, D."

"My crew ain't a part of the club."

"Your business is. A percentage goes into the club coffers, D. So really, it is."

D grunted. He knew she was right.

"I told him it wouldn't work from the beginning. He kept pushing. Then reality hit him and he pushed me away instead."

"Ain't pushin' you away."

Bella sighed. "D, he already did."

Diesel shook his head, planted his palms on his desk and leaned forward. "That man ain't pushin' you away. Saw it with my own two eyes."

Bella sat back and studied her cousin. The one who always had her best interest at heart, even though he could be the biggest, most unfeeling asshole out of all the brothers. "Why are you telling me this?"

D sat back, too, running a hand over his short dark hair. He frowned. "Hate what his blood did to Z, freezin' him out. Hate they turned their back on the club. Hate they didn't do shit when Z went inside. But hate it even more that I fuckin' had no clue what Rebel was doin' to you. Hate that Rebel had the opp to fuckin' do you wrong. Hate the fact I didn't get the chance to take 'im out 'cause I woulda gutted the fucker." His eyes got hard and his body went solid when he growled, "Really hate the fact you kept that secret from me, Bella. Shoulda told me."

He slammed his palm on the desk and Bella jumped.

"An' it pisses me off that he took that life from you. From all of us. Good thing Rocky took the fucker out. Woulda loved to filet our colors off Rebel's back with the knife he stabbed you with."

"D—"

He raised his palm and shook his head. "Hate the fact you love a cop. An' hate that he loves you. But, woman, that's the fuckin' facts. You love each other as much as I hate it."

"You're getting all mushy. You getting soft now that Jewel's got you wrapped around her finger?"

D grunted.

That wasn't a no.

"The *fact* is," Bella stated, "it's not going to work. We're too different."

"Got DAMC blood runnin' through his veins. He's a biker at heart."

Bella shot up straight in her chair, surprised. "You *are* getting mushy!"

"Shut the fuck up," he muttered.

"*Fact* is I love you, you big asshole. And I'm lucky that you have my back."

D grunted, but she didn't miss his eyes softening just a touch.

He jerked his hand toward the door. "Get the fuck outta my office. Got work to do."

Bella pushed up from his chair and hid her smile until she faced away from him. Then she beamed as she reached for the door handle.

"Expect the fucker at the party. Time for this club to start movin' forward in all ways."

"Can't promise that," she said over her shoulder, without looking at him.

"Get it done," was the last demand she heard before heading down the corridor and back out to her car.

She had no idea how she was going to do that. She wasn't leaving the club, not that anyone would let her, anyway. So Axel was either going to have to accept her as she was… DAMC. Or she was just going to have to disappoint Diesel.

And Sophie.

She sighed. That reminded her that she needed to go apologize to the woman for freaking her out.

BELLA FROWNED at her brother Dex. "You are supposed to be keeping an ear out for the stolen toys."

"We are," he insisted as he made change. He shoved the cash register drawer shut, then thanked the customer. "Need help takin' that to your car?"

The man grabbed the stereo speakers and told Dex he didn't.

After watching the customer walk away, Dex turned his dark brown eyes to her with a frown. "Why're you here, besides bein' a pain in my ass?"

Bella looked over her brother's shoulder to see their sister behind the glass in the back office. Ivy made a face at her and Bella made one back. "I came to talk to Ace."

"He ain't here."

She groaned. "Thanks, Captain Obvious. So now I'm talking to you."

Dex twisted at one of the large clunky silver rings that he wore on his fingers. "We're keepin' an ear out."

"Did Axel stop by here to talk to Ace yet?"

"How the fuck would I know?" he snapped.

Bella narrowed her eyes at him. "Don't you work here?"

"Bad enough I gotta work with Ivy," he lifted his chin toward their sister, "but now you're in here pestin'."

"Dex, this is serious. Thousands of dollars' worth of toys went missing." Not missing, swiped by those asshole nomads.

"Know that."

"Don't you care?" she asked him.

If anyone would care it should be him. Their mother was a single woman raising three children on her own. If anyone knew what it was like to not get a lot for Christmas, it was the three of them. They probably would've gotten nothing if it wasn't for their uncle Ace and their aunts helping out. So she understood the need for a charity like Toys for Tots.

"Yeah. Of course, I do."

"Then act like it."

"Fuckin' bitches," he grumbled.

Bella jerked her eyebrows up. "Really?"

"You hardly ever talk to me unless you want somethin'," he grumped.

"'Cause you're a pain in the ass, too. Ever think of that?"

Suddenly he grinned and leaned back against the counter, crossing his arms over his chest. "Was gonna give some info to D…"

Bella's ears perked. "What info?"

"Gotta call from a shop in Baldwin."

"Baldwin!" she exclaimed. The Dark Knights were expanding into Baldwin, so it surprised her that the Warriors would dare step a foot into the other outlaw club's territory. And the Knights had a great dislike for the Warriors, wanting to see them obliterated as much as the Angels did.

"Will ya let me finish?"

Bella struggled to pin her lips together.

"Asked if we were gettin' a high influx of kids' electronics in. New shit. This is the time of year people are buyin' presents for kids, not sellin' 'em."

"Right. Have the name of the shop?"

"Yeah. Baldwin Pawn."

Well, that wasn't obvious. "Thanks."

She began to turn to leave when his brows furrowed and he jerked out his hand to stop her. "Hold up. Whataya gonna do?"

"Just go take a ride up there."

"Uh. No. Tellin' D to check it out."

"No. Hold off on D. I'll go talk to them and if I find out anything useful I'll give it to him."

"Uh, no," Dex repeated, shaking his head. "Ain't happenin'."

Now her brother cared what happened to her? "*Ain't* got a say in it, *Dexter*."

His face became stormy at her use of his full name, which he hated for good reason. "Okay, *Izzy*."

"Dex," she warned.

He lifted his palms. "Shouldn't have told you then."

She sighed. "I got it. I'm just going to go talk to them and see if they know anything else."

Her brother stared at her for a few seconds, then sighed, too. "Look, I'll call 'em an' tell 'em you're headin' up there. Then you gotta promise to tell D if you learn anythin', got me?"

"Got you." She smiled at him and turned to leave. She stopped and looked over her shoulder, blowing him an exaggerated kiss. "Love you, brother."

He grunted in reply.

Bella headed out to the parking lot and before she got to her car, Ivy was rushing out of the shop in her high-heeled boots, pulling on her leather jacket. "Hey, wait up."

She hit the automatic locks on her Challenger and looked over her shoulder as Ivy caught up with her.

"Where are you going?"

"Why?"

Her sister shrugged then smiled mischievously. "I'm bored to death. Dex can handle the pawn shop's customers until Ace gets back."

"Heading to Baldwin to check out a lead."

"For the theft?" Ivy asked.

"Yeah. You should stay here."

"Fuck that!"

They heard a screamed "Hey!" from above them.

Both their heads turned up to the apartment over the pawn shop. Jewel stood at the top of the landing with her hands on her hips. "What are you sexy bitches doing?"

Ivy snorted and Bella sighed.

"Going to Baldwin," Bella yelled back.

"For what?" Jewel jogged down the metal steps and approached the car.

"Dex got a lead that someone might have pawned some shit at a shop in Baldwin."

"Cool. Can I go?"

"Diesel going to have a shit fit?" Bella asked.

"Probably."

Bella turned to her sister. "Jag going to have a shit fit?"

"Probably" was Ivy's reply.

Bella smiled. "Mount up, ladies. We're heading to Baldwin!"

All three laughed as they climbed into the Dodge. Bella turned the key and the big block roared to life.

Chapter Twelve

BELLA LEANED back against the brick building and eyeballed the man who was obviously a biker but not wearing any colors. He had pulled into Baldwin Pawn's lot a few minutes before in a piece of shit van of the multi-color variety. As in the van had been wrecked and been patched back together with parts of several other pieces of shit vans.

Hurry the fuck up.

Though, she said it silently, she really wanted to shout it in the direction of that asshole. Her leather jacket wasn't warm enough to allow her to brave the elements for any length of time, especially during December in Pennsylvania.

Shit, this fucker was slow as he dug through the back of the van.

Two days ago, when her and the girls stopped in Baldwin to talk to the pawn shop owner, he'd been very cooperative. Since it was now Knights territory, she should've given them a heads up, but she hadn't. And she wasn't planning to, either.

If she told her plans to the Knights' enforcer, Magnum, he was sure to call Diesel and snitch on her. And she was determined to get the stolen toys back from those fuckers.

All she needed to do was find out where they were being kept. Then she could formulate a plan to steal back what toys remained.

She was sure both Axel and Diesel would be supportive of her idea. She snorted.

And that's why she wasn't giving them a heads up, either. If she did, the PD would go riding in like the Cavalry, then seize the toys as evidence until after Christmas, which would do the needy families no good. Or D and his crew would just go in and create chaos. This needed to be a stealth operation. There was no way she was letting those nomads get away with stealing shit. Not on her watch.

She also didn't tell the women she'd be coming back to Baldwin to "hang" out and hope that the Warrior, who had been stopping in every couple of days with new merchandise, would show up.

She also had to trust that Jewel hadn't told D anything they learned the other day.

Bella pushed away from the wall as the Warrior finally pulled a box from the back of the van and kicked the door closed with his boot.

She moved past him, avoiding eye contact as she went back to her car. The shop owner said he'd purchase any toys that the nomad club brought in and then donate them back to Toys to Tots, and that Bella could stop back next week to pick up anything he bought.

As she climbed into her Challenger, she wondered where else the fuckers were selling the stolen goods.

The earth would be a better place if the Warriors didn't exist, but she'd leave that to D's crew to deal with. Right now, she had to find out where the stolen toys were.

Bella sat in her idling car with the heat blasting for ten minutes until the asshole came back out of the shop, sans the box of toys. When he finally pulled out of the lot in the van, she rolled out to follow the vehicle.

Good thing somebody had a leaky valve gasket. The smoke rolling out of the exhaust pipe helped her track him from a distance without being spotted. She only hoped the dickhead headed back to wherever he was stashing the toys.

The Warrior headed north out of Baldwin toward the city of Pittsburgh and she made sure that she stayed far enough behind him where she could keep track of him, but not close enough to get made.

When the vehicle turned right, she went straight, then sped around the block, coming out a few streets down. They were no longer in Baldwin but another town nearby that she'd never been in before named Whitehall. Luckily, she spotted the van up ahead and began to trail him again.

When the van pulled into a driveway of an abandoned house—it had to be, because no one in their right mind would live in a house with busted out windows in winter—she pulled over to the curb quickly, parking behind another car.

Shoving the shifter into park, she leaned toward the windshield, watching as the dirt bag biker entered the house. Now, she just needed to wait until he left so she could enter the house and see if her loot was in there.

She hoped to hell it was...

Her heart skipped a beat, and she squeaked in surprise when her door was ripped open and a big body filled the opening. At first, she thought it was Diesel but as a bald head popped into her doorway, there was no doubt it wasn't. The massive man, a hell of a lot darker than D, was pissed. And that was putting it mildly.

"Move over to the passenger seat," he barked.

Fuck!

"Magnum," she pleaded, gripping her steering wheel tighter.

"No fuckin' lip, woman. Get into the passenger seat now before we're spotted."

With a grumble and a last reluctant glance toward the house, she awkwardly climbed over the center console and ended up on her knees on the passenger seat, while Magnum jammed his bulk into her driver's seat, shoved the seat back, and slammed the door shut.

His head spun toward her like he was possessed. "What the fuck, woman?" His shouting was way too loud in the now much smaller interior of her Dodge.

"I was just—"

"Just!" he barked. "Just? Just nothin'. Fuckin' first of all, you're in Knights territory without an invite or permission. Second, you're fuckin' up what we're tryin' to find out with those rat bastards. Had that shit under control an' you almost fucked it up."

"I—"

"*I* nothin'. Takin' you directly to Diesel. Fucker's gonna be pissed."

Shiiiiit. "You don't need to do that. I can head home myself."

He shook his dark head, the gold skull earring in his ear flashing as he did so. "No fuckin' way. In our house now. Gonna make sure you get outta here in one piece. Fuckin' Warriors would like nothin' better than to snag your ass an' torture the fuck outta you like your other sisters."

He shoved her car into reverse and backed down the street into a side alley, then he shoved it into drive and smashed the gas pedal down. Squealing the tires and fishtailing, he tore out of town toward Shadow Valley.

"What the fuck you thinkin'?"

She had a feeling she would be asked that several more times before the day was over. "I'm getting those toys back. They aren't going to get away with that shit. Stealing from kids!"

"No shit! Said we're workin' on it. Ain't a woman's job."

Bella sighed as he drove her car balls to the wall down the road. "Can you slow down?"

He only grunted, which she assumed meant "fuck you."

"Do you know if they're storing them in that house?"

No answer.

Jesus, he was like a Black version of Diesel. Just what the world needed: two grunting meatheads.

"If they are, are you planning on going in and getting them back?" she asked.

Bella's answer was silence. No, that wasn't true. It was Magnum turning up her stereo to drown out her questions. She reached over and turned the volume back down.

"Hey, don't be turnin' down Black Sabbath."

"My car. My rules," she muttered as the sign welcoming visitors to Shadow Valley whipped past them in a blur.

Magnum opened his mouth to bark something at her, but closed it quickly and flicked his gaze up to the rearview mirror. "Fuck," he grumbled.

Flashing lights and a screaming siren chased them down the road. Bella glanced over her seat to the SVPD cruiser following on their tail at the same high rate of speed. She turned to Magnum, "Going to pull over?"

He grunted.

"If I were you, I'd pull over," she suggested. "Like soon before this turns into a pursuit."

He grunted again and mumbled something under his breath before yanking the car over to the side of the road and hitting the brakes. Bella braced in case the cop behind them couldn't stop in time and rear-ended the car she loved so much.

As it was, the cop had to lock up his brakes and swerve over quickly to park at an angle behind her Dodge.

"Let me do the talking," Bella suggested, hoping Magnum wouldn't be a complete asshole to a cop she might know.

Magnum cocked a brow at her.

When she twisted in her seat, she saw exactly who was getting out of the cruiser.

"Oh fuck," she whispered, making Magnum check the rearview mirror a little closer.

"Know him?"

Bella closed her eyes and sighed. Did she ever.

Axel approached the driver's side door, and it was hard to miss his surprised face morphing into what she could only describe as dark and angry when he saw who was behind the wheel. He rapped his knuckle on the window and pointed his finger to the ground. "Roll it down," he ordered.

"Fuckin' pig," Magnum muttered under his breath but hit the power window button. No one said a word until the whir of the window silenced.

Then Axel took a step back from the car and bent over to shoot Bella a look. And it wasn't a good one. "Thought it was your car. There a reason why someone else is driving it?"

Magnum opened his mouth, but Bella quickly squeezed his thick, muscular arm. A move Axel caught if the sharp turndown of lips was any indication.

"Just giving Magnum a ride," she kept her voice light and as innocent sounding as possible. Like she normally went on joy rides with members of other MC's.

"Magnum." Axel repeated.

"Gotta problem with my name, cop?"

Bella squeezed Magnum's arm tighter.

Axel's frown deepened. "Looks like he's giving *you* a ride instead."

"You know how these guys are about having a woman drive them."

It was Axel's turn to grunt his answer. Ignoring Magnum, he caught Bella's gaze. "Are you okay?"

"Don't she fuckin' look okay?"

"Bella?" Axel asked, shifting in an attempt to look past Magnum's bulk.

She sighed. "No, I'm not okay. He's taking me to Diesel and I don't want to go."

Magnum's arm tensed under her hand and she released him.

"So, he's taking you somewhere against your will?"

Oh fuck.

"No, takin' her back where she'll get a lesson about stickin' her nose where it don't belong."

Axel blinked and then tilted his head like a dog whose curiosity had been piqued. "And where was that?"

Magnum stared forward through the windshield and ignored him.

Axel straightened and stepped closer again. "Okay then. Need your license."

Magnum twisted his neck to look at her. "See what happens when bitches meddle? Shit. Shit happens."

"Are you going to give me your license or do I need to call for backup?"

Totally ignoring Axel's question, Magnum asked her, "This your prez's brother?"

"Yeah," she muttered.

Magnum scratched his chin in thought but didn't reach for his license.

"You have a license?" Axel asked him.

"Fuck! You were driving my car without a license?" Bella shouted then whacked him in the arm.

He grunted and frowned at her. "Got a license, just suspended."

Axel held out his hand. "Let me see it."

"Don't got it on me."

"Out of the car."

Magnum cocked an eyebrow at Axel. "Want me to get out."

"Yep. Step out."

Axel stepped back a couple steps as Magnum opened her driver's door and untangled himself from the seat. Once he was out, Bella could only see him from his ass down. She wondered if Axel was now wishing he called for backup.

Bella scrambled out of the passenger side to see Axel escorting Magnum back to his car.

"Are you arresting him?" she yelled.

"Just putting him in the back of my car while I run him for warrants," Axel yelled back over his shoulder.

"Oh fuck," Bella mumbled. D was going to kill her. If Magnum had warrants, Axel was going to arrest the Sergeant at Arms of their ally and she would be blamed for it.

She jogged after Axel. "Do you have to do that?"

Axel stopped Magnum at the front of his marked car. "Hands on the hood. Legs spread... Back farther. Just going to pat you down for weapons."

Surprisingly, Magnum complied without argument. He probably knew the drill very well.

"Are you sure?" she asked Axel as he patted the bigger man down, checking his waistband for anything that could hurt him or illegal items.

"Bella, get back in your car."

"But—"

"Bella," he said in a bossy cop voice. "Get back in your car." He opened the back door of his cruiser, placed a hand on Magnum's head and guided the large man into his back seat.

"You have warrants?" she asked Magnum.

"Fuck no," he grunted before Axel slammed the back door shut.

Oh, thank fuck.

"See? No warrants," she said to Axel as he moved up to the driver's side door of the cruiser. "You can let him go now."

Instead of getting into his car, he locked the doors, grabbed her elbow and escorted her back to her Dodge.

"Are you crazy?" he asked a little too loudly, then dropped his voice low. "You're driving around with... No. A Dark Knight is driving *you* around in your car. What the fuck, Bella?"

"It wasn't my choice."

"So, should I charge him with kidnapping?"

"No."

"Then what?"

"Just let him out."

He shook his head like he couldn't believe she just asked him that. "I'm going to take him back to the station and one of his guys can pick him up there. Now you won't have to go to Diesel."

"You're not going to arrest him?"

"As long as he doesn't have warrants."

"What about his license?"

"I'll give him a citation for driving on a suspended license."

Relief flowed through Bella.

Axel's gaze bounced from his patrol car back to her. "Want to explain how this all came to be?"

"Not really."

He cupped her cheek and tilted her face up to him. "Bella, I love you, but it's this shit that I was talking about. Bet that guy has a record as long as my arm. *And* he was driving your car like it was stolen *on* a suspended license. Or so he says."

Since she couldn't argue with any of that she asked instead, "Got anything on the stolen toys?"

He blinked at the change in subject. "No, not yet."

"Right." If she waited for the PD to find them, they'd all be sold by then.

"Go home, Bella. Whatever trouble you were looking to get into, just don't."

"Who said I was looking to get into anything?"

His eyebrows shot up his forehead. "If ol' *Magnum* there is taking you to Diesel to teach you a *lesson* about sticking your nose where it doesn't belong... then..."

Yeah, that.

She lifted her palms up in surrender. "Fine. Going to go home."

His blue eyes narrowed. "Right. Don't make me swing by later to check."

She turned away from him and got into her car, having to adjust the seat so she could reach the pedals again. "No need to check up on me," she said before slamming the door closed.

She powered up her window and watched his chest heave in the side mirror. He was probably sighing in frustration. Then he shook his head and headed back to his cruiser.

She couldn't resist watching his ass in the mirror as his long strides took him quickly back to his patrol car.

As soon as the traffic was clear, she pulled back out and headed toward home.

When she finally couldn't see his police car in her rearview, she took a sharp right on the next side street and headed back to Whitehall.

Chapter Thirteen

"Got a fuckin' text an' know you couldn't be so fuckin' stupid as to try to handle this shit yourself."

"Who texted you?" Bella had a fifty-fifty chance of being right. And she couldn't imagine Axel had D's cell number. It wasn't like they were best buds.

Had to be fucking Magnum.

Bella sat in her car at the curb, staring up at the run-down house. She winced when Diesel boomed in her ear, "Don't fuckin' matter who texted me! Where the fuck you at?"

She pursed her lips. She could lie and say she was home, but that would be too easy for someone to check.

"I... uh..."

"Better not be in Knights territory. Tellin' you now, gonna cause problems between the clubs that we don't need, Bella. Bad enough you got Magnum taken into custody."

"He was arrested?"

"No, the pig let 'em go with a fine."

Bella let out a breath of relief. "He didn't have to drive me back."

"Yeah he did. 'Cause now you're back out where you probably shouldn't be. You better not be in Baldwin."

"I'm not in Baldwin." Which was true. Whitehall was not Baldwin.

She peered out of the windshield at the Warrior's stash house again. "D, I gotta go." And then she hung up before he could bitch at her anymore.

Oh yes, he would be pissed that she did that. The proof was him calling her right back. She ignored her ringing phone and decided to leave it on the passenger seat as she got out of the car.

Looking around, she noticed nobody was outside on the block, no one was parked in the driveway. The street remained eerily quiet. She hurried up to the house and went around back, sticking close to the overgrown bushes that surrounded the former dwelling. But because of those bushes, she couldn't peek in the damn windows. At the back of the house was an equally run-down porch and she carefully made her way up to the back door.

The screen was missing from the outer door and it hung crookedly off its rusty hinges. It squeaked loudly as she opened it, making her wince. So much for being stealth. She peered through the door's filthy glass pane into what used to be a kitchen. The appliances were all missing, the linoleum floor destroyed, and the counter tops coated with a layer of dust so thick that it had to be at least a half inch deep.

Trying the knob for shits and giggles, she was surprised to find it unlocked. After opening the door, she listened carefully.

Nothing.

She practically tip-toed through the kitchen and down the hallway, peeking into doorways to see if she spotted the toys.

Nothing.

Fuck!

At the front of the house a stairway led to the second floor. Though they looked like they'd seen better days, she'd gone this far, and wasn't turning back now. She took one tentative step, then another, putting her weight carefully on each stair-step. They moaned and creaked but held her weight as she climbed to the upper level.

Peeking into the first doorway she came to, she gasped.

The room was packed full of the stolen toys. The toys she'd collected, the toys the PD had collected, and more. She didn't know whether to be pissed even more at the Warriors or elated she found them.

"Fuckers," she muttered.

She checked the other two bedrooms and only found one partially filled with more of the stuff they took from the storage unit.

However, there were so many toys that there was no way she could carry everything herself and, if she could, they wouldn't all fit into her car. She cursed.

She would need to return with more people and more vehicles or get someone with a truck.

Axel had a truck.

But she doubted that he would do a little breaking and entering even in an abandoned house. Not to mention, there was a little issue called trespassing.

Hawk had a truck, too, but then she might as well tell D what she was doing, because Hawk would not let her come back here with his truck. She'd have to think of a good excuse why she needed it.

Crash! Crash might have a vehicle at the shop that she could borrow. He might keep his mouth shut or not ask any questions why she had to borrow it.

Yeah. She was going to hit up Crash and maybe drag Diamond back with her since she now worked in the office at the body shop.

After grabbing as many toys as she could carry, she hurried down the steps and back out the kitchen door.

She rushed around the side of the house and back out front only to stop dead.

Fuck!

There was no way!

No fucking way!

She groaned loudly, no longer having a reason to rush back to her Challenger.

Parked behind her was a truck. And leaning against that silver Dodge truck with his arms crossed over his chest and shaking his head was Axel.

Though, the man was no longer in uniform.

How the fuck did he know where she was?

Again with fucking Magnum! Had to be.

"Are you fucking kidding me?" he asked, or more like shouted at her.

She frowned and ignored his outburst, walking with fake calmness to the back of her vehicle. "Reach into my pocket? My keys are in there. Pop the trunk for me, will ya?"

Axel pushed away from his truck, his lips drawn thin, his eyes narrowed. "Are you asking me to assist you with B and E, as well as theft? A fucking burglary, Bella!"

"No it's not." With a sigh, she put the toys on the ground, since he apparently wasn't going to help her, and grabbed her keys to unlock the trunk. She opened it and loaded the few toys she had nabbed.

"I beg to differ," Axel growled.

"So arrest me," she said, slamming shut the trunk lid. She swung around to face him, hands on her hips.

"Not my jurisdiction, but it would just take a call to the local PD for that to happen. That what you want?"

"No. What I want is to take back what was stolen. From me, from you, from us. Jesus fuck! From the kids who are supposed to have a nice Christmas!"

"Bella—"

She swung a hand toward his pickup. "You have your vehicle here. That's what I need. A truck to haul it all back to Shadow Valley, Axel. There's a room and a half full of toys up there. I need help getting them before one of those asswipes comes back. You in?"

His blue eyes widened, and he looked at her with incredulity, scrubbing a hand over his military-short hair. "No, I'm not fucking in! I can't just go in there and steal the shit back! I'll need to notify Whitehall PD and they'll need to get a judge to sign a warrant to enter the premises." He glanced up at the house in thought. "Unless they can get permission from the property owner." He shook his head. "But who knows where that person is from the looks of it."

"We can't wait for that. They'll sell this shit soon. Or they might move it. We can't risk it."

"Bella, it's fucking toys! It's all replaceable. You put yourself in harm's way by coming here, by entering that house, by being anywhere the Warriors are or hang out."

"I don't think they hang out there. I think it's just a stash house."

He groaned as he scrubbed his palms over his face in frustration. "*A stash house*," came muffled from behind his hands.

"Axel..."

He dropped his hands. "Get in your car. I'm following you home."

"Axel—"

"Bella, get in your car now."

She pinned her lips flat as she stared at him. He was not going to help her. And now he'd tell Whitehall PD, and they'd go in and take all the toys. And they probably wouldn't even get an arrest out of it.

"And if I don't?"

His jaw tightened and his blue eyes darkened as he stared at her for a long moment. Then he reached into the back pocket of his jeans and pulled out something shiny and silver and very metallic.

Handcuffs swung from his index finger.

"You just said this isn't your jurisdiction!" Bella exclaimed, her heart thumping wildly.

"If I cuff you it won't be in an official capacity."

She smirked as his words sunk in. "So you're going to cuff me and have sex with me?"

His mouth opened and then shut closed. He stared at the toe of his boot and shook his head, dropping the cuffs by his side. She could have sworn she heard him mutter, "Fuck me."

Then he lifted his head, looked her straight in the eye and said, "No. I'm going to cuff you, shove you into my truck and take you directly home."

She lifted a finger. "Just to be clear, you're going to kidnap me like you accused Magnum of doing."

His expression became dark and stormy. "Unlike *Magnum*, I have your best interests at heart."

She crossed her arms over her chest. "Right." She tilted her head and studied him. "Tell you what. I'll get into my car and head back to your apartment with you if you use those cuffs on me in an *unofficial* capacity."

His body went completely solid and his lips parted with a rush of breath. His eyes quickly turned from angry and frustrated to heated. She could even see his Adam's apple bob from where she stood. A smile crept over her face.

"What's the catch?"

She shrugged. "Help me load the toys into your truck."

He scowled. "No. I'm not going to break the law just to have sex with you."

She shot him a fake pout. "Even with the cuffs? And the promise you can do whatever you want?"

"I... uh..." He shook his head as if to clear it. "No! Damn it. No."

Suddenly, he was there. Toe to toe with her. His hands cupping her face and tilting it up. He lowered his head until his lips were just barely above hers. She could feel the warmth of his breath on her lips and she was tempted to stand on her tip-toes to close the slight gap between them. Her nipples beaded under her sweatshirt as a thrill shot through her.

She couldn't deny the pull he had on her.

"Go home, Bella. Get in your car and go home. Leave this shit to law enforcement."

"Axel," she whispered, holding his gaze. He was so close but yet so far away.

"Yeah?" he asked softly.

"Take me home," she murmured, fisting the front of his jacket in her hand. "I'll still let you cuff me an unofficial capacity and let you have your way with me."

After a long pause, he stepped back, nodding. "I'll follow you."

Her pussy clenched hard and her breathing shallowed as she broke away from him and climbed back into her car. Before she pulled away, she picked her phone off the passenger seat and glanced at it.

Three missed calls. All from Diesel.

She pulled up her texts and read the furious ones he sent that were all misspelled because he was probably so pissed that he was fat-fingering them. She ignored them and typed in...

Get Magnum 2 grab stuff out of house b4 Whitehall PD gets warrant.

She hit Send. Turning the key in the ignition, she took a last look in her rearview mirror at Axel sitting in his Dodge truck waiting for her to pull away and she smiled.

Chapter Fourteen

AXEL SAT in the driver's seat of his truck with both hands on the wheel, tapping his finger.

His eyes flicked down to the passenger seat where his handcuffs sat there mocking him.

Mocking him.

Because he wanted to do this. He did.

But he shouldn't.

He'd told her they couldn't be together, that it would never work. Because of his job. Because of her affiliation with the club and their skirting of the law.

He wasn't willing to bend. Neither was she.

He should've just left her alone all those times she told him to. She had begged him to "let her go." He didn't. He couldn't.

And then the kiss happened. The sex in his truck. The sex in the storage unit. Then the sex...

Yeah.

He wasn't lying when he told her that she was like an addiction. She was.

She was all he could think about. Whether at work, watching football, hanging out with his fellow officers, driving by the bakery...

And he always worried about her.

Not that it helped to pull her car over and to see the Sergeant at Arms from the Dark Knights, one of the infamous outlaw MCs from the greater Pittsburgh area, driving her car.

Driving her fucking car.

The man had been on his way to hand her over to Diesel because she had done something crazy. Enough so that Magnum reluctantly cooperated with him on the way back to station, giving him the information he needed to find her.

The Knights' enforcer knew she'd head back to Whitehall and explained why. Even told Axel he'd texted D to give him a heads up. And stupid fuck that Axel was, he told this *Magnum*, this huge badass biker, to text D back and tell him that Axel would handle it.

Yeah, *he'd* handle it. Like he wanted to get in the middle of whatever bullshit Bella was getting herself entangled in.

He didn't know why she couldn't let the stolen toys go, let the PD handle it the right way.

Nope. She couldn't do that.

So now there he sat, in his truck, in front of his apartment building while his handcuffs mocked him for being weak and agreeing to come back to his place for sex. It wasn't just the cuffs mocking him, his cock was, too.

The whole drive back from Whitehall to Shadow Valley Apartments, he couldn't get rid of the picture of Bella cuffed to his bed as he did wicked things to her. So, his cock was steel hard, jammed cockeyed in his jeans and dripping like a leaky faucet.

"Fuck," he muttered.

He sucked in a breath when the passenger door was flung open. "Having second thoughts?"

He blew all the air back out as he studied her. Her long dark brown hair hung loose in waves around her shoulders and down her back. Her cheeks were flushed from either the chilly weather or the anticipation of having sex, and her eyes... Fuck, her dark brown eyes held a lot of promise of what could happen in the next hour. "Want the truth?"

"Always," she answered with a nod.

"I am."

If he went upstairs with her, he was going to get sucked right back in. And he would have a tough time pulling himself back out again. It was difficult enough last time when he finally admitted that he couldn't be with her. Especially after wanting her so much for so long.

"I'll go home, then," she whispered. Her expression might have been unreadable, but her voice couldn't hide her disappointment.

He closed his eyes and gripped the steering wheel tighter.

Was he going to let her go? Let her just walk away?

When she slammed the door shut, his eyes popped open. Tagging the cuffs and shoving them into his jacket pocket, he scrambled out of his truck, and hurried to snag her arm before she rounded her car to leave.

"Hold up."

She stared down at his fingers wrapped around her forearm. Then slowly she raised her gaze until she met his. "Changing your mind again?"

"I don't know what I want... No, fuck! I know what I want. Goddamnit, Bella, I want you. I've always wanted you."

"But not enough to look past my involvement with the club," she said softly, a hint of sadness tinging her words.

"It's not that simple."

She bit her bottom lip for a moment, then admitted, "I know it's not, Axel. I know."

Her gaze bounced to her car then back to him. Now her eyes held something... He could only guess it was regret. Maybe even the harsh reality of the situation.

She continued, "I'll make the decision easy for you. I'll just go."

As she began to move away, he tightened his grip on her arm. "Fuck... Don't go."

"I don't want you compromising your integrity by being with me. I've said this a million times, Axel, I'm DAMC and always will be. Even when I climb into your bed, that fact doesn't change. It never will."

His gaze dropped to where he held onto her. He could release her and let her go. Or hold on and pull her back into his apartment, into his bed, into his life.

Her warm, husky voice drifted over him. "You need to choose carefully. I don't want you to ever regret your decision."

"I don't want to risk my career, but I don't want to risk losing you, either."

"I told you before, there are other women out there that would fit better into your life."

"Do you think it'd be that easy for me? To just find someone else? Would it be that easy for you?"

"We're not talking about me. I'm not looking for a man, ol' man or otherwise. And, anyway, I'm damaged goods."

He shook his head vehemently. "You are *not* damaged goods. Fuck, Bella, that's bullshit. It kills me that you think that way, that you sometimes try to cover yourself when you think I'm looking. I love the way you look. Everything that's happened in your past has made you who you are... scars and all. I love everything about you."

"Except my being a part of the club."

Axel sighed and ran a hand over his chin. "I can't ignore that part."

"Right. And that's why I should go."

"Then why did you come here in the first place? Why did you say I could do what I wanted with you? Were you just trying to distract me enough that I wouldn't call Whitehall PD? So you could give Diesel or Magnum or whoever time to break into that house and clean it out? Is that what you were doing? You didn't want to be with me, you were just playing me?"

"No. There's nothing I want more than to go upstairs with you, Axel. Nothing."

"I think you're lying."

With wide eyes, she said, "Do I need to prove it to you?"

His nostrils flared as the blood rushed through him, landing back into his cock. "Yes, prove it. Prove to me how much you want me. That I mean something to you. That this wasn't just a play to get me away from that house."

"You could've called Whitehall PD on the way here. Nothing stopped you from doing that."

She was right. He could've, but he didn't. The truth was, he wanted those toys back as much as she did. He didn't want the Warriors to get away with ruining Christmas for a lot of needy kids. It stuck in his craw that the outlaw MC kept fucking with the DAMC and the PD's donations got caught up in the beef between the clubs.

And he had to admit, bringing her back here was just as much as a distraction for her, to get her away from that house and her mind off those kids' toys. Did she call or text someone from DAMC or the Knights to go in and get them? Most likely. But he didn't hear the call or see the text, so he couldn't be sure. His hands were clean if something happened and the toys were miraculously recovered.

It was an abandoned house that no one lived in. No one would be hurt. Nothing would get damaged. He would wait an hour or so and make the call to Whitehall to give them a heads up. If the toys were still there, then great. If not, then so be it. Either way, some kids were going to have a nice Christmas, for fuck's sake.

But right now, he was holding on to a beautiful woman he loved and had a pair of handcuffs in his pocket he was itching to use. He wasn't going to worry about how the stolen toys got returned as long as they got returned.

He released her arm. "If you want me, and this wasn't just a ploy, then I'll let you lead the way."

"Where are the cuffs?"

"In my jacket pocket."

She smiled, then reached into his pocket and pulled them out to study them. "They're a little cold."

"We can warm them up."

She swung them on her fingers, her eyes heated. "I was never into wearing clunky silver jewelry."

His dick kicked in his jeans. "First time for everything."

"I'm sure you're an expert with them. They won't hurt?"

"I'd never hurt you, baby," he whispered.

She nodded, then glanced toward his apartment building. "Why are we still standing here?"

With a smile, Axel swept an arm out. "Lead the way."

He stood still only for a second as she walked toward his place, her hips rocking and rolling as she approached the entrance. She didn't even bother to look back to see if he would follow.

She knew he would.

Fuck him, but he could not let this woman go.

Ever.

"To the bed or behind your back?" he asked her, his breathing ragged, his cock raging as he held the handcuffs in his hands. Bella slowly stripped off her clothes and as much as he'd like to do it for her, he'd rather sit and watch instead.

"Do you have to watch me?" she asked, her lips turning down at the corners.

"Yes."

"Why?"

"Watching you takes my breath away, baby."

The frown quickly disappeared and her eyelids got heavy as she shimmied out of her jeans. She had already shed her jacket, boots and socks, which laid in a pile on the floor.

"Hopefully in a good way."

He grabbed his erection and squeezed. As soon as they'd hit his bedroom, he had quickly stripped down to nothing in his excited anticipation of what was to come. "This leave you any doubt?"

Her burning gaze dropped to his cock, which made a drop of precum bead at the opening. She didn't bother to answer. Instead, she tossed her jeans onto the pile and yanked her sweatshirt over her head.

"Fucking beautiful," he murmured, when she tossed that aside and then stood in only her black cotton panties and matching plain bra. Even in her generic underwear, she did it for him a thousand times more than any Victoria's Secret model in a skimpy, overpriced lingerie set.

She traced her fingers over the scar on her chest subconsciously, then brushed her hand over her lower belly.

"C'mere," he encouraged, holding out his hand to her. He separated his thighs to make room for her to step between his legs.

She slowly did so, and when her warm skin brushed against his, he had to resist throwing her onto the bed to take her hard and fast. Fuck the cuffs.

He forced himself to take a breath, to slow his rapid heartbeat, to stay in control. Dropping the handcuffs onto the mattress, he grabbed her hips and pulled her even closer. Close enough so he could brush his lips over the pale scars that decorated her abdomen. The long horizontal one, and the smaller, thicker ones. While he did that, he slid his hands around her to cup her ass under her panties. He groaned against her warm skin as he squeezed.

Sliding her panties over the globes of her ass, they fell to her ankles, and he pressed his face into her belly and inhaled her scent.

She smelled ready for him. Warm, musky but sweet. He ran his fingers between the cleft of her ass, then up her back to unhook her bra. When it fell forward, she let it drop off her arms to the floor. He nuzzled his face between her full breasts, kissing the curve of one, then the other.

Her nipples were hard, peaked, begging for his mouth. When she brushed her fingers over his hair, he tipped his eyes up to see her staring down at him with a look on her face that made his heart squeeze and his chest tight.

No matter what outside forces might want to keep them apart, it was clear they were meant to be together.

No matter how many times she insisted there was a better woman out there for him, there wasn't. The only woman for him was Bella.

Without her, he'd be missing a piece of himself. He only hoped she felt the same.

He flicked one peaked nipple then the other with the tip of his tongue, then released her.

"On the bed." His voice sounded gruff even to his own ears.

Without a word, she moved from between his legs and rounded the king-sized bed, climbing on and settling in the center. He got to his feet and snagged the cuffs. "Now, I'll ask again. To the bed or behind your back?"

She cupped her own breasts and strummed her thumbs across the tips of her nipples as she contemplated her options. "Have you done this before?"

That was a loaded question. Would she really care if he had? "Not with you."

She grinned. "Good answer."

He snorted a laugh as he moved to the side of the bed. "Well?"

She glanced over her shoulder at the headboard. "Will it hold?"

"Are you planning on becoming a wild cat?"

"Absolutely."

His brows shot up his forehead. "I like the sound of that."

"Then what are you waiting for?"

With another chuckle, he raised a finger. "Hang on, I have an idea." Without waiting for her response, he rushed from the room into the kitchen and dug through his junk drawer. He found a heavy-duty zip-tie and a knife, along with his spare cuff key and hurried back into the bedroom.

He stopped short. Bella now sat against the headboard, knees cocked and spread, her fingers busy between her sweet, supple thighs.

With heavy eyelids she stared at him, her lips parted and a slight flush running from her chest, up her neck and into her cheeks.

"How wet are you?"

"Very," she whispered, her voice catching.

Axel swallowed the lump in his throat and moved forward. "As much as I hate to stop you from what you're doing, I need your hands out front."

She studied the items in his hands and, with a start, he quickly put the knife aside on the nightstand. He wouldn't need that until later and it only hit him then that she might get uncomfortable around a man with a knife.

He groaned silently at being a dumb fuck. "Sorry."

She shook her head, her dark hair sweeping across her shoulders.

"If I fell apart every time I saw someone holding a knife, I'd never get through life. A lot of the guys carry a knife on their belt."

He didn't want to remind her that she completely splintered apart by simply feeling Sophie's baby move. But then he didn't know what it was like to be in her head. He never had to deal with the tragedy she had, so he had no room to judge her reactions. But even so...

"Are you going to be okay with me restraining you?" he asked carefully.

Bella pulled her hand from between her thighs and raised it to him. "See that?"

Her fingers were slick and shiny with her arousal and he groaned. Leaning over he captured them in his mouth and sucked them clean, savoring her taste on his tongue.

"There's more where that came from," she whispered, her eyes heated, her legs spread apart and inviting.

"Hands out front," he ordered, donning his official cop voice.

She did it, holding them up and pinning her wrists together. He carefully cuffed her, making sure they weren't too snug against her skin.

He grabbed the zip-tie and told her to put her hands behind her along the headboard. When she did, he slipped the zip-tie through the slats and hooked it to the chain on the handcuffs. By using the plastic tie, he'd be able to turn her over without twisting her arms uncomfortably. If they even got that far.

Seeing her restrained to his bed, naked, pussy wet, nipples pebbled hard, he might not last as long as he'd like.

He needed to go slow, take his time, and savor her.

BELLA'S HEART pounded in her chest. Even her pulse throbbed in her neck, as well as in her pussy. She was soaked. Seeing Axel's lean, muscular body leaning over her as he fastened her cuffed hands to the headboard made her want to come right then and there. She tilted her head just enough to nip at his nipple and he jerked back, rubbing it where she made contact.

She thought he'd make her slide down onto her back, but he didn't. Instead, he moved until he was laying between her spread legs. He kissed from her knee up to the top of her inner thigh on one leg, then moved over and did it again on the other side.

He only touched her with his lips. Nothing else. It drove her crazy. She wanted not only his mouth on her, but his cock inside her and his fingers creating chaos everywhere else.

But he wasn't rushing. Oh no, he wasn't.

She closed her eyes as the tip of his tongue traced the same path where he'd laid the soft, gentle kisses previously. She sighed as his hot breath swept over her throbbing pussy.

His mouth, hot and wet, took her, his tongue sweeping through her swollen folds up to her clit, to tease her, to torture her. Lifting her hips slightly off the bed, she moaned, wishing she could grab his head with her hands and hold him tightly against her. But she couldn't. She was under his control.

She had told him earlier that he could do whatever he wanted to her. And that was true. She trusted him completely. Axel would never hurt her.

At least on purpose.

He might do so without meaning to.

She pushed that thought out of her mind and concentrated on what he was doing right now, which was bringing her extraordinary pleasure. He licked along her plump lips, sucking each one, then flicked her clit before dipping his tongue inside her.

"Yesss," she hissed. "Yes, Axel, yes..."

She opened her eyes and saw his tipped up to her, watching every response of her body, every reaction on her face.

He watched her intently as he plunged two fingers deep inside her, curving his fingers, stroking her gently. Tilting her head back, she gasped as he sucked on her clit. Her thighs began to tremble at his non-stop onslaught. She knew he wouldn't stop until she came.

At least once.

She hoped twice.

When her toes curled, she felt it coming. Approaching. Sweeping through her body. Then it hit her core like a tidal wave. Intense. Powerful. From deep within. She cried out his name, arching her neck as her hips shot off the bed. He stayed with her as she rode out the surge. He hung on and kept up his endless barrage against her sensitive skin.

As she caught her breath, and as the throbbing subsided, she groaned, "You're so good at that."

He pulled away slightly. "More?"

"Oh, fuck yes."

He chuckled against her heated flesh and started all over again, driving her quickly to the peak once more. This time when she came, she jerked at the cuffs, her whole body twitching in response to her strong climax. Her nipples ached for his attention. She needed him inside her, filling her, completing her.

She dropped her head forward and as he pulled away from her, his smiling lips were shiny from her arousal. He grabbed her ankles and she gasped when he jerked her down the bed until she was flat on her back. Then he stalked back up on his hands and knees until his face was directly over hers.

He lowered his head to take her mouth, parting her lips with his tongue, making sure she could taste herself. She groaned as he took the kiss deeper, rougher, their tongues tangling, fighting to get the upper hand.

Finally, he pulled away, pressing his forehead to hers. His breathing was as fast and ragged as hers. Then he shifted down enough to snag one of her nipples into his mouth, sucking hard, scraping her flesh with his teeth, pinching the other one between his fingers, rolling it, plucking it, twisting it, until her back arched beneath him.

She wanted more. She couldn't get enough of him.

In a flash he was gone, and she found herself quickly flipped over onto her belly, the cuffs clanking loudly with the sudden move.

He was up and over her, his heat and weight covering her as he pressed his mouth to her ear. "You said I could do whatever I want, right? Is that still true?"

She didn't even think twice. "Yes. I'm all yours."

"All of you?" His warm breath tickled her ear, causing goosebumps to break out all over her body.

"Yes."

"Baby, you don't know how good that sounds to me. You're mine, Bella. No matter what we say, no matter what we do, no matter who tries to come between us. You're mine. You'll always be mine."

She lost her breath at his words.

"Tell me," he growled.

"I'm yours."

"For always."

"Yes, always," she answered on a breath.

"I want you, baby, like you can't even imagine."

She closed her eyes and let his words wash over her. Warmth radiated out from her center. "I want you, too."

Her eyes burned with unshed tears. She needed to keep them at bay. She didn't want to cry. But, hell, this man moved her to tears time and time again.

She loved him so much that she ached deep inside.

How could her life turn out so differently? A lifelong biker chick with a rough, violent past, ending up with a straight and narrow cop?

From being with someone she only knew a few short years to someone she'd known a lifetime.

From being with someone who turned out to be completely evil, to one who was such the opposite. Someone who loved her for who she was and not what she was.

When Axel nipped her earlobe, she gasped, then he worked his way down scraping his teeth along the skin of her neck, alternating sharp bites and soft kisses from the top of her spine all the way down her back to right above her ass. He sucked her flesh hard, then swirled his tongue over the damp skin before moving down even farther.

His tongue tickled along the cleft of her ass and even lower. He circled her most secret spot with the tip of his tongue. Even though it was shocking to her, it made her nerve endings tingle.

She tensed as he got more aggressive, more daring. He pulled away enough to say, "Anything I want, right?"

Now she was rethinking her careless words. But again, she trusted him and he would never hurt her or do anything she wouldn't like or couldn't handle.

That wasn't him. That wasn't Axel.

He slipped two fingers inside her slick folds once more, while he continued to tease her tight hole, bringing about sensations she hadn't expected. She tilted her hips up to give him better access.

With one hand, he tapped her hip. "On your knees."

Using her elbows for leverage, she pushed to her knees, his fingers still buried deep inside her, working their way in and out, making her even wetter than before. He bit then kissed each ass cheek before whirling his tongue around her hole once again.

"Axel," she whispered, unsure where he was going to take this.

"You can tell me to stop."

She wasn't sure if she wanted him to stop. She was willing to let him continue, to see how far he'd go. Though, she believed if she told him to stop, he would.

Instead, she relaxed her muscles and let him continue his exploration.

Then his fingers were gone, and she felt empty.

"I want you," she whispered.

"I know," he murmured back.

"I need you."

She meant that in more ways than one.

The bed shifted under her and then she felt the hot, bulbous head of his cock at her entrance. He pushed forward just enough to separate her swollen lips. Just enough to make her want to push back, driving him inside her.

But she waited. She would let him do what he wanted, to be in control.

Then he tilted his hips enough to enter her barely an inch. Not enough for her. Not nearly enough.

But again she waited. And that wait made her jaws clench and her fingers twist harder into the sheets.

Suddenly, he was pressing on her anus, pushing through her tight ring with a slick finger. Up to a knuckle, then two, before hesitating.

Did he groan? She did, for sure.

It was crazy, the sensation was different but in a good way. She wanted him to continue on this new journey for her.

"Okay?" he asked, sounding strained.

She couldn't answer but moved her head in a nod against the sheets. She wanted to shout for him to keep going. To fuck her. To fill her up.

She opened her mouth, but before she could even get a word out, he thrust his hips forward and did exactly what she wanted. She took the whole length of his cock, accepted the whole length of his finger deep inside her.

Yes. She was his.

She. Was. His.

The outside world no longer existed. In this room, in this bed, their differences disappeared. They were only Bella and Axel.

Simply two people who loved each other. Two people who wanted nothing but to belong to each other completely, no matter what anyone else said or did.

This was how they were meant to be. Two halves of a whole, where one ended, the other began.

Her eyes rolled back in her head as he worked himself in and out of her at an unhurried pace. His warm breath swept along the skin of her back, his fingers dug into the flesh at her hip.

She heard him murmuring something low, raspy. "We'll do this again... next time take it further... I want you everywhere... I want you completely... Only mine, Bella... Only mine... Promise me... you'll only be mine..."

She didn't know if she should answer him, if he would even hear her, but she did anyway. "Only yours, Axel... I promise."

His pace quickened, his breathing became even rougher, and she just let him make her feel good, whole, loved. Having him in both places at once pushed her to the edge so much faster. She allowed him somewhere she never thought she'd let anyone. But it was Axel.

Her Axel.

She groaned into the mattress as she met him thrust for thrust. His hand on her hip slipped down and around her, his thumb pressing on her clit and that was all she needed for her to let go...

A grunt escaped him as she clenched around him hard, his finger, his cock. His rhythm stuttered. Then he drove himself deep and her name tumbled from his lips as he came. He throbbed and twitched deep inside her as cum spilled from him. And then he stilled. His breathing loud, his skin damp against hers.

"Holy fuck," he groaned, sliding his finger from her gently. He pressed his lips to the center of her back, giving her a soft kiss. "Are you okay?"

She smiled at his concern. "Yes. Perfect."

"Can you wait for me to release you until I've cleaned up?"

She twisted her head as he pulled out and moved off the bed. But before she could answer, he was gone, heading down the hallway to the only bathroom in his small apartment.

She could hear the water running, the toilet flushing and then before she knew it, he was back, releasing the handcuffs with a long, narrow key, cutting the zip-tie free from the bed. After throwing the items on the nightstand, he took her into his arms, gathering her close.

"I need to clean up, too," she reminded him.

"I know. Just let me hold you for a minute."

She sighed with exaggeration. "Just a minute, then," she teased. But honestly, she was in no rush to leave his embrace. She pressed her hand to his chest over his heart to feel the strong beats beneath her palm.

"That beats for you," he whispered, placing a kiss along her temple.

She felt the sharp sting once again behind her eyelids and she blinked back her tears.

"I love you, Bella. No matter what happens, always remember that."

Unfortunately, she knew love didn't solve everything.

Chapter Fifteen

"Fuck me," came in a low grumble beside her. Bella followed Zak's gaze to see what he was commenting on.

"Fuck me," she repeated under her breath and tossed the small towel she was using down onto the bar.

Z started to push to his feet and Bella quickly reached out to him, shaking her head. "No. Let me handle this."

Z's eyes narrowed on her, but he gave her a nod.

All the raucous carousing, the smack of the pool balls, the hooting and hollering—except for the loud music being piped into the common area of church through the speakers—suddenly lowered to a dull roar. Nash's band, Dirty Deeds, continued to play hard rock Christmas tunes on the public side of the building in The Iron Horse. Of course, they had no idea the end of the world was upon them.

Bella grimaced as she rounded the bar. Eyes were either pinned to her as she moved quickly through the crowded floor space or they were on Axel as he stepped inside the clubhouse by the way of the back parking lot.

Bella's heart began to race and worry ate at her gut.

She ignored the low insults, curses and unkind comments that were shot his direction as she met Axel about three steps into the room.

She got as close as she could, stopping his forward progress by grabbing a hold of his jacket at the waist.

"Maybe this wasn't such a good idea," she said, staring up at his serious poker face and tight jaw as he surveyed the room before dropping his gaze to hers.

"Didn't I tell you that?" he asked stiffly, his lips hardly moving.

"Yeah, I know. But—"

She felt the presence of the two extremely large bodies behind her before she saw them, though she had a feeling she knew who was at her back, especially by watching Axel's face. His reaction disappeared as quickly as it had come. He certainly was good at gathering his courage and hiding his rightful concern.

Suddenly, those two men flanked either side of her. She sighed but refused to step away from the subject of their attention. She refused to let him face them alone.

Magnum leaned close to Axel and sniffed loudly, his nose wrinkling. "Smellin' pork." His dark eyes flipped to Diesel. "Didn't know we were roasting two pigs tonight."

"Any night's good for a pig roast," D mumbled.

"So, what's he doin' here?" Magnum asked, as if Bella and Axel were deaf.

D's eyes slid from Magnum to Axel and back. "Fuckin' my cousin."

Bella closed her eyes and inhaled deeply through her nostrils before letting the air escape through her lips in a rush. She was not going to go postal on those two meatheads. She wasn't. But it didn't help that Axel was as stiff as a board under her hand. He needed to keep his shit together, too, for this to work.

They were just toying with him. And he couldn't let their attempt at intimidation pressure him.

"Then take the fucker out," Magnum suggested with a shrug and a smile.

"You know, I'm fucking standing right here. I can hear your threat."

Diesel and Magnum both grunted as they grinned at each other.

"Ain't gonna do nothin' about it. Already met this one," D held out his fist that said "Dirty," then raised his other one that had "Angel" tattooed on the fingers. "Might meet this one, too."

Magnum put his head down and chuckled, his big body shaking.

A sudden whirlwind hit them. Jewel, hands on her hips, stood toe to toe with Diesel, her eyebrows raised as high as the stars and stripes on a flagpole. Her face was flushed, her eyes snapping. "Are you fucking serious? This is a fucking Christmas party! Are you really threatening to hit Axel when he was *invited* here by Bella? Why are you acting like a fucking beast?" She shook her head and scowled at him.

"Woman," D grumbled in a low warning.

She jabbed a finger into his chest and screeched, "Don't you 'woman' me!"

His head jerked back as he stared down at his ol' lady. "Woman, back the fuck off."

She stabbed his chest again. "You start shit tonight..."

"What? What you gonna do?"

"It's what I'm *not* going to do," Jewel huffed.

Diesel grunted, then shot a look at Magnum. "My woman needs a fuckin' lesson."

Magnum's full lips drew into a wide, knowing smile. "Best kind."

Then before anyone could react, D had Jewel thrown over his shoulder and was taking long strides toward the stairway to the second-floor rooms. His shouted "Be back" promise was drowned out by her bitching at him to put her down and slapping at his back.

A bunch of hoots and whistles followed them as he disappeared up the steps taking two at a time.

Axel glanced at Bella, his brows raised. "Uh... Is she going to be okay?"

Bella snorted. "Yeah. But we might want to turn the music louder, so you don't hear your cousin howling like a cat in heat."

"Jesus," he muttered.

She nodded, fighting a grin. "Trust me, it isn't pretty."

He winced. "I'll take your word for it."

"Yeah, I'd highly suggest that. Let's go get as far away from the stairs as possible." She moved to Axel's side, still holding a handful of his jacket, and gave Magnum the eyeball. "Not that it's your club and you shouldn't have shit to say, but do you mind getting the fuck out of our way? We have a Christmas party to attend, booze to drink and good food to eat."

Magnum's lips twitched at her little speech.

"Now," she continued, as she held the larger man's dark gaze. "I appreciate your brothers bringing back the stolen toys. And I'm sure this representative of the Shadow Valley PD does as well and he's about to say thank you for that." She looked at Axel and tilted her head toward the pine tree decorated with Harley ornaments, bike parts, and random paraphernalia that was propped up in the corner of the room. His eyes slid that direction and then widened.

When Magnum and his crew had arrived earlier, they all came in carrying the shit they "confiscated" from the Warrior's stash house. Because there was that much stuff, it all didn't fit under or even around the tree, so she had them stack some of the toys there, but the rest ended up stored in the club's meeting room until the prospects would be able to deliver everything to the Toys for Tots representative the next day.

Watching the Dark Knights bringing in all those toys almost made her fall to her knees in relief. Hell, why she was down there she would have even kissed Magnum's feet for cooperating with her plan for his club to get the toys out of the house before Whitehall PD did.

It worked and from what Z said, everything had gone smoothly. No run-ins with either the PD or the Warriors.

But she was sure the Warriors weren't happy. Nor was the PD for taking the time to get a warrant, then showing up and not finding shit after Axel called them.

But, to Bella, that was neither here nor there. A large chunk of the donations was recovered. Which meant it would be a merry Christmas for a lot of families who needed it and for kids who normally went without.

"So now Axel's going to thank you." She tugged on his jacket.

His blue eyes narrowed at her for a split moment before he turned to face the Knights' overly large Sergeant at Arms. His face got a pinched look, and it looked as though he had a bad taste in his mouth as he said, "Yeah. What she said."

Bella bumped her hip into him and whispered, "Try again."

Axel grimaced, brushed a hand over his head, then choked out, "Thanks."

Magnum smirked and cupped a hand to his ear. "What was that?"

"You heard him," Bella said, frowning.

The Dark Knight bellowed out a laugh and lumbered away.

She sighed. "Let me get you a beer."

"I think I should stay one hundred percent sober."

"You need a beer to loosen up."

"Not sure if that's going to happen tonight."

She bit back a smile. "Come. Sit by the bar while I serve."

"Why are you working?"

She shrugged. "I don't know. It keeps me busy and I'm used to it. And bartenders always hear the best shit."

She slipped her hand into his and intertwined their fingers before tugging him behind her toward the front of the crowded room.

He tilted his head as he followed her. "That a band playing?"

"Yeah, Dirty Deeds set up over at The Iron Horse."

"Bar closed?"

"To the public, yeah."

He nodded his approval. "Probably for the best. Safer that way. Front entrance locked?"

"Yes, Axel, everyone has to come around back to get in."

He nodded again.

Before he could ask the next question, she interrupted him. "Can you shut that shit off?"

"What?"

"The cop shit. If you think anything's going to go down with all these bikers in here tonight..." She let that ride.

"I sure as fuck hope nothing goes down."

She let her gaze drift down to his boots and wondered if he did what he said: strapped a gun to each ankle. If he was double packing, she couldn't tell.

Suddenly he lurched forward, knocking their hands loose.

"Look at that, thought the only pig here tonight was on the spit outside," Zak exclaimed, going toe to toe with Axel.

"Z," Bella said in a low warning.

Suddenly, Sophie was between the two brothers, shooting Bella a look and a secret smile. She grabbed Axel in a hug, squealing, "I'm so glad you came!" She took his hand and put it on her belly. "Feel your niece? She's rocking and rolling tonight to the festive music!"

Axel's eyes went from hard as he stared at his brother to soft as he dropped his gaze to his sister-in-law's rounded belly.

Then they widened as he said, "I feel her. Damn! She's a busy little thing."

"Ain't a girl," Z grumbled.

Bella pinned her lips together in amusement until it hit her that she'd never be pressing Axel's hand to her belly to feel their child move.

Sophie looked over at her tentatively. "Want to feel?"

Bella hesitated and then shook her head. "Another time."

Sophie nodded and went back to beaming at Axel, keeping his hand glued to her stomach. She winked at him. "If you want to get her something, little pink onesies with elephants would be cute."

"Ain't a fuckin' girl," Z grumbled again, a little louder. Both Axel and Sophie ignored him.

With a smirk, Axel asked, "And if I can't find a pink one with elephants?"

"Any cute animal will do," she assured him.

"Ain't gonna be a fuckin' girl," Z griped louder one more time as Ace and his wife, Janice, approached. Ace snorted and slapped Z on the back.

"Don't matter if it is. Just want her healthy," Janice told Zak.

"Stop sayin' *she* an' *her*," Z complained. "Gonna jinx it."

Ace chuckled and pointed to Zak's groin. "Whatever came outta that nut sack of yours is what the sex's gonna be. If it's a girl, it's all your fault, son." Ace turned to Axel and put a hand on his shoulder.

"Glad to see you here, Axel. 'Bout time you come hang out with the dark side of the family."

"Well, he had a good reason to, right, Bella?" Janice asked, giving her a sly look.

"It's nice to see you two boys gettin' along," Ace said, his eyes crinkling at the corner like he was trying to contain his amusement. "Should sit down an' have a beer together."

Sophie gasped. "That's a *great* idea!"

Z and Axel's gaze slid to the other and then slid away quickly.

"Gotta go check somethin'," Z grunted, then disappeared.

Sophie patted Axel's arm. "It's going to take a little while. Don't worry."

Bella contained her snort. She doubted Axel was worried about it. Though she did have to admit that at least he took a step forward by showing up here tonight.

Sophie leaned against Bella, wrapping an arm around her when she whispered, "Thank you."

Bella gave her a small smile. "Too early to thank me."

Sophie nodded. "I'm going to head over to The Iron Horse and get some food. I'm starving!"

"Kiki and Hawk over there?" Bella asked.

"I think so," she answered over her shoulder as she walked away.

"I'll pop over there in a bit."

"Don't wait too long. Get some of the food while it's fresh."

She watched Sophie walk away with Janice following in her wake.

"Coming, ol' man?" the older woman called out.

"In a minute," Ace answered.

Bella started as her uncle unexpectedly cupped her cheek and turned her to face him, his eyes soft. "Proud of you," he said quietly.

"For what?" she asked, surprised.

"Overcomin'. Pickin' a good one this time."

Her eyes flicked to Axel, who pretended like he couldn't hear what Ace was saying.

"Ace," she breathed.

"Know it's all new…"

Ah, fuck.

"Ace," she began again, a little firmer this time.

"Just gotta work on bringin' Mitch 'round. With Mitch, will come April. No need to work on Jayde, she's here tonight."

"She is?" Bella asked, surprised.

"Yeah. Saw her headin' over next door."

"As long as she isn't heading upstairs with anyone," Axel interrupted.

"Nah. You know Z would bust a gut if that happened. He'll see after your little sister."

Axel scowled as if he was worried about Zak taking over his job protecting their younger sister.

"An' my boys won't let anyone take advantage of her, either."

That was for damn sure. Both Diesel and Hawk would keep an eye out on their president's sibling.

"All right, 'nough talkin' to this old man. Go have some fun. It's fuckin' Christmas for fuck's sake!"

With a whack on Axel's back, Ace wandered the same direction as his wife.

"C'mon," Bella said, yanking Axel toward the club's bar. "I'll buy you a beer."

AXEL WATCHED Bella move down the bar, pouring beers, opening bottles and handing out shots. Even when she was busy, she'd pause and give him a smile that would shoot the blood straight down into his cock.

He wasn't planning on leaving the party until she did because he was taking her back to his place. He wanted to kiss that sweet mouth of hers. And that was just for starters. His cock twitched in his jeans at the thought of her wrapping those lips around it.

He sipped at the draft beer she had slid in front of him twenty minutes before. He'd hardly made a dent in it since he needed to stay on top of his game. He was in enemy territory and most of the time he was at the bar, he'd sat at an angle because he hated putting his back to the crowded room.

Though, he was pleased to see that the club members, both Angels and Knights, as well as various prospects and club hang-arounds, didn't give Bella any shit. She was super comfortable around all the bikers and their women. But then she should be. This shit ran in her blood. She knew no different.

As he sat there trying to keep to himself for the most part, he tried to imagine how his life would have been if his father hadn't broken away from the club. Hadn't raised him and Jayde, and even Zak, away from the club family. Though, as soon as Z could, he slipped right back into the fold.

That's when the split occurred. His father had been—and still was—pissed that the effort he put into raising his children "right" went to the wayside when it came to his oldest child.

Z and Axel had always been close when they were little, it wasn't until Zak turned ten or so when he decided he wanted to ride motorcycles, whether dirt bikes or just riding on the back of Ace's sled.

Every time Z would take off with Ace on the back of his bike, Axel would feel the jealousy biting at him. But every time Z got dropped back off he had to deal with Mitch's wrath. Year after year, Z pulled slowly away from the family, sneaking off whenever he could to hang at the club, to learn about Harleys, to entrench himself into the biker lifestyle.

Axel knew Z had hid his prospect vest under his bed. The fucking guy was a prospect when he wasn't even old enough to vote yet. He was patched in the day he turned eighteen and was the club president before he was even old enough to drink legally.

This club was his brother's life. At least until Sophie walked into it. Now, his life revolved around the MC, his wife and his future kid.

Axel felt a little bit of jealousy nipping at him again as he watched his blood brother surrounded by club brothers. They all respected him, loved him, and had his back. The allegiance ran deep in this MC.

It also hit him how their brotherhood was even stronger than Axel's own, the "blue line." The DAMC members were more loyal to each other than his fellow officers at the station. Yes, his fellow officers were a family in a way, but not as tight as this MC or even the Dark Knights.

Axel's head spun toward Bella as he heard her striking laughter rise up from the other end of the bar. She was leaning over, whispering with Crow. Her eyes were alight and her smile wide as the tattoo artist knocked her hand away from his long, black pony tail with a smirk. They clinked their whiskey glasses together, took a sip, then she headed back toward Axel, her eyes still smiling.

Axel studied Crow at the other end of the bar and wondered how the hell the man ended up a part of the DAMC. From what Axel knew, the man had no blood ties to the club and he wondered how a man with Native American blood would even land in such a normally non-diverse club like this.

Bella stopped in front of him.

"What's his story?" he asked her.

She glanced back down the bar. "Crow?" She shrugged.

"How'd he end up in the club?"

"I don't remember. It seems he's always been around."

"But he didn't grow up in the club."

"No. But neither did Crash, or Rig. Or even Dawg and Nash. Not all of us were DAMC kids."

He was well aware of that fact. Especially since the club was actively recruiting. None of the current prospects had blood ties from what he could tell. It wouldn't be until their generation's children grew up and joined would the Doc and Bear bloodline continue.

That bloodline ran strong and was pretty much the tie that bound the club in general. That's why he was surprised that Pierce was voted in as president after Z went away to prison.

He had no idea why Ace hadn't stepped up. But then, he knew Ace had a lot on his plate. And still did.

When he heard Bella make a disgusted sound, Axel shook himself out of his thoughts. He glanced up at her.

"What?"

Bella tilted her head toward one of the prospects who was rounding the bar to approach her. Axel read his name patch.

The prospect named Weasel pointed to his groin and asked Bella, "Gonna kiss me under the mistletoe?"

Axel's gaze dropped to where he was pointing, and his hackles rose. The asshole had a piece of plastic mistletoe hanging from his belt buckle and he was holding back his leather prospect vest to show her.

He was ready to leap over the bar to thump the twenty-something year old idiot when he realized Bella could handle herself just fine. She was probably used to obnoxious behavior like that, especially when she tended bar for years over at The Iron Horse.

Bella wrinkled up her nose and rolled her eyes. "Seriously? Does that work with other women?"

Weasel shrugged. "Yeah."

"Right. You think I'm stupid?"

"All bitches—"

"Careful," Axel growled. There was only so much he was willing to take, though.

Weasel's head swung his direction. "What the fuck are you doin' here?" He turned wide eyes to Bella. "What the fuck's that pig doin' here?"

Bella's eyes narrowed as she slapped a hand on her hip. "He's with me. Got a problem with that?"

He frowned and shook his head, muttering, "Crazy bitches."

As he stomped away pissed, Bella yelled, "Still want me to kiss you under the mistletoe, Weasel dick?"

As the prospect shot her the bird, he stepped from behind the bar and slammed directly into Crow, who scowled down at him. "You just give 'er the finger, *prospect?*"

Weasel scowled back. "What's it to you?"

Crow straightened to his full height, his dark eyes narrowed on the prospect. "Let me see that finger you like to flash around. Must be an important one."

"Fuck you," Weasel grumbled, trying to skirt the bigger man.

Crow shifted, blocking his escape. "First, fuckin' disrespectin'

Bella, now disrespectin' a patched member. Can see your time's limited in this club."

"Ain't gotta say in it."

"Ever wonder why you ain't fully-patched yet?" Crow said in a low, dangerous voice.

"Startin' to wonder since they patch in people like you." Weasel spat on the floor at Crow's feet.

"Like me," Crow echoed softly.

"Yeah."

Weasel tried once more to step around Crow, but the ink slinger widened his stance to block the open end of the bar. "Still waitin' for you to show me that important finger of yours."

Weasel slowly lifted his hand, giving Crow the middle finger. As he shoved it in Crow's face, Crow grabbed his hand lightning fast and snapped the extended finger.

"Fuck," Axel muttered and winced as the prospect screamed in pain.

"Gimme your cut," Crow demanded, ignoring the man's hollering as he held his injured hand.

"Fuck you!" Weasel yelled, doubling over.

"I need to break your other one?"

Then Z was there, moving Crow to the side with a hand on his back. "Gimme your colors, you fucknut, before I get D to take 'em from you."

"Don't need D," came a deep voice behind Crow and Zak. Hawk reached through them, grabbed Weasel by the collar of his vest and yanked him through the two other men as they moved out of the way quickly.

The prospect ended up on his knees at Hawk's feet. And since Hawk was six-foot-four, not counting his mohawk, that was not the best place to be.

"I feel like I should be stepping in," Axel murmured to Bella.

Her eyes slid to him as she shook her head, but said nothing.

Axel sighed, taking another sip of his beer and then decided he'd only intervene if things got too out of hand. He had to remind himself that he was outnumbered here, and he didn't want to end up as the piñata he worried about becoming.

Crow moved behind Bella and put his hands on her shoulders, leaning close to her ear. "Okay, baby?"

"Yeah, he's just a weasel dick."

Axel stared at Crow touching his woman. Crow's dark eyes slid to him and he gave him a grin, then wrapped his arms around Bella even tighter, pulling her against his chest.

"Really?" he mumbled.

Crow cocked a brow at him. "Gotta problem with it?"

"Yeah, I do," Axel responded.

Bella patted Crow's forearm, then peeled his arms from around her. "C'mon, Crow."

The man shrugged, shot Axel another smile and wandered off to the other side of the bar. Once he was gone, Axel's attention went back to what Hawk was doing with the prospect, or former prospect, apparently.

When he turned his head that direction, he realized they were gone. Axel shot up from his stool and turned around to see Hawk dragging Weasel toward the back door. He no longer wore his prospect cut, instead Zak was holding that. But Hawk still had him by the collar as the smaller man was being slid along the concrete floor.

Dawg rushed to open the steel door and once Hawk got him to the threshold, he got behind the former prospect and shoved him out the door with his big-ass boot. As soon as Weasel tumbled outside, Dawg slammed the door shut and made a big show of dusting off his hands.

"Good fuckin' riddance," the strip club manager shouted.

A yell rose up from the crowded room. Then Hawk bellowed, "Down an' dirty..."

"'Til dead!" came the answering cry.

Zak jumped up on a nearby pool table interrupting their play and held up the prospect's cut in one fist. "Listen up!"

The room's noise level lowered. "This is a warnin' to all you prospects an' wannabes. When you're a prospect you're lower than dogshit. You disrespect any one of us, includin' our women, an' your ass will be outside lickity-fuckin'-split."

"You hear your prez?" Hawk hollered.

"Yeahs" and "fuck yeahs" were shouted around the room.

Hawk nodded, then looked back up at Z.

"Now we got lots of pussy, food an' booze here to celebrate Christmas right. So, eat, fuck an' be merry!"

Axel shook his head at his brother's speech. "So fucking eloquent," he mumbled.

"Gets the job done," Bella said.

Axel's attention was drawn to the swinging door of the kitchen. He was hoping it would be his sister, Jayde, coming through it. He couldn't help but be worried about her being amongst bikers from two MCs. He doubted any of the Angels would fuck with their president's sister, but he wasn't sure about the Knights.

Unfortunately, it wasn't Jayde coming through the doors, but Grizz with a plate piled high with food. Axel's stomach growled. It actually looked and smelled good.

Imagine that.

But it was time he found his sister. "I'm going to head next door and check on Jayde."

"I have a feeling I know why she's been over on that side."

"Why?"

"Two reasons really. And both are pretty good-looking."

Axel's brows shot up. "Who?"

"Well, Slade for one."

"That new guy that hit on you? The one that Diamond's chasing?"

"Yeah."

"And who else?"

"Well, last time she was here—"

"Last time? When the hell was that?"

"That time she came into church to say hello to her brother who just got out of the slammer. Remember that?"

Axel frowned, but nodded.

"She was eyeballing Linc. And those two were having a little chit-chat at Z's wedding, too."

"Great," he grumbled.

Bella laughed. "She's old enough to make her own decisions, mistakes or otherwise."

Axel's frown deepened. "Still my little sister."

"Understood," Bella said with a smile. Her eyes twinkled with amusement. "I'll go with you."

"Why? You worried about me?"

She hesitated. "Yes. But I could use something to eat, anyway. And Grizz's plate looks good."

Axel snorted. He met her at the end of the bar and held out his hand to her, which she accepted right away. He raised their clasped hands and kissed her knuckles. "Lead the way, baby."

Chapter Sixteen

AXEL SAT BACK with a full belly and groaned. Grizzly's wife Mama Bear certainly knew how to put out a spread. And the woman could keep the sweet butts and prospects on task when it came to keeping the food coming out fresh and hot. He wouldn't be surprised if she had a bullwhip hanging curled up on her belt.

Music, the sounds of people playing pool, loud, rowdy conversation, and smoke swirled around him. He didn't think he ever heard Nash's band, Dirty Deeds, play before, but he was impressed with how good they were. A temporary stage had been set up in a corner of The Iron Horse and Nash sang and played the drums like a pro.

He was also impressed on how they made Christmas tunes rock out, giving them a heavy metal/hard rock vibe.

Axel kept one eye on Jayde as she flirted with this newer patched member, who went by the name of Linc, near one of the pool tables. His other was focused on Bella as she danced in the middle of the bar with some of the other DAMC women. Before deserting their corner table, she announced she was going to dance to work off all the food she just ate.

She was kind enough to drop off a fresh draft for him before leaving him on his own. He felt a lot more comfortable where he currently sat because his back was to the corner and he could survey the whole bar without worrying about anyone sneaking up from behind.

This Christmas party didn't seem to be any different from any of the other parties the club had on a regular basis. Besides the Christmas tree strung with orange blinking lights that was propped in the corner inside church.

Hell, it wasn't as though the club needed much of an excuse to throw a party, anyway.

Suddenly, Jewel broke off from the ladies at the center of the room and sank into a chair next to him. She wiped a bead of sweat off her brow and blew out a breath.

He cocked an eyebrow at her. "You okay?"

She gaped at him in surprise. "Yeah, why?"

"D didn't look happy when he carried you kicking and screaming upstairs."

Color rushed into her cheeks and she dropped her gaze from his. "Nothing new."

"He didn't hurt you?" He lowered his voice even though the bar was so loud no one could hear him unless they were standing right next to him, anyway. "You can tell me if he did."

She frowned at him. "Axel, he'd never hurt me."

He stared at his cousin. He had a hard time believing that beast of a man with a short fuse wasn't capable of hurting her even if he didn't mean to. She was less than half his size.

"I just want—"

"Axel," she cut him off, sweeping her long dark hair out of her face. "He loves me; he'd never hurt me. I promise. But I appreciate your concern."

He nodded, but wasn't so convinced. "How are things going at the warehouse?" The warehouse as in the In the Shadows Security business Diesel owned and ran.

"Great. I'm getting him organized and helping him grow the business in the direction he wants it to go."

"And what direction's that?"

Jewel closed her mouth and looked away. Axel followed her gaze toward the bar. Both Hawk and Diesel were behind it, watching the two of them with great interest.

Her head swiveled back toward him. "Just expanding the security part, that's all."

Right.

"They keep shit on the up and up there?"

"Of course."

And if it wasn't on the up and up, there was no way Diesel and his crew would tell Jewel, a woman. Or if she knew, she probably wouldn't tell him. Even so, he had to ask.

"I just don't want to see you get entangled in any bullshit. You're family."

"Ax, we're *all* family. When are you and Uncle Mitch going to recognize that fact?"

"I can't speak for my father, Jewelee."

"But you can speak for yourself. You're with Bella, right? And she's part of the club. You're not only Bear's grandson, you're our president's *brother*. Can't get any more family than that."

"You know the issue."

"Yeah, but the club has come a long way since we were all kids, Ax, you know that. You've seen it yourself."

He sat back and regarded his cousin. She was young, beautiful, and had a head for business, which was apparent when she ran the office at the club's body shop and towing company. He believed she limited herself by being Diesel's ol' lady and his glorified "secretary." By being with him, she was tying herself tightly to the club and limiting her options. "This thing going to last?"

"What thing?"

"You and D."

She pursed her lips in thought, then asked, "You and Bella going to last?"

"The truth?"

Jewel nodded.

"I don't know. I just know I don't belong here tonight." His gaze landed on Bella while she swung her hips and arms around the dance floor with Diamond and Ivy. "She does."

"Yes, she does. And we don't want you taking her away from us."

He sighed. "I'd never do that."

"D and Hawk would never let you, anyway."

Right. His eyes bounced from Bella to her two overly large, overly protective cousins still watching him and Jewel closely. Diesel now had his arms crossed over his chest, emphasizing just how big and bad the fucker was.

Axel did not want to get up close and personal again with the man's fist anytime soon.

Jewel laughed when she saw who he was staring at. "He's a complete kitten."

Axel snorted. "I've known him just as long as you, Jewelee."

"But I know him better," she said with a smirk.

"Yeah, well, there's a reason for that and we don't need to go into details."

She leaned closer. "I think you're good for her."

"As much as we both want it to work, I don't know if it will."

Jewel nodded. "I get it. I do. I love being DAMC. I love being an ol' lady. I was born for this. But I see your side of it, too."

"Do you really?"

"Yeah, I do."

"When did you go and grow up, Jewelee?"

She laughed. "You should be asking Jayde that. Hard to believe she's the baby of the family and look at her now. College graduate. Bet she makes your parents proud."

Axel's gaze roamed over to where Linc and Jayde were standing a little too close for his liking.

"She wouldn't be making my father proud right now, cozying up to that guy."

"Linc? He's a good one."

He'd reserve his judgment until he got a better read on the guy. "Has she been seeing him?" Because if she had, she'd been sneaking around to do it.

"I don't think so. Though whenever she shows up, they tend to gravitate toward each other."

"Fuck. My father would pop a blood vessel if he knew."

Jewel jerked one of her shoulders up slightly. "Don't tell him." She laughed again. "She can tell him when she comes home knocked up by a club brother."

"That's not even funny."

"Against his will, Mitch would be granddaddy to the next generation of Angels. First Z's kid, then Linc's kid and then...." She drifted off, her face becoming sad. "Fuck. Sorry."

Axel traced the lip of his pint glass with his finger.

"You two could always adopt," she said softly.

"Jewel..." He sucked in a breath, his chest getting tight. "We have a long way to go before we'd be even close to talking about kids."

"You'll get there."

"I hope so," he murmured.

"You should go dance with her."

"Just like you should go dance with your man."

Jewel threw her head back and laughed. "Look, the—"

The sharp, rapid crack of gunshots ringing out had Axel up and out of his seat, dragging Jewel to the ground. She struggled underneath him, calling out Diesel's name.

"Stay down," Axel yelled at her, covering her body with his, while covering his own head with his arms as shots continued to spray the building, shrapnel raining over them.

He had no idea what caliber ammo or what type of firepower the shooter or shooters were using but whatever it was was big enough to make decent holes not only through the hollow steel door, but the walls. Pieces of drywall, wood, insulation came raining down around them.

Suddenly, Axel was ripped off of Jewel and thrown to the side. He rolled onto his back and saw Diesel grab Jewel.

"Get down, you asshole. You're going to get shot."

"Nothin' new," D grumbled, picked Jewel up in his arms and

rushed to tuck her behind the bar. How he wasn't hit, Axel would never know.

The bullets went whizzing over his head at a rapid rate. Whoever was out front had something automatic for sure.

He looked around to see if anyone was hit nearby and when he didn't see anyone bleeding or writhing in pain, he searched for Bella. Keeping low, he snaked his body on knees and elbows toward the back of the bar.

"Bella!" He got no answer and ducked his head when another hail of bullets began. "Fuck!"

As soon as there was a slight pause, he crawled forward some more, seeing Jag dragging Ivy toward the kitchen door. A quick look to his left showed that Linc had his body curled around Jayde, a gun in his hand, as they remained behind a pool table.

"What the fuck?" Axel shouted their direction. "Get her out of here."

Linc gave him a look, then nodded, but didn't move since more bullets went flying.

Axel crawled forward again and saw Diamond hiding behind another pool table. "Where's Bella?"

She turned wide eyes to him and shrugged.

"You got a phone?"

She nodded. "Yeah!"

"Call nine-one-one." When she hesitated, he screamed. "Now!"

Even from where he was, she could see her digging a cell out of her back pocket with trembling hands.

Where the fuck was Diesel and Hawk?

He peered up toward the bar and couldn't see anyone. Hopefully they were taking cover.

When he finally reached the bar, the shooting had slowed down some, but it wasn't over. Keeping low, he rounded the bar and saw Slade ducked behind the bar. And with relief he saw Bella. But she was pinned against Slade.

"You got a weapon?" Axel asked the former Marine as he finally got a chance to pull his revolver from his ankle holster.

"Just a knife."

"Fuck. Can you help clear everyone out of here? Take them into the kitchen. I don't know if they're shooting up the backside of the building, too. Kitchen is the safest right now until we get units on scene." Axel looked at Bella. "You okay?"

"Yeah," she answered, her face pale, but he was proud of her since she wasn't freaking out.

"Get yourself into the kitchen. Make sure everyone stays in there."

She nodded and moved away.

"Stay low, Bella. I'll be there as soon as we get everyone clear or the shooting stops."

She nodded and as he watched the woman he loved crawl away on her hands and knees to the swinging door, he realized just what kind of life he'd be living if they continued their relationship.

Chapter Seventeen

"Well, merry fuckin' Christmas to us." Hawk stood in front of The Iron Horse, hands on hips as he surveyed the damage to the front of the building.

"Warriors are the gift that keeps on fuckin' givin'," Zak muttered and spat on the ground.

Axel let his gaze roam the front parking lot. It was hard to miss that Diesel was nowhere to be found. And it wasn't like he took Jewel home. She was still in church with the rest of the women.

Luckily, the Warriors didn't do any damage around back. Maybe they thought everyone was in The Iron Horse since they could hear the band playing.

Nash ended up with a graze along his ribs from a stray bullet. Two of his band members had minor cuts from shrapnel hitting them since the stage was set up by the front wall of the building.

Linc had gotten Jayde to safety as did Slade with Diamond. Then the former Marine came back to help Axel get everyone else to cover.

By the time they were done clearing the bar area, the Warriors were gone. But Axel had a feeling D and some other Angels were on their tail. And he was sure D had called in his "Shadows" for assistance.

Axel wasn't going to ask since he figured it was better not to know the details.

There were enough cops on scene between Shadow Valley PD and the Pennsylvania State Police that he didn't need to get involved in the investigation.

In fact, a few of his fellow cops were surprised to see him already on scene when they arrived code three. He didn't bother to clear up their curiosity.

But he couldn't wait for them to be done. He wanted to get to Bella. Even though he knew she was okay, he wanted to see for himself.

Axel groaned when he saw his father beelining in his direction, his face a mask of fury, his body tight, his hands clenched into fists.

This wasn't going to go well.

Mitch's eyes landed on Zak who stood about ten feet away from Axel, then bounced back to him.

Joy.

"Did you know your sister was here? Did you know she was inside when those... those *motherfuckers*," he spat, "shot up this place?"

Axel's eyebrows rose at his father's uncharacteristic cursing. He was in his civvies, so he wasn't on duty, but still... it had been awhile since he'd seen the man this angry.

Mitch shoved a finger in Axel's face. "You knew, and you didn't get her the fuck out of here. What the fuck is wrong with you?"

"Pop..." Axel started.

"Don't fucking 'Pop' me!" Mitch swung an arm toward the bar. "Things like this were why I kept our family away from this club. The last thing I wanted was my boys to get caught up in this violence or my daughter to become an old lady!"

"Jayde isn't becoming an ol' lady," Axel reassured him calmly and hoped that was true.

Mitch's eyes snapped as he scowled at his youngest son. "She better not. It's bad enough Zakary's a bad influence on her by being a part of this club, but you...," he shouted, "I expected better of you. Have a fucking sense of pride, boy. There are plenty of other women who you can stick your—"

"Pop," Axel growled a warning.

Mitch inhaled deeply and then blew it out in a rush. His bluster quickly disappeared, the red in his cheeks faded a little, and he began to talk much more calmly. "Look, I like Bella. Honestly, I do. But she comes with baggage, son. A lot of it. And some of it remains because she won't break free of this life. This is not *your* life. You have a good life. You're a fucking police officer."

Axel's jaw tightened. "You don't need to remind me of that."

Mitch shook his head. "And I assume you want to remain one."

Suddenly, Z was standing next to Axel. "Got a good life. There ain't nothin' wrong with bein' a part of this club, this brotherhood, this family."

Mitch's gaze landed on his oldest offspring, his eyes hard. "Right. Kidnapping, rape, assault, theft... *prison*," he swept an arm around again, "having your place shot up and people almost getting killed... Yeah, what a life. One that you're going to be raising my grandchild in. You want to continue to put your wife and child at risk like this? Is it worth it?"

Axel watched as something crossed Z's face. In a blink it was gone. Reality. That's what it was. Reality that his wife and future child could be killed with the chaos that Warriors kept bringing.

As much as he didn't want to admit it, he understood where Z was coming from. This club *was* a large part of his older brother. But so was his wife and unborn child. He could imagine the internal struggle Z was having because Axel was living it himself right now.

The disappointment was clear in their father's face as he studied Zak. Then Mitch shook his head and sighed. "I'm getting your sister and getting her out of here." He turned toward Axel. "I don't want her here; do you understand me? I can't tell you what to do but she still lives under my roof and she's *not* to come here. She's *not* to hang out with these bikers. If you want to risk your career hanging out with this club, that's on you."

With that, he stomped away, shoving his hands deep into his jacket pocket and shaking his head.

"I guess inviting Bella to Christmas dinner is out?" Axel shouted at his father's back.

Mitch raised a dismissing hand over his shoulder at him.

"Fuck," Axel muttered. He looked at Z. "Couldn't have one fucking night where crazy shit didn't go down."

"You didn't have to fuckin' come. Why don't you just leave Bella the hell alone an' leave us all alone. Go with Mitch an' Jayde back to where you belong."

Axel tensed, and a muscle popped in his jaw. "Shut the fuck up, *Zakary*."

His older brother turned to face him bringing them eye to eye since they were the exact same height. And pretty much the same build. So, if Z wanted to get "down and dirty" Axel was ready. There was no way this would be a one punch knock-out like D gave him.

Hell no, it wouldn't.

"You're in my house here," Z grumbled, his fingers twitching at his side.

"And I've got my brothers at my back right now, too," Axel reminded him. There were plenty of cops still in the parking lot and inside The Iron Horse. "So think about that."

"Need your pig buddies to get your back?"

"Nope. You want to go at it?" Axel raised his arms out. "Bring it."

Z spat at Axel's feet. "You'll have me arrested."

"No. Want to take a shot? Do it. It's been a long time coming. They all know you're my brother. I won't press charges." Axel raised his arms out again, wagging his fingers, encouraging Z. "C'mon, brother, take your best shot."

Axel ducked as Zak took a swing. He felt the rush of air as Z's fist just missed him. He straightened, and Zak caught him under the chin with an uppercut. Axel grunted at the impact.

Widening his stance, Axel lifted his fists in a defensive position to match Z's. Then he took his shot, nailing Z in the chin and when his brother's head flew back, Axel came in with his left fist and punched him in the gut.

Z stumbled back another step with a grunt and then recovered, bringing his body up to full height, his fists ready to strike.

They rounded each other, breathing heavily, eyes and feet active, watching for the slightest movement. Zak swung again, this fist making contact with the side of Axel's eye.

Fuck. That hurt! Not as much when D hit that eye, but even so...

Axel reacted with a quick one-two punch. The first one directly in the gut, the second one glancing off Z's cheekbone.

"What the fuck!"

The scream came from a distance, but Axel kept his attention on his brother as they kept rounding each other, waiting to deflect the next strike or jump on an open opportunity to land one of their own.

"Stop it!"

"Will you separate them?"

"Zak!"

"Axel, stop it!"

Axel took another punch, but Z dodged it. Z got another uppercut in and got Axel in the stomach. All the air rushed out of him and he gasped for breath.

"Separate them, goddamnit!" It finally sunk in that it was Sophie's voice. "I'm pregnant! Don't make me do it myself!"

Those words made Zak turn his head slightly toward his wife and Axel took advantage by doing a leg sweep and taking Z down to the ground. Zak landed on his back with an *oof*.

Breathing hard, Axel wiped the blood off his mouth with the back of his hand and backed up.

He stared down at his brother, who was struggling for breath, whose nose was bleeding, his eye swelling, and his knuckles busted.

Axel lifted his right hand. His were busted, too. And he could already feel his eye bleeding and swelling, as well.

Fuck.

Fuck. Fuck. Fuck.

He looked over his shoulder and saw a line of cops just standing there watching them, amused. He turned back and saw a line of Angels watching, as well. Though, they didn't look so amused.

Not one person interfered besides Sophie.

And next to Zak's ol' lady stood Bella, her arms crossed over her chest as she took in the two of them.

With a sigh, Axel stepped up to his brother and offered his hand. Zak clasped it without hesitation and Axel helped pull him to his feet.

"*Brother*," Axel said.

"*Brother*," Zak answered. He swiped at his bleeding nose, then laughed. "Fuck that felt good."

"Damn right," Axel said with a smirk.

"So glad you thought that 'felt good,'" Sophie shouted at Zak. "What the hell?"

Z grinned at his wife, then threw an arm around her shoulders. "Let's go, woman. You need to clean me up."

"The hell I do. What the hell's wrong with you two?"

Z swung her around and they headed around back to the private side of the building.

The onlookers began to disperse. Angels whacking Z on the back as he passed, the cops going back to their cars or heading back inside the bar to finish their investigation, shaking their heads and chuckling.

Bella remained with her hands now planted on her hips, staring at Axel. "What the hell was that about?"

"Nothing."

"Wasn't nothing."

"You're right. It was something."

She tilted her head as she studied him. "A breakthrough, maybe?"

Axel shrugged. "Maybe." He wiped at his lip again and stared at the blood smeared on the back of his hand. Then he glanced up and let his gaze roam over the front of The Iron Horse. Hundreds of rounds had been aimed at the bar which was full of people enjoying a Christmas party.

This was life in an MC.

This was reality.

He couldn't imagine the long-term beef between the two clubs would ever come to an end. Even if the DAMC wanted it to. The skirmishes weren't petty crimes or minor clashes, like a simple fist-fight. No. These were life-taking, life-altering circumstances.

Jazz would never be the same again after falling into the Warriors' hands.

Then there was Kiki and Jewel. As well as Diesel getting shot.

And everyone who died before them.

This ongoing rival between the two clubs had resulted in actual deaths.

How could he go off every day to work as a police officer and not worry that his woman could be kidnapped, raped, shot at, or even murdered because of who she was or who she considered her family?

He would worry about her every minute of every day.

He grabbed Bella's bicep, and she flinched. He almost released her immediately, but he wasn't going to hurt her, and she had to understand that. He just needed to show her reality. The truth of the situation.

He pulled her along with him as he took long strides to the front of the bar. He lifted the yellow police tape and pulled her inside. A few of the remaining cops looked up, saw who it was, and put their heads back down to finish their reports.

He dragged Bella to the middle of the bar to the exact spot where she had been dancing not even a couple of hours before.

He pointed to the debris on the floor. "Look." He pointed to the bullet holes in the walls, the overturned tables, and the pool tables. "See that?" He pointed to the blood on the floor near the band's stage. "And that?" Then he turned her to face him. "Is this how you want to live?"

She didn't answer.

He shook her. "In constant fear of being shot or kidnapped? Or worse?" He let her arm go and scrubbed a hand over his hair. "Fuck!"

"Nobody wants to live like this!" she shouted back at him. "We're still paying for shit that happened decades ago."

"This is exactly why my father pulled us away from the club, Bella. Can you blame him?"

"No."

"It's this shit... This shit..." He shook his head and pointed pleading eyes at her. "Bella, I can't lose you. I can't."

"You're not going to lose me, Axel."

"How do we know they won't take pot shots at you in the parking lot out back? Or at the bakery? Or, hell, even at your house?"

"We don't. But I'm not going to live in constant fear that they're going to do something to me. I'm not going to let them win like that." She flattened her palm on his stomach, then curled her fingers into his shirt. "You go every day to a job that's dangerous. Every day you could be injured or killed. Did you ever consider that?"

"That's different."

"No, it's not. Axel, I don't want to lose you, either. But I would never ask you to give up your job, your career. I know the risks. None of us want or encourage what the Warriors bring on us. They keep this alive, not us. Zak and the others are doing what they can to keep this club legit. Warriors keep trying to bring us down. We can't just sit back and do nothing. Can't allow them to destroy this club, to destroy us as a family. We can't." She looked directly into his eyes. "We won't," she finished with a determined tone.

For fuck's sake, he loved this woman, but it scared the shit out of him that something could happen to her at the hands of that outlaw club. Just by being a part of DAMC, she became their target.

"I see your mind spinning. And I'll tell you right now, I'm not going to leave this club, Axel. Not even for you."

Axel closed his eyes and drew a long, slow breath through his nostrils. He needed to calm his fears. He needed to look at the two of them together with clarity.

He needed to do what was best for not only Bella, but for himself.

The club might be her priority, but it wasn't his.

His career might be his priority, but it wasn't hers.

However, they needed to make themselves priority to each other.

No matter what.

And he didn't know how they could do that. Not with how things stood.

"I'm taking you home," he said finally.

"I have my car here."

"I don't care. On the way, we'll stop by your place to make sure everything is okay there, then you're coming home with me."

Chapter Eighteen

"After tonight, I guess Christmas dinner with your family is no longer on the table," Bella said, as she watched Axel pace in his kitchen.

After checking her house to make sure everything was okay there, they headed back to his apartment. And after grabbing a beer from the fridge and downing it without coming up for air, Axel had started the restless pacing.

She could only imagine that he had a million things running through his mind.

Tonight was once again a wake-up call that the Warriors weren't going to stop with their strikes on the DAMC. The occurrences were getting closer and closer together.

And that wasn't reassuring at all.

She tried to look at the situation through Axel's eyes. Not only as a cop, but also as an outsider. Though, he could never truly be an outsider. Not with his grandfather being one of the founders, not with his brother, his future nieces and nephews, and his cousins as part of the club.

He'd never be truly free of his connection, unless he moved away and turned his back on them all.

He would never do that because he wasn't that type of man.

"No," he finally answered.

"Should we try again next Christmas?" she asked, trying to put a humorous spin on it. Though, she was sure he didn't find it funny.

"Right," he answered, then stopped abruptly in front of her, where she leaned back against the kitchen counter.

"That shit didn't scare you, Bella?"

"You know it did."

"Let me tell you, that scared the fuck out of me. Not the being shot at part. I knew that was possible when I took the job. But the part where people I knew and loved could've been taken out like that by a bunch of crazy-ass, irrational motherfuckers. My parents could have lost all three of their children tonight."

"I'm sure underneath all of Mitch's anger was fear, too. He probably realized his family could have been wiped out..." She reached out and ran a finger down his arm. "I'm sorry."

Axel blinked at her. "For what? None of this was your fault."

"For dragging you into the club mess. We both know this isn't going to work, Axel. We know it deep down inside, no matter how much we want it to. Neither one of us is willing to give up what makes both of us who we are."

He grabbed both of her wrists and wrapped her arms around his waist. He leaned into her, cupping her cheeks with both hands. He pressed his forehead to hers and inhaled deeply. "I don't know the answer, Bella. I wish I did. And I'm sorry that I don't."

Bella closed her eyes and also sucked in a breath, inhaling his scent. She wrapped her arms around him tighter and she was helpless to stop a tear that slid out of the corner of her eye. She had no desire to wipe it away, to hide it.

Because if there was a reason to cry, this was it. The thought that she had a man who loved her but they just couldn't find a way to make things work killed her. She couldn't see the conflict and turmoil of both the club and between their families ending any time soon.

Her heart squeezed, and her chest became tight at the thought of not having Axel in her life.

"I love you, baby," he murmured.

"I know."

"I wish there was a way."

"I know," she repeated, trying to swallow the lump in her throat.

"I don't know what to do."

"Yes, you do," she said softly.

He didn't say anything for the longest time. They held each other close and neither wanted to be the first one to let go.

"I can't do this," Axel said.

"I know," she whispered, her heart cracking painfully into two pieces.

This was the second time she tried to love someone.

And the second time she failed.

He pushed away from her. "No, I mean I refuse to let you go. You're mine, Bella. Fuck everyone else. Fuck everyone. Just fuck everyone!"

"Axel—"

"No, we deserve to be happy. *You* deserve to be happy. I want the rest of my life to be about making you happy. I want you to never doubt you're loved. I will tell you every day when I wake up that I love you. I will tell you every night. No one's going to take that away from us. No one."

"Axel—" she tried again.

"No, baby. We're going to make this work. Everyone else is just going to have to get over it. We belong together."

She reached out and snagged one of his flailing hands. She intertwined her fingers with his and raised it to her lips, brushing a kiss over the knuckles he split having a fight with his own brother. His own blood.

"I don't want you regretting your decision. I don't want you to wake up one day and realize you wanted kids and be bitter. I don't want you to blame me for a split with your father. I don't want to cause problems with your job. I don't want to be the reason to *ever* make you unhappy. I'm afraid you'll never forgive me."

"Every couple has problems, Bella. Every single one. We won't be any different. We're going to have some hills to climb, yes. But fuck it... I'm dragging you to the top. We're going to do this."

Bella wished she could be as enthusiastic about it as he was. It felt as if tonight was one step forward when Axel actually showed up to the party, then two steps back when the Warriors reared their ugly heads. Then there was that bit of a shift when Axel and Z got into a fist-fight, though it seemed as if that was what they needed to move past their... past.

Bella had no idea where that relationship would head. But with Mitch still not accepting his oldest son's life choices, then the struggle to bring the family back together would still be an issue.

One that she and Sophie—and maybe the new baby—could help with.

"I'm getting rid of this apartment. I'm moving my big bed into your house until we find something more permanent."

"Axel, you need to be completely sure of this."

"Baby, I'm sure. I've never been so sure about something in my whole life."

She shook her head. "You're crazy."

He nodded, grabbed her face in his hands and planted a big, wet kiss on her lips. "Yep. You're damn right I am. Crazy in love with you. And you're just as crazy for being in love with me."

"I just want you for your body," she said in a serious tone.

Axel grinned. "You've got that."

Bella fought back her laughter. "Can I have it right now?"

"You can have it whenever you want. It's yours."

"Hmm. I like the sound of that. But Axel, are you *sure*?" The feeling that he was going to regret this decision still niggled at her.

His blue eyes twinkled. "Yep. I'm sure we're going to go fuck."

"No, about all of this..."

"We're going to go fuck, then everything else we'll take it as it comes. We'll deal with it."

She arched an eyebrow at him. "Did you drink some Red Bull or something?"

"Nope. Just excited about our future."

"Our future," she repeated softly.

"That sounds good on your lips, baby," he murmured, then kissed her again.

As soon as he broke it, he grabbed her hand and dragged her toward his bedroom.

He stopped in the middle of the room and faced her. He tugged his long-sleeve Henley over his head and threw it to the side.

"Now you."

Bella grabbed the bottom of her loose top and yanked it over her head. She threw it in the direction of his Henley.

"Bra, too," he said with a crooked smile.

As she reached to unclip it in the back, she thought how funny it was that she was no longer self-conscious of her body, of her scars, of how her body had changed after that fateful night. She was now completely comfortable with Axel seeing her as she was.

He accepted her, scars and all.

She let the bra fall off her shoulders and then threw that, too.

She bit her bottom lip as his gaze swept over her. Her nipples pebbled hard when he licked his lips.

Oh yes, that mouth was going to be busy soon.

Without taking his eyes from her, he unsnapped and unzipped his jeans. She did the same, mirroring his actions. Then they both kicked off their shoes, and yanked off their socks, throwing them with disregard.

When they both straightened up, their hands went to their waistbands. As if coordinated, they pushed down their jeans, taking their underwear with them. Axel's steely length bobbed when his boxer briefs released his cock. Bella's pussy clenched in anticipation as she shoved her panties down her legs.

They stepped out of their pants and underwear, then moved closer to each other. But they didn't touch.

They were close enough to feel one another's heat, to feel the sweep of the other's warm breath along their skin.

"Are you going to get the cuffs?" she asked.

His Adam's apple bobbed. "No. Tonight, I want this to be a

meeting of the minds, a meeting of our souls. A coming together of the two of us."

She tilted her head and studied the beautiful, naked man before her. "Hmm. Poetic."

He grinned. "Tonight, I want to appreciate everything that is you, Bella. Tomorrow we can explore our kinky side."

"I'm not going to argue with that plan."

He released a soft laugh. "I didn't think so."

"So, why are you so far away then?" she teased.

She squealed when he swept her up into his arms and then laughed as she bounced onto the mattress, landing in the center where he tossed her. He quickly followed, climbing over her on hands and knees, until he stared down into her face, his inches from hers.

He settled his hips between her thighs, and she felt the crown of his cock along her slick folds. She loved foreplay, but right now she wanted him to be inside her. To complete her. She didn't want to wait any longer.

As he thrust slowly inside her, she sighed, "I love you, Axel," cupping his cheek.

He stilled and his expression got serious. "We'll make this work; I don't ever want you to worry about that."

She nodded, but she would still worry no matter what he said. It would be impossible not to. There were too many outside forces in their lives that would test their relationship.

"We just need to stay strong. Stay together," he continued. His hips tilted and he began to move at a slow, steady pace, sliding in and out of her with great care. As if she was breakable. "Tell me you're willing to do that."

She gasped as he thrust a little harder. She angled her hips higher so the head of his cock would slide over just the right spot.

Yes, there. That was the one.

"Axel..."

"Yeah, baby?" he whispered by her ear.

His honey smooth, low voice made her shiver and moan while the gliding movements of his hips drove her mad. "Ax..."

"Yeah," he breathed.

"Oh, fuck," she groaned.

"That's it. Let go," he encouraged softly. The tip of his tongue traced the outer edge of her ear, then he sucked her lobe into his mouth for a second. "Come for me."

"Ax, I'm going to come."

"I feel you. So fucking hot and wet. Squeezing my cock so hard. That's it..." He dropped his head down to her breasts, sucking one nipple in deep, scraping the tip with his teeth.

She cried out, arching her back, her nails drawing along his muscular back and sinking into his ass, encouraging him to move faster, harder.

She was right there. She needed just a little push.

Just a little...

She dug her heels into the back of his thighs and lifted her hips to meet him. Tensing, an orgasm rocked through her, making her gasp out his name. Her core pulsated around him, drawing him deeper as he blew out a ragged breath.

"One more before I come, baby. One more," he encouraged her.

She wasn't going to argue that.

AXEL'S MIND spun as he tried to keep himself together. He wanted to give Bella one more orgasm before he let himself have one of his own. He loved being inside this woman, being a part of her. They fit perfectly.

At least here they did. In the outside world, maybe not so perfectly. But he would make it work. *They* would make it work. No matter what.

His balls tightened as her wet heat squeezed him tight. He wasn't going to be able to take too much more.

She needed to come soon. He clenched his jaw to not only keep himself together but from the pain of her digging her nails into the flesh of his ass. But he wouldn't tell her to stop. No way.

Shoving his face into her neck he licked along her throat, then laid a kiss in the hollow. He shoved one hand into her hair, bending her neck back, exposing more of her throat so he could kiss and lick and bite along it. Her groan vibrated under his lips.

He snagged one of her nipples between his thumb and forefinger, rolling it roughly, making her jerk beneath him.

"That's it, baby. C'mon."

"I don't want this to end," she said on a breath.

"It's not going to end. This is only the beginning," he assured her. Because that was the truth. "Don't hold back. Give me all of you."

Her hips thrust up to meet his and he increased his pace, his rhythm becoming faster, more frantic. But he needed to stay together... just a little while longer.

He wanted to cry in relief when she moaned, "Come with me."

Her gasp filled his ear, and as her core squeezed him tight, he grunted and spilled deep inside her. Her pussy pulsated around him, milking every drop of cum from him until he was depleted, boneless and ready to drop.

As much as he didn't want to break their connection, he knew she wouldn't be able to handle his weight, so with a groan he slipped out of her and to her side, gathering her into his arms.

He pressed a kiss to her forehead as she released a satisfied sigh. She combed her fingers over his short hair absently and stared up at the ceiling as she tried to slow her breathing since it was as ragged and rapid as his.

"Tell me everything is going to be all right."

His heart squeezed at her words. He traced a finger over the pale, puckered skin that would be a permanent reminder of when everything had not been all right for her.

"Everything will be all right. I promise." He sure hoped he could keep that promise. He'd do his damnedest. "It's going to be a new year soon, baby. We're going to make the most of it."

And he knew just where to start.

CROW GLANCED up and his eyes widened slightly as Axel came through the door of In the Shadows Ink. Slade was lying on his stomach on the plastic wrapped tattoo chair. He turned his head to watch Axel walking in their direction.

Axel approached the man who had hit on his woman, then lifted his gaze to the dark-eyed man who liked to flirt with her, too.

"Whataya here for, pig?"

"See your busy," Axel replied, studying the pattern that Crow was tattooing onto Slade's back.

The man was getting the DAMC colors inked onto his skin. The rockers, the emblem, everything. It was part of being in the club. The mark of loyalty and brotherhood.

Axel understood it.

Would he ever do something like that? No.

But he had a similar idea to show his loyalty.

To Bella.

To his woman.

To hopefully his future wife.

Possibly the mother of their children, depending on how they decided to go about that. *If* they decided that's what they wanted. He would leave that up to her. Whatever she wanted, he was good with.

"Was hoping you weren't busy," Axel murmured, taking in the excellent work Crow was doing on Slade's back. The lines were sharp, the shading perfect. The man was a pro at slinging ink. And that's exactly why he came here.

He wanted the best.

"Am. So what the fuck do you want?"

"Want you to do a big piece for me."

"Where?"

"Across the top of my back."

"Gonna cost you. What do you want?"

When he told Crow exactly what he wanted, Slade jumped off the table willing to wait for his piece to be finished at a later date. He planned on sitting there watching while Axel had his tattoo done.

His excuse was he wanted to see how much of a pussy Axel was. See if he could take the pain without flinching or taking breaks.

Axel was determined to take it like a man. Prove to these guys that his love for his woman was as strong as their loyalty to the DAMC.

He showed them both.

Epilogue

Bella gasped and Axel winced as he pulled off his shirt. She was leaning back against his headboard since his big bed was now stuffed into the small bedroom of her rental house.

She rolled to her knees as he approached the bed. "Holy shit, Axel, what did you do?"

He grinned at her. "I didn't realize tattoos hurt so damn much."

She grinned back. "Yeah, they can. Depends where you get them and how long you sit for."

"Seemed like forever. My skin felt like it was being burnt by lava."

"Well, yeah, that's a helluva lot of black ink. But you didn't need to do that!"

He turned his back to show her and looked over his shoulder. "I know the brothers get the club's rockers inked onto their backs to show their loyalty to the club, to their brotherhood. I got your name because I want to prove my loyalty to you, Bella. You are a part of me forever. You've been under my skin almost my whole life and now you're on it, too."

"You know that's permanent, right?" She let her gaze roam over the large black block letters that spelled out BELLA in an arch at the top of his back. His skin was both red from the tattoo being fresh and shiny from the ointment that was smeared over his irritated skin.

"That was the point." He might as well have added a "duh" onto the end of that sentence. Even though he didn't, she heard it in his tone.

"You're crazy," she muttered. "You need to put a clean cotton T-shirt over that until it's healed, honey."

"I know, Crow told me how to take care of it."

"Crow!"

"Yeah, of course. He's the best."

"You really are crazy!"

"In love with you," he finished for her.

She climbed off the bed and dug into the dresser drawer she had cleared out for his shirts. She dug a worn T-shirt out and held it to her nose.

His eyebrows rose. "Are you sniffing my clothes?"

She grinned into the soft cotton. "Yep."

"Do you do that often?"

"Yep."

"And you call *me* crazy."

She laughed as she gathered up the tee and pulled it over his head. He tucked his arms through the sleeves and she pulled it down over his torso, making sure to drag her fingers over his warm belly as she did so.

"Keep touching me like that, you're going to make me hard."

"That's the point, officer."

"I don't think I'm up for playing with cuffs tonight."

She pouted. "And you'll have to be on top for a while, too. At least until that heals."

"There's always doggy-style. I'm sure we can come up with other creative positions. Like against the wall, remember that one?"

"Mmm. How can I forget?"

He slid his fingers into her hair on either side of her face and tipped her head up. She sighed as his lips met hers and he took advantage of her open mouth to explore it thoroughly with his tongue.

She groaned and grabbed at his waist to keep her knees from buckling. He was a great kisser. She was lucky that he was so skilled with his mouth. And not just with kissing.

He pulled away just enough to murmur against her lips, "When's the next executive committee meeting for the club?"

She pulled back a little, her eyes wide. "Why?"

"I'm not done declaring my love for you."

"Have I told you today yet that you're crazy?"

"I think you have that covered, but you can tell me again as soon as you're done telling me how much you love me."

She smiled.

So did he.

"SOME OF YOU might not like me, and I don't give a shit. The truth is, I want to make this work with Bella no matter what. I don't care if you spit on me, hit me, call me pig. You're not going to get me to give up Bella. She's mine and I'm here to tell you all that."

No one said a word in the meeting room. He had busted in on their executive committee meeting knowing that he might get thrown out on his ass, or even get his ass beaten. But he didn't care. He was doing this no matter what.

He cleared his throat and widened his stance. "I'm here to claim her," he stated more loudly than was necessary. But he wanted to make sure everyone sitting around that table heard him loud and clear.

Dex snorted. "You can't claim her."

Axel planted his hands on his hips and looked to his right, directly at Bella's brother. "I just did."

To his left, Ace's head dropped, and Axel saw the older man's body shake with laughter. Finally, Bella's uncle looked up, slammed his palm on the table and said, "Boy, you got balls the size of watermelons. That's for damn sure."

Axel nodded. "That's right. Watermelons. If any of you have a problem with it, you let me know directly. Don't go to Bella about it. I won't tolerate it."

Dex snorted again, then mumbled, "He won't tolerate it."

"She ain't leavin' the club," Diesel growled, his eyes hard.

Axel stared at the man who he knew would push back the hardest. It wouldn't be his brother, Zak, and it wouldn't be her brother, Dex. No, it would be that monster of a man, Diesel. He would be their biggest obstacle.

"No, if she wants to leave the club that would be her choice." He lifted a palm to stop any of them from interrupting. "I'm not going to encourage it, but I'm not going to stop her if she ever decides that."

"Your bitch ass can't ride along on our runs," Jag spoke up, leaning back in his chair and crossing his arms over his chest.

Axel shrugged, swinging his gaze to the club's Road Captain. "I wouldn't ask that, anyway. You forget that I'm VP of the Blue Avengers, we have our own runs."

Someone chuckled. Could have been Hawk, could have been Zak, Axel didn't know nor did he care. The Blue Avengers MC wasn't out to prove that they were more badass than the Dirty Angels MC. They weren't, and they weren't trying to be.

"She gonna be accepted by the rest of your type?"

His type. He sighed silently at Hawk's question.

"Yep. And she agreed to wear my colors," Axel quickly raised his palm again when Hawk slammed a fist on the table, his big body tensing, his dark eyes narrowing. "On the runs only. She's DAMC. I get it."

"Can't see my sister wearin' anyone's cut after Rebel," Dex muttered with a frown.

A few grunts rose from around the table in agreement.

"Look, the reason why I'm here is that I'm asking for you all to just respect what Bella and I have. That's it. We don't need to drink a beer together. We don't need to play a game of pool. Just let me take care of her." He directed his gaze to D. "We both want what's best for Bella."

He grunted.

"We both want to protect her and see her happy."

D grunted again.

"You've got your hands full with Jewel," Axel told him.

Axel was sure the big man did not appreciate that little reminder when D's eyes narrowed on him and his jaw got tight.

"She's my cousin and I know she's your ol' lady. But I also know she probably doesn't make life easy for you. Plus, I know you thrive on the challenge. So why don't you let me take care of Bella. Leave the worry to me. Let me protect her."

D's shoulders squared off and pulled back. "My job to protect her."

Axel shook his head. "Not anymore."

"We gonna let this pig come in here an' claim one of our own?" Diesel said, his gaze bouncing around the table from one brother to the next.

Ace nodded. "I think that's for the best, son. For Bella."

Dex nodded, too. "Yeah, for my sister."

Axel eyeballed his older brother at the head of the table. "Are you going to bring it to a vote?"

The corners of Z's lips curled up slightly in a smirk. "That what you want?"

"Yeah," Axel answered softly.

Z nodded and announced, "Motion to make Bella this asshole's woman."

Ace shook his head with a grin. "I second."

"All in favor?"

"Ayes" went around the table.

From every one of them.

Every. Fucking. One.

Axel smiled.

Life was sure going to get interesting.

Sign up for Jeanne's newsletter to learn about her upcoming releases, sales and more! http://www.jeannestjames.com/newslettersignup

Down & Dirty: Slade

Welcome to Shadow Valley where the Dirty Angels MC rules. Get ready to get Down & Dirty because this is Slade's story...

He thought he liked easy. Until she showed him easy was boring.

Right out of the Marines, Slade's first mistake was patching into a club that was headed down a destructive path. His second was rolling into Shadow Valley on a search for answers. He had no plans to patch into another club, even one like the DAMC, and he certainly wasn't looking for an ol' lady. Especially a ball-buster like Diamond, who could singe the hair off a brother's nuts with just a look.

DAMC born and bred, Diamond was ready to give up on becoming an ol' lady until the heavily tattooed biker rolled into town on his Harley. Problem is, months later Slade's still a mystery. He never talks about himself or his past, and Diamond wants answers. But she's not quite ready for what's uncovered: secrets that could very well implode the club. It doesn't just bring Slade's loyalty into question, but forces Diamond to make a choice she doesn't want to make. A choice that affects not only Slade, but the whole MC.

Turn the page to read chapter one of Down & Dirty: Slade, Book 6 in the Dirty Angels MC series

Down & Dirty: Slade

Chapter One

"C'MON, brother, wake the fuck up."

Slade groaned as the annoying voice disturbed his peaceful rest.

"Slade. C'mon, brother. You gotta get the fuck outta here."

For some reason, the disturbance sounded a lot like Dawg. Why the fuck would the strip-club manager be giving him an unwelcome wake-up call?

Slade popped one eye open.

Probably because he had passed out at Heaven's Angels Gentleman's club. *Again.*

That wasn't a pillow under his head. Nope. It was a stripper's lap.

He tipped his eyes upward. Not surprised at all, she was passed out, too. Her head rested against the back of the red velour love seat, her neck bent cockeyed and her mouth wide open.

She didn't look so hot right now.

But then, he probably didn't look much better.

With a groan, he lifted his head off her fishnet-stockinged thighs. Hopefully, she didn't mind the little bit of drool that had escaped his gaping mouth during his snooze-fest.

Fuck.

He wiped the back of his hand over his mouth and groaned.

"Seriously, brother, you gotta get the fuck outta here. Wanna lock up. Take 'er with ya, if you gotta. But just get gone."

He blinked. His brain felt like a whole lot of cotton had been shoved between his ears.

He sucked in a deep breath, then grimaced.

Fuck. He wouldn't be eating that snatch any time soon.

Fuck him. That was deadly.

He pushed himself upright faster than he should have, and his head wobbled. No, that wasn't his head, that was his pickled brain.

"Want me to get one of the prospects to take you back to church?"

He blinked again, hoping his vision would clear. He turned his head to find Dawg standing about five feet away, hands planted on his hips, an unhappy expression on his bearded face. The six-foot-two biker had dark smudges under his eyes. He was probably ready to get some shuteye of his own after working all night.

Slade tried to shake his head, but that made things so much worse. "No," he finally got out, his voice croaking like a sick frog.

"Either that or Diamond. Take your fuckin' pick. If I were you, I'd take door number one. Number two might just shriek your head right off, an' then slam your dick over an' over in that door. 'Specially since your usin' one of my girls as a fuckin' pillow."

Door number one sounded like a good option. There was probably a prospect still in the club that could drag his ass home.

Slade forced out, "Where's Moose?"

"In the back, restockin'. Gonna get him to haul this passed-out bitch home in a few an' can get 'im to drop you off, too."

Slade started to nod but thought better of it.

His brain felt like soup; no point in sloshing it around more than necessary.

"Don't get why you're gettin' fuckin' plastered here every night instead of The Iron Horse. Drink free there, here you don't."

He drank here because most of the club members didn't come out to the strip club. It wasn't a typical hang-out for them. They preferred drinking in church or the public side of the bar, so they could just walk upstairs to their room to pass out.

If he had any sense he'd do the same, but after working a shift at The Iron Horse slinging drinks for Hawk, the club's VP and bar manager, and helping contain any out-of-control customers, he didn't feel like serving himself. He wanted to sit on the other side of the bar, enjoy himself, and not be bothered.

It also didn't hurt that most of Dawg's girls were easy on the eyes and came with big-ass tits.

Not to mention, soft laps to pass out on. And sometimes pussy that didn't smell like death warmed over.

But that wasn't the main reason he'd been ending up here. Fuck no, it wasn't.

The main reason was to lay low. Get his drink on without that bitch harping at him.

A bitch he hadn't even banged yet.

A bitch who had tried to get her claws in him. Take a permanent seat on the back of his sled.

He wasn't ready to have an ol' lady, for fuck's sake.

And even if he was, it certainly wouldn't be Diamond. While they had a bit of fun last summer during some of the club runs, that was all it was... fun. To an extent.

At least until she wanted to become his regular piece.

Worst part about her was the woman didn't listen. No fucking way was he putting up with backtalk and attitude.

He didn't mind claws as long as they only came out while fucking. Screw that everyday shit, though. That would give a brother a headache. Worse than the hangover he would have tomorrow.

Was the bitch hot? Fuck yeah, she was.

Long dark, dark, dark brown hair that was typical for the Dirty Angels MC women, and great for digging his fingers into. Bright blue eyes that could pierce him to his soul. Plump, red lips that would be perfect for wrapping around his cock and sucking him like a fucking Hoover vacuum. And the fucking tits on her... Damn, they'd been pressed to his back during the runs a couple times. He couldn't forget those curvy hips of hers, either. Perfect to sink his fingers into, whether he was fucking her from behind or she was riding him like a bucking bronco.

All stuff he had planned on doing with her until he found out she was fucking crazy, too. She could flip the bitch switch in an instant.

Could have something to do with Di's father, Rocky, doing time in SCI Greene for murder. She was the kind of woman who needed a firm hand and apparently didn't get it growing up with her mother, Ruby, from what he heard. The only father-figure she had was Ace and that poor man already had his hands full with his own two sons, Diesel and Hawk, as well as his nieces and nephews, Dex, Ivy and Bella.

But it wasn't like he'd had a father-figure in his life, either.

No matter what, Slade certainly wasn't going to be filling in for her "daddy" and giving her some life lessons. Especially now that she was about to turn thirty.

No. Fucking. Way.

Though... some of those so-called life lessons could be fun. Her sister, Jewel, got a lot of those from her ol' man, Diesel. It always seemed D, the club's Sergeant at Arms, was throwing his ol' lady over his shoulder and hauling her ass either home or upstairs to his room at church to "teach her a lesson."

His lips twitched. Those were the best kind.

Slade wasn't sure if that's what Diamond needed. But if she did, he wasn't the one willing to give them to her.

Though, he normally didn't mind a challenge, right now he wanted easy.

No lip. No attitude. Fuck, tuck, and go.

Another reason he kept landing face down on Dawg's girls. Couldn't get easier than that. For the most part, anyhow.

They knew better than to cling afterward.

"What's 'er name?" Slade asked Dawg, who was coming from the back room with Moose on his heels. Slade had been so caught up in his thoughts, he hadn't even noticed he'd left.

Damn.

"Don't think it's gonna matter when you wake up tomorrow mornin'."

"It *is* tomorrow mornin' already," the prospect told Dawg.

"No, once he lands in his rack, he ain't wakin' up 'til tomorrow mornin'."

Moose laughed and nodded.

Nope, that couldn't happen. Slade had to work The Iron Horse tomorrow night... tonight... what-fucking-ever. "What time is it?"

"Three."

"Fuck," Slade groaned.

"Yeah, an' I wanna hit my own rack. So get the fuck outta here."

Slade tilted his head toward the still passed-out stripper. "Didn't fuck 'er, right?"

"No. Didn't make it off that couch 'fore you both passed out. Got a sloppy lap dance an' then you were both out fuckin' cold."

"Fuck," Slade muttered again.

"Yeah, owe me a hundred bucks."

Slade's eyebrows shot up his forehead. "For the lap dance?"

"No, owe *her* for the lap dance. Owe *me* for the loss of tips since she missed her last dance on stage."

"Shit."

Dawg nodded. "Yeah, *shit*. This shit's gotta stop, brother. Bad 'nough when you're gettin' wasted, but gettin' my girls wasted ain't good. Got me?"

Slade sucked in a breath. "Yeah. Got you."

"Gotta carry her, Moose. Make sure she gets inside her place an' it's locked up 'fore you leave."

"Got you, boss."

"An' don't be copin' a feel, either. Got me?" Dawg said louder than what was necessary, which made Slade wince.

The heavyset prospect lifted his palms in front of him. "Ain't takin' advantage of some unconscious lady."

Dawg snorted at the prospect's use of "lady." But no matter what Dawg thought of his "girls," he treated them well and made sure they stayed safe. That's why he never had a lack of talent on stage.

"An' that's why I pay you well, prospect. Now get 'em both outta here so I can go crash."

Moose leaned over, picked the stripper up like she weighed nothing, even though she was dead weight, and Slade reluctantly climbed to his feet. His head spun for a second but once he leveled out, he was good to follow Moose out of the club's back door to the employee parking lot.

However, out in the parking lot on the way to the prospect's vehicle, he had to take a quick pit stop and rid his gut of its liquid contents.

And that didn't make him feel one fucking bit better.

"THE BIG THREE-OH!" Jewel practically screamed in her ear.

Diamond winced at her sister's loud enthusiasm. Who the hell was excited when they turned thirty? Not her. Di was not looking forward to her thirtieth birthday. No way, no how. Thirty and still single. Thirty and still not an ol' lady. Thirty and still didn't have anyone in her bed on a regular basis. Thirty and her steady boyfriend took batteries. And a lot of them.

She frowned.

"Okay, so what are we planning?" Bella asked, leaning back into the counter at Sophie's Sweet Treats.

They were having an impromptu meeting of the DAMC women. Somehow, whenever that happened they always ended up at Sophie's bakery.

Well, the reason why was simple.

Fucking awesome, sweet, fattening cupcakes. The best in western Pennsylvania if you asked Diamond. But that was neither here nor there...

The point was the women wanted to do something for her birthday.

"We could do a ladies' night out!" Kelsea chirped.

"Where?" Ivy asked.

Kelsea shrugged. "Find some hot club in the 'Burgh?"

"I'm not going to some club," Bella muttered.

"Why not? It would be fun!" Kelsea exclaimed.

"Well, that would leave me out," Sophie said, holding onto her huge belly. "All I need is my water to break in the middle of the dance floor."

Sophie looked like she was about to pop out Zak's kid at any second. Di wrinkled her nose. It actually looked painful with her body stretched enormously out of its natural shape. It looked like she shoved an overfilled beach ball under her maternity top. She couldn't imagine Sophie's former hot body would ever be the same again.

The woman waddled over to the display case and groaned as she tried to lean over to pull out a tray of cupcakes for them to devour.

"Oh!" Sophie gasped.

"What?" Kiki yelled, eyes wide.

Sophie straightened, making a face. "I think I just peed myself a little. Freaking kid is riding on my bladder like it's a Harley."

"Let me get that," Bella said, putting a hand on Sophie's back and gently moving her out of the way. She pulled out a tray of cupcakes that looked mouth-watering.

"What are those?" Diamond whispered in awe, mesmerized by the hip-widening confections.

Bella did an elaborate hand sweep over the tray. "S'mores cupcakes. Chocolate cake filled with a swirl of fudge and marshmallow filling, topped with toasted marshmallow frosting and graham cracker crumbles on top."

Ivy sighed as she stared at the baked goodies.

Di felt the same way. "Give me one of those right now!"

Bella laughed and handed them out. Everyone got very quiet as they shoved all the sugary goodness into their cupcake holes. Eye rolls, passionate groans, and lip smacking ensued.

Then the bells over the door jingled and they all turned their attention in that direction.

"How'd you know we were pigging out on the newest cupcake flavor?" Bella called out.

Axel pushed through the door, wearing his uniform and a heavy patrol jacket since it was March and winter still hadn't completely vacated Shadow Valley. He smiled and shrugged. His gaze bounced from the tray of cupcakes to Bella.

"I've been thinking about them all morning. Especially since you mumbled something about S'mores cupcakes in your sleep."

"I did not," Bella scoffed.

"I swear you did! Give me one of those." He approached the display case and Bella handed him a cupcake.

All the women held their breath as Axel peeled the baby blue paper baking cup off the bottom of the cupcake and waited for him to tongue the icing in the sensual way he was known to do. But he didn't. He just took a big bite.

All their breath rushed out at once.

"What the fuck, Bella? You ruined it now that he's in your bed every night," Ivy muttered under her breath to her sister.

Bella smirked and shrugged.

After swallowing his bite, he cocked an eyebrow toward the group of women behind the counter. "Am I interrupting an important meeting?"

"Yes, since your cousin's turning thirty in a couple weeks. We're making plans."

"Oh fuck," Axel muttered. "Like what?"

"Going clubbing or male strippers. Or," Kelsea shrugged, "something fun."

Axel frowned. "Male strippers?"

"Yeah, why not?"

Di didn't miss it when Axel's gaze hit Bella's. Something went unsaid between the two.

"We're not doing male strippers," Bella said softly, rolling her lips inward to contain her amusement.

"Says who?" Kelsea asked, disappointed.

Diamond was surprised she didn't stomp her foot for good measure. She was known to do that on occasion.

"I could tell you who would have something to say about it." Axel's gaze landed on Jewel. "Diesel." It moved to Sophie. "Z." It bounced to Ivy. "Jag." Then finally landed on Kiki. "And Hawk. Maybe that's who."

"But not you, right?" Kiki asked, just as amused. "You'd be fine with Bella going to see male strippers?"

Axel's inhale of breath and his chest puffing out was unmistakable. He yanked up his duty belt. "I have no problem with it."

Kelsea's laughter peeled through the shop as she slapped her palm on her thigh. "Right!"

"I wouldn't. Bella's free to do what she wants!" he exclaimed.

"Riiiight," Kelsea said again, still laughing.

Bella moved around the counter and up to Axel, slipping a hand into his open patrol jacket and planting it on his belly. "Maybe it's best if you leave us women to finish our little pow wow. Go fight some crime or something."

He planted a quick kiss on her lips before shoving the remainder of the cupcake into his mouth. He nodded, chewed and swallowed before saying, "Can I take one to go?"

Kiki grabbed another cupcake and held it out to him. He moved to snag it and then leaned into Bella, putting his mouth to her ear.

Diamond wondered what he whispered to his woman and felt a pang of jealousy. It wasn't that she wanted Axel, hell no, she didn't. He was her cousin, for fuck's sake. But she was envious of what those two had.

Hell, she was envious of what all the women in the room, who had hooked up recently, had with their men. All but her. Well, and Kelsea, too.

Bella beamed up at him and after another quick kiss to her forehead, Axel left.

Bella turned to the group who was staring at her and she clapped her hands together sharply. "Now, let's get down to the business of planning Di's thirtieth birthday bash!"

The women hooted and held up their cupcakes, tapping them together like champagne glasses.

"I know part of my plan is that I'm getting laid for my thirtieth," Di declared with a nod.

"Easy enough," Ivy said, licking icing off her finger.

"No, seriously."

"We believe you, sis," Jewel assured her. "All we have to do is plan a pig roast and there'll be plenty of dick to choose from."

"Like who?" Di asked and before anyone could answer, she added, "And don't say Slade."

"Okaaay. I won't." Jewel frowned. "Like hang-arounds. And... we can invite the Dark Knights. I'm sure one of them would drag you by your hair upstairs and bang the shit out of you."

"Yeah, I'm sure our brother would love to watch me being dragged upstairs by a Knight. Your ol' man might have something to say about it, too."

Jewel waved a dismissing hand in the air. "Then don't do it at church. Take whoever it is back to your place."

Di tilted her head as she considered her sister's suggestion.

"Okay, but we still need to plan what we're doing," Kelsea said.

"I think we need to do it somewhere other than church," Kiki said. "We want it to be special. You only turn thirty once and we don't want it to turn into a club party just like any other."

"True," Ivy said, tapping her bottom lip with her finger.

"So we don't want to do it at The Iron Horse, either..." Kiki said, clearly giving it some thought.

"No. Plus, do we really want the men busting in and being all up in our business? Making sure we're not doing something *they* don't approve of?" Jewel said, reminding them all of how bossy and domineering the club members can be.

"Right. I thought you liked driving your man so crazy he gives you those "lessons" of his?"

Jewel smiled, her eyes sparkling. "I do. But still..."

"Right. They'll spoil it. It has to be elsewhere."

"So we go to a club and go dancing. Simple as that," Kelsea said.

"Somebody *really* wants to go out clubbing," Kiki murmured.

"What else is there to do?" Kelsea, the youngest of all the club sisters, asked.

"Not goin' out dancin'," came the deep grumble from the direction of the bakery kitchen.

"Ah, fuck," Kelsea muttered next to Di as Zak came through the door.

"Ain't goin' out runnin' 'round puttin' yourself in danger with the fuckin' Warriors on the warpath," he continued.

"The Warriors aren't going to be at a night club in Pittsburgh," Kelsea huffed.

Z shook his head, making his dark shoulder-length hair swing, and stepped up to his wife, curving a hand along the bottom of her extended belly. "How's he doin'?"

"*She's* doing fine," Sophie corrected him.

"Why didn't you guys find out the sex?" Kiki asked with more than a little exasperation in her voice.

Sophie waved a hand around, then laid it over Z's. "We want it to be a surprise. And I already know it's going to be a girl."

"Ain't gonna be a girl," Z grumbled.

Bella snorted at the argument that kept being repeated for almost the last nine months. And it was driving them *all* crazy.

"What are you going to do if it is?" Kiki asked, her eyes crinkling with amusement at his stubbornness.

Z opened his mouth and shut it. His eyes narrowed, and he frowned. Then he said, "You women wanna party, do it at church."

"Z! No!" Kelsea yelled.

"No, we're not doing it at church," Jewel seconded Kelsea.

"No lip. Ain't gotta choice."

"The fuck we don't!" Kelsea cried.

Z raised his brows and swung his head toward her, laying down the law. "Church or nothin'. Got me?"

"What the fuck," Kelsea muttered. "We're not having our meetings here anymore."

Di sort of agreed with Kelsea. It was difficult to have their meetings at the bakery now when it always seemed that Z was around. Instead of working in any of the other club businesses, he decided he'd help "manage" the bakery, which, to him, pretty much meant he got to boss his wife and Bella around and *sometimes* do paperwork.

But really, Diamond thought the reason he wanted to "work" in the bakery was to keep an eye on and protect his pregnant wife.

Sophie cupped her man's cheek as she grinned up at him. "Then you men have to promise to stay out and we can have male strippers come in."

His blue eyes swung back down to his wife. "What?"

"You heard me," Sophie murmured, her grin widening to a smile.

His eyebrows hit the top of his head. "Strippers?"

Di tried not to laugh at the way he spit that word out of his mouth.

"Yeah, you know, like the ones that are always at all the club parties, except these have dicks instead of tits," Kelsea said, crossing her arms over her chest. "Shouldn't have a problem with that, right? With equality and all that."

Z's eyebrows dropped low and his expression turned dark and stormy. "Equality? Have you lost your fuckin' mind?"

"Nope. Time for this club to come into the twenty-first century. We're demanding equality," Kelsea declared as she stomped her foot. *Ah, there it was.*

Z snorted, dropped his head to stare at his boots and shook it. "Brain musta got scrambled," he muttered to the floor. He raised his gaze to his wife. "You ain't goin' nowhere with my kid in your belly, got me?"

Sophie pinned her lips together as she patted his chest reassuringly. "First off, I'm not going out dancing in this condition."

"In any condition," he corrected her in a mutter.

"And your concern with our safety is duly noted."

"Reason for it."

"Right. I get it, baby," she whispered. She glanced toward the rest of the women. "But it's Di's thirtieth birthday and we *are* going to celebrate it, whether you like it or not."

"That so?"

"Yep, that's so," Sophie repeated with a nod.

Di rolled her lips under in an attempt not to beam at Sophie's control over her husband. As club president and badass biker, he wasn't normally willing to bend for a woman, but Sophie had him wrapped around her little finger. And right now she was wiggling that powerful pinky.

The rest of the women were pretending not to notice Sophie's control over her old man. Di eyeballed Kelsea, hoping the younger woman kept her trap shut and didn't blow it for them.

Kelsea's eyes slid to hers and she bugged them out in a silent message. Di gave her a slight nod.

Zak finally sighed. "Gonna get Hawk to close down The Iron Horse an' get Dawg to book you some male strippers. Ain't gonna let any of the brothers over there to bother you. Drink, dance, eyeball some strange dick, have fun. Still safe. Got me?"

"Got you," Sophie whispered, her eyes sparkling.

"Invite Dawg's girls."

"No," she said firmly with a shake of her head.

His eyebrows furrowed. "The sweet butts."

"No."

"The Knights' ol' ladies," he muttered finally.

"Fine."

"Gonna set the prospects out front to guard the door. Keep an eye out for trouble."

"Fine. As long as they don't come in."

His nostrils flared. "Whatever," he muttered, pressed a kiss to her forehead and moved back in the direction he had come from. No one said a word until the door to the back kitchen swung shut. Then they even waited a few more seconds until they knew he was out of hearing range.

Then they all looked at each other and beamed. Di rushed up to Sophie and gave her a high five. "Good job."

"Now, I just hope I don't pop until after the party. I want to see the results of my negotiations."

"Strange dick?" Ivy asked, quoting Z.

"Hell yes!" Kelsea crowed.

Ivy snorted. "Dawg should have connections to find a hot traveling troupe of male strippers on short notice."

"Up to him, he may find the ugliest ones."

"I'll call him and make sure he doesn't," Jewel assured Kelsea. "And I'll make sure there's a lot of them. One for each of us."

"Oh, brother. You know Z was only the first obstacle. Some of us will have one of our very own," Kiki said.

"Like Hawk?" Jewel asked.

"Mmm. And remember that big, serious, overly protective brother of his?" Kiki asked her with an arched brow.

"How can I forget?" Diesel's ol' lady answered with a frown.

"Right."

"Bah," Jewel answered, waving a dismissing hand. "They'll all get over it."

Di was suddenly glad she didn't have to worry about a possessive man like most of them did. She was free to enjoy her birthday and hot, naked men as much as she wanted.

And she was going to make sure she took full advantage of her birthday celebration. Maybe she'd even be able to talk one of the strippers into a private dance. At her place. With both of them totally naked. And horizontal.

No batteries required.

Yeah, that sounded like a great idea.

She couldn't wait.

Get *Down & Dirty: Slade* here:
mybook.to/DAMC-Slade

If You Enjoyed This Book

Thank you for reading Down & Dirty: Axel. If you enjoyed Axel and Bella's story, please consider leaving a review at your favorite retailer and/or Goodreads to let other readers know. Reviews are always appreciated and just a few words can help an independent author like me tremendously!

Bear's Family Tree

- **BEAR Jamison** — DAMC Founder
  - **MITCH Jamison** — Blue Avengers MC
    - **ZAK Jamison** — DAMC (President)
    - **AXEL Jamison** — Blue Avengers MC
    - **JAYDE Jamison**
    - **JEWEL Jamison**
  - **ROCKY Jamison** — DAMC
    - **DIAMOND Jamison**
    - **JAG Jamison** — DAMC (Road Captain)

Doc's Family Tree

		DIESEL Dougherty DAMC (Enforcer)
	ACE Dougherty DAMC (Treasurer)	**HAWK Dougherty** DAMC (Vice President)
DOC Dougherty DAMC Founder		**DEX Dougherty** DAMC (Secretary)
	ALLIE Dougherty	**IVY Doughtery**
		ISABELLA McBride
	ANNIE Dougherty	**KELSEA Dougherty**

Also by Jeanne St. James

Find my complete reading order here:
https://www.jeannestjames.com/reading-order

Standalone Books:

Made Maleen: A Modern Twist on a Fairy Tale

Damaged

Rip Cord: The Complete Trilogy

Everything About You (A Second Chance Gay Romance)

Reigniting Chase (An M/M Standalone)

Brothers in Blue Series

A four-book series based around three brothers who are small-town cops and former Marines

The Dare Ménage Series

A six-book MMF, interracial ménage series

The Obsessed Novellas

A collection of five standalone BDSM novellas

Down & Dirty: Dirty Angels MC®

A ten-book motorcycle club series

Guts & Glory: In the Shadows Security

A six-book former special forces series

(A spin-off of the Dirty Angels MC)

Blood & Bones: Blood Fury MC®

A twelve-book motorcycle club series

Motorcycle Club Crossovers:

Crossing the Line: A DAMC/Blue Avengers MC Crossover

Magnum: A Dark Knights MC/Dirty Angels MC Crossover

Crash: A Dirty Angels MC/Blood Fury MC Crossover

Beyond the Badge: Blue Avengers MC™

A six-book law enforcement/motorcycle club series

COMING SOON!

Double D Ranch (An MMF Ménage Series)

Dirty Angels MC®: The Next Generation

WRITING AS J.J. MASTERS:

The Royal Alpha Series

A five-book gay mpreg shifter series

About the Author

JEANNE ST. JAMES is a USA Today and international bestselling romance author who loves an alpha male (or two). She writes steamy contemporary M/F and M/M romance, as well as M/M/F ménages, and has published over 63 books (so far) in five languages. She also writes M/M paranormal romance under the name: J.J. Masters.

Want to read a sample of her work? Download a sampler book here: BookHip.com/MTQQKK

To keep up with her busy release schedule check her website at www.jeannestjames.com or sign up for her newsletter: http://www.jeannestjames.com/newslettersignup

www.jeannestjames.com
jeanne@jeannestjames.com

Newsletter: http://www.jeannestjames.com/newslettersignup
Jeanne's Down & Dirty Book Crew: https://www.facebook.com/groups/JeannesReviewCrew/
TikTok: https://www.tiktok.com/@jeannestjames

- facebook.com/JeanneStJamesAuthor
- amazon.com/author/jeannestjames
- instagram.com/JeanneStJames
- bookbub.com/authors/jeanne-st-james
- goodreads.com/JeanneStJames
- pinterest.com/JeanneStJames

Get a FREE Sampler Book

This book contains the first chapter of a variety of my books. This will give you a taste of the type of books I write and if you enjoy the first chapter, I hope you'll be interested in reading the rest of the book.

Each book I list in the sampler will include the description of the book, the genre, and the first chapter, along with links to find out more. I hope you find a book you will enjoy curling up with!

Get it here: BookHip.com/MTQQKK

www.ingramcontent.com/pod-product-compliance
Ingram Content Group UK Ltd.
Pitfield, Milton Keynes, MK11 3LW, UK
UKHW021640160226
10734UKWH00007B/18